D1488741

A
NOVEL
CALLED
HERITAGE

A NOVEL CALLED HERITAGE

Margaret Mitchell Dukore

CHARLES SCRIBNER'S SONS
New York

Copyright © 1982 Margaret Mitchell Dukore

Library of Congress Cataloging in Publication Data

Dukore, Margaret Mitchell.
A novel called heritage.

I. Title.
PS3554.U398N6   813'.54   81-21336
ISBN 0-684-17428-6   AACR2

1 3 5 7 9 11 13 15 17 19   F/C   20 18 16 14 12 10 8 6 4 2

Printed in the United States of America.

For Bernie

A
NOVEL
CALLED
HERITAGE

430 Pacific Avenue
San Francisco, CA 94133

May 1, 1974

Martin Goldsmith
Senior Editor
HASTINGS, HEARTE & DANIELS
118 Avenue of the Americas
NYC, N.Y. 10013

Dear Sir:

Enclosed is a short story for your con-
sideration. Since it's really worth looking at,
I do hope you actually read it.

Sincerely yours,
Anne Sarah Foster

P.S. Sometimes what publishers say to aspiring
authors, I'm told, can make or break a
great writer. Please do not send me a
form letter. Thanks.

I WASN'T THERE
By Anne Sarah Foster

When I was sixteen years old, we lived in San Francisco on Pacific Avenue in a huge house my mother had bought with the money from her deceased aunt's estate. I lived with my father, my father's ex-wife Janet, my father's mistress Linda, my sister Holly, and my father's ex-wife's mother Ruth.

Since my mother was dead, it wasn't really as sick a situation as it sounds. Mother killed herself when I was ten years old. I thought it was rather inconsiderate of her to do it at that exact point in my life. When you are ten, you are too old to get used to *not* having a mother, but you are too young to get along without one.

Another reason it was inconvenient was that we had only moved to San Francisco two weeks before her death, and I had sort of thought she might take time out from introspection to take Holly and me to school on the first day. She was a great one to dwell on the state of the world, on (in her words) "how fucked America was," and on how she really wanted to "change things." My sister Holly once observed that the closest Mother ever came to changing the world was to bare her breasts in an anti-war play, which not only didn't stop war but doesn't count in my book. Mother's introspection just made her sorry she was alive. Because Mother had been an actress before I was born, she spent a lot of time trying to justify theatre by saying that the plays she was in didn't always attack whatever it was she was against at the time, but that they attacked the mentality that allowed such things to go on.

Her sudden demise was also hard on us because everyone was so *nice* to us. Since Mother had taught us that people are only nice when they want something or when a relative dies, it made me kind of want to puke when she was proved right. Everyone was very careful to keep away from the subject of our dear deceased mom. They waited around for us to scream, cry, or carry on the way people always do in movies, in Greek tragedies, or on "Young Dr. Malone." If we didn't do that, everyone expected us to be in shock or to regress or to do *something* besides just shake our heads. Even Mother would have wanted some hysterics. If you take all the trouble to kill yourself, it seems to me, it should accomplish *something*. When telling the story, the six o'clock news didn't even use her name. If she had heard herself called merely "a local woman," Mother would have been furious.

Now, I don't want you to get me wrong. I was always reasonably fond of my mother. I was fond of her in a sort of detached way, and at the age of ten, I thought I was very capable of getting through this "difficult period" (as my father's ex-wife Janet called it). My father thought we could use some help from the ex-wife.

My father had been married to Janet for something like twenty years before he married my mother, and Janet was just a little too eager, I thought, to come to his rescue. Okay, if she wanted to come to *his* rescue, that was all right, but I really hated people who used kids as an excuse. Janet's excuse for flying in to San Francisco the very day after my mother conked was to "help Annie and Holly through this difficult period." Now, if she just *said* her sole purpose was to put the move on my father again (even before Mother cooled off) that would have been okay, but, as I've said, I really hated people who used kids as an excuse for anything they either wanted to do but were too lazy to do, or anything they didn't want to do but everyone thought they should.

4

Before we moved to San Francisco, we lived in Lake Oswego, Oregon, a suburb of Portland where all the rich people live. My father always professed to hate Lake Oswego, but he couldn't have hated it too much because he had lived there for eleven years with my mother, and he lived there with Janet before he even met my mother. He said it had a goddamned good school system (the "kids excuse" again).

The only reason he moved to San Francisco was because my mother's aunt bit the dust and left my mother the money to buy her "childhood home." She said she had had it "fucking up to here" (pointing to her nose) with Lake Oswego. She was always saying that Oregon was no place for a Yale graduate, and my father would agree, but since it had been her idea to come back there in the first place, he said he didn't feel a bit sorry for her. She was always getting on his ass about how he hadn't accomplished anything in life, but I felt that throwing away what you *do* accomplish, which Mother did, is just as bad as not doing anything at all.

Now, I haven't had much experience in love, but it seems to me that when people are in love, they are never practical. My mother said that she loved my father more than the theatre; she could always do stuff at the Portland Civic Theatre; she had done her undergrad work in Oregon, so she already had lots of friends there; and there was nothing she wanted more than to be a professor's wife. Shit, giving up the lights of Broadway to live in Utah with Robert Redford is one thing, but for my father? That fact alone points out that she kind of got off on self-destruction. She said it was sex. Because a kid can't ever know about her parents and sex and all, I had to buy it. However, I did make a mental note not to let sex screw things up for me. Life's too valuable to throw it away just for some man—especially if that man is a loser like my father.

I really *do* feel sorry for him, though. You're really in for it when you fall for a neurotic. Well, I shouldn't make generalizations. You're really in for it when you fall for someone like my mother. Most people, I guess out of self-preservation, get scared off or get fed up with someone as "dramatic" as my mother. Once you get attached to a personality like hers, I guess regular people are just boring. He even went so far as to *say* that once you're loved by Kate, everyone else will be second best.

Sounds like the hot, steamy, sexual marriage of all time, doesn't it? Perhaps it was, but the fact that the more my mother loved someone, the more she raked them over the coals puts a slight damper on the fantasy.

Actually, Holly and I were both grateful that Mother never really cared all that much about us. As long as we didn't do anything that might be a bad reflection on her, we were okay. Now, that sounds like a pretty bad situation, but Mother had such a wide spectrum of beliefs, it was pretty hard to do *anything* that couldn't be tucked into *some* niche.

For example, Mother hated plastic flowers, greeting cards that said things like "the burden of life is love," and anything in general that represented what she loved to describe (with great detestation in her voice) as "suburbia America." *Yet*, she thought all that junk was just hysterically funny. She would go shopping at Newberry's with our "Uncle" Hollistor (really her best friend, not a relative), and they would buy plastic hula girls for each other, key rings shaped like waffles, and the most ugly postcards they could find. Did my mother hate junk? A typical comment of hers was, "That was the most terrible movie I've ever seen, the acting really stunk, the screenplay really sucked eggs, the direction was jack shit . . . I just loved it!"

She believed in (and practiced, as far as I know) monogamous relationships, but it was rumored that she had one of the most exotic sexual histories of any faculty wife or any known resident of Lake Oswego. So, to sum it up, there was really not much we could do to offend Mother.

After we moved to San Francisco, Holly and I had our rooms on the very top floor of the house. It was one of those straight up and down houses with two levels of rose gardens in the back. You had to go upstairs to get to the living room, and on the ground floor was the library. My mother's aunt had been an artist, so the bathroom between our bedrooms was painted with birds. Mother had told us not to be obvious and call it "The Birdbath." She thought that was the "tackiest, el-suck-o" thing you could say about a bathroom with birds on the walls. Naturally, for the two weeks we lived there before she died, we *always* called it The Birdbath.

The evening before she died, Mother made herself a Tanqueray martini, put on long rhinestone earrings and an old ratty bathrobe, and held me on her lap. Since she had just finished lecturing my silent father on what things were *really* important to her, she wasn't in too red hot a mood. One great desire she had stressed (between tears and harsh criticism of my father) was that her daughters would grow up in the true family tradition.

"And what's that?" my father had asked.

"Never to think small," she had answered.

She rocked me, said nothing, and then suddenly pushed me off her lap so hard that I hit the floor with a thump, which caused my father to call up from downstairs, asking if anything was wrong.

"Shut the fuck up!" was Mother's answer to him. Because Mother was always doing weird things, I didn't really consider her behavior odd.

"Oh, God, Annie! Look what I did," she said in tears. While helping me up, she apologized and asked where Holly was.

"She's in The Birdbath," I said just to torture her. The expression had really gotten to her in the last couple of days.

"Why do you do that, Annie?" she asked, picking the olive off the rug, wiping it off on her bathrobe, and expertly tossing it into her mouth.

"Because it pisses you off," I said, not thinking fast enough to tell her that torture was as much a part of our family tradition as "not thinking small."

She held me and put her wet cheek next to my neck. "Only I, my darling," she said, "am allowed to operate that way in this house."

"Okay, okay," I said. "She's in the goddamn bathroom!"

The day after my mother did the old suicide routine, I walked through The Birdbath into Holly's room to have a conversation about the turn of events. For an eight year old, she was very logical. She said the world wouldn't change. Poor Mother, we thought. We realized she had hoped it would.

I was more like my mother than Holly was—a little on the flaky side—but what saved me from being a complete loony was that I *knew* I was like her. Because of this knowledge, I could rest easy that I wouldn't end up dead at thirty-six with nothing to show for it but a scrapbook of reviews and a painfully sick family.

When I was six or seven, I can remember happening into my parents' bedroom one Sunday morning and seeing my naked mother sitting cross-legged on the bureau. "The only thing," she said to my father, who was doing his usual trick of pretending sleep—"The only thing," she repeated, "you are good for in this world is making very sensible and very logical decisions about things, and that is the *only* thing."

"Kate," he said, sitting up in bed, "you've pointed out my failings before. Just come back to bed."

"Why?"

"Because I want you."

"Bullshit."

"Kate," he said. "Please stop."

"Why?"

"Because I want you," he said. My father wasn't very original with words.

"And you *got* me," she said softly, went into the bathroom, and slammed the door. As usual, my father sat there and did nothing.

Mother was really the one who told me I was more like her than my father. One night she was nearly ready to go out to a rehearsal, I asked her if I should be an actress too.

"Annie," she said, "being an actress is the most incredible waste of a good brain there ever was—saying other people's words. You're smart enough to make up your own." Because she hung around people who believed in "natural beauty," she put on her eyeliner very lightly so it would look as if she weren't wearing any eyeliner at all.

"You're an actress," I said. "You've always considered yourself smart . . . *and* talented."

"Our family, Annie, isn't very smart, and we are not talented."

Since I was only seven years old at the time, I figured there was no real way she could make such a rash statement about *all* of us. All I could say was, "How do you know?"

"Your father thinks he has read just everything, and I think I know just everything, but Christ, if that were true, we wouldn't be rotting here in Lake Oswego hoping for our *big* break at the Portland Civic!"

"You wanted to be here—you didn't have to be."

"I had to," she stated and then looked startled. "Go be a clinical psychologist, Annie, and it will save you a lot of ego deflation and heartache . . . the arts . . . forget it."

Because I didn't exactly understand what she meant by that, I decided to start over.

"Well, should I?"

"Huh?" She looked at herself in the mirror for a long time just to make sure she looked as if she had casually thrown herself together in a couple of seconds. "What was that, Annie?"

9

"Well, should I be an actress?"

"Don't you want to be a nurse? All seven-year-old girls want to be nurses."

"Not particularly."

"Well, ask your father. Ask Holly. Ask someone else. You and I are both much too unrealistic to have this conversation to begin with."

"Huh?"

"Annie," she said, sucking in her cheeks and checking out the effect in the mirror, "what I meant was that you should ask your father about *logical* things. It is dangerous to follow your heart. Look at me: I followed mine, and ended up part of his mundane existence."

I didn't know much about my father's first wife before Mother kicked off. When she wanted to be, Mother could be a very cruel and sarcastic person, and she sometimes referred to Janet as "having a disgustingly good personality." She never liked anyone who had anything that could be considered a better quality than she possessed. Also, the fact that Janet had been married to my father before Mother had waltzed into the scene and done the cheap, age-old trick of being young and beautiful while Janet looked like Porky Pig didn't help her feelings about Janet in the least.

Now, I consider myself a rather rational person (in comparison to my mother, Jack the Ripper would seem rational), and I, even at the age of seven, sensed that anything my mother seemed to feel guilty about was something she had developed a contempt for. Because she was always putting Janet down, we knew she felt *super* guilty about taking my father from her.

Janet was one of those people who was a product of her background. She married my father while they were both young, had been the working wife of a graduate student, stayed home while my father was at rehearsals, and limited her friends to the people my father worked with.

Even before he met my mother, my father was not exactly what anyone would call easy to get along with (my Uncle Hollistor once made the comment that my father deserved *anything*—even Mother). My mother used to love to tell stories about how everybody in the drama department at Portland City University hated him. Since she was never one of those college coeds who fell for the king of the campus, I guess my mother must have loved him just to be different. I mean, how "different" can you get—falling for a married, reasonably ugly professor, who wasn't even a very good director, whom everybody disliked working with?

I figure Janet cooked dinners for his friends, and I know my mother had late-night ("after the theatre") cocktail parties for *her* friends. When you got to know him, my father was a halfway likable person, so my mother became his public relations person. She was his contact with the outside world. *He* had been Janet's contact when they were married, and he was a lousy contact. So Janet and my father had lived for twenty years in their own world.

Since Janet worked at the Bureau of City Records, and my father was the head of the most dog puke drama department in the country, you can imagine how exciting their "own world" was. Janet's work made it possible for them to do things together like go to Las Vegas and lose everything she earned at the Bureau of City Records.

Aside from being nuts, my mother was energetic, had millions of friends, and hated Las Vegas; and if my father didn't want to go out to her never-ending circle of parties, she simply would take the car and go herself. This fascinated my father. Suddenly he was married to someone who wasn't a duty.

Even though Janet had been a job and an obligation, he loved her. But she had gone along with anything he thought of, and she had never added anything new. Because my father was not a very inventive person, their life had continued on the kind of even keel that *most* people strive for: security, conferring, and existing.

Kate, my mother, was not "most people."

This was perfect territory for her to get her claws into. Although he lived a boring life, my father was a man who dreamed of something more. Kate was slender, wide-eyed, dependent on my father because of her youth and erratic behavior, but also totally *in*dependent because of her youth and erratic behavior.

Because she was still young, she truly thought she was acting out of love and not self-destruction.

When you asked my mother how she got my father to give up his "life" for a bittersweet unbalanced existence, she would say, in her most convincing and sincere voice, "I loved him, you idiot."

I don't know. I wasn't there.

I do know that Mother graduated from Yale Drama School in 1952 and came back to Oregon and told my father she still wanted him. While she was still an undergraduate, he had thought that she wanted his security because she didn't know what she wanted to do with her life. So, she went to Yale, received the Sybil Sykes Acting Award, became what Walter Kerr once described as "one of the finest young American actresses" for her Broadway performance in *Young Victoria*, turned down a role with Elia Kazan, came back to dumb old Lake Oswego, Oregon, and asked my father what else she had to do to prove that that was where she really wanted to be.

Because my mother was very good at pretending to be tender, was very beautiful, had been to Yale, had been described by Walter Kerr as "one of the finest young American actresses," and told my father that the only reason she had gone to Yale was to prove to him she could do anything she wanted to, but he was what she wanted, he was fooled into thinking the mistake of his life was the one big bonanza card that life ever handed to him.

What my father should have said was, "Now you have a life, so why don't you just buzz off and go live it, and let me live the one that I have had a fifty-one-year start on." But what loser turns down a second chance? He couldn't ignore my mother. He couldn't tell "one of the finest young American actresses" who was "giving it all up for him" that he didn't want her.

The sad thing was that he *did* want her. I guess. But then, I wasn't there.

The two weeks before Mother died were not exactly what I would call the two greatest weeks of my life. The first one was spent moving out of our house in Lake Oswego, two days of the second were spent driving down to San Francisco, and the rest was spent putting our things away in the house and hoping Mother would get better.

Since the house in San Francisco was so much bigger than our house in Lake Oswego, moving in wasn't that bad. It was four stories high, had Persian rugs and a butler's pantry. The living room, dining room, kitchen, and sitting room were all on the second floor, so when you came in the front door, you had on your left the library (appropriately wood-paneled with a fireplace and library ladder, as all libraries are supposed to be); in front of you a curved staircase; and next to the stairs, a mysterious door that led to a downstairs apartment. In the grand days of my mother's childhood, this had been servants' quarters, but after Mother died and Linda—my father's mistress—came down from Portland, it became her apartment (a level of sophistication his ex-wife Janet said she wasn't quite ready for).

The two floors above the living room were filled with oversized bedrooms with fireplaces in them and lots of closets, corners, and dormer windows. My father had hoped this would make Mother happier, so he was disappointed when she continued to pace at night; look nervously over her shoulders; reread her reviews; and finally come to him, in a state of terror, and weep in his arms. He would kiss her ears, her neck, her hair, and then lead her to the bedroom.

"I wanted this to make you happy," he said.

13

"Nothing will *ever* make me love life," she answered, "but I can act here, so maybe life will be easier to bear."

Horseshit. If Mother had settled into happiness, she wouldn't have known what to do with herself.

"I need creative energy," she had said to me, but obviously, speaking other people's words for the reward of applause wasn't enough.

The two weeks before Mother bumped herself off were bad because we were moving. The *moving*, we said, was responsible for all the tensions. Actually, Mother was her usual self: stuffing glassware into boxes while Holly and my father removed them piece by piece and wrapped them carefully; saying she'd rather lose three deposits than bother to clean up the place; giving her usual anti-Lake Oswego, anti-suburbia speeches; talking about her possibilities for getting a job with Actors' Rep Theatre when she got to San Francisco; telling us about her childhood memories of the house we were moving into (she said that she used to pretend it was in Venice instead of San Francisco, and she would sit upstairs in the living room and look down at Pacific Avenue and watch the gondolas go by); dance to the music of Elvis Presley's "Treat Me Mean and Cruel"; and in general, do exactly what we would expect my mother to do if she were faced with moving. *Naturally*, she complained, bitched, screamed at us, talked endlessly about how she hated to be tied down by "things" but couldn't escape them, about what "one of the finest young American actresses" was doing cleaning the sink, and about how the educational system in America was designed to destroy anyone's individuality. But these were all common topics for her—what we expected. Even the crying fits after we moved were anticipated. We knew all that would come with a major change in her life; what we didn't expect was her death.

She went through her collection of books before packing them and weeded out the rotten novels. Because she didn't want anyone to know she loved rotten novels, she never had any of them on the shelf. Her favorites were the kind about the career girl in New York who has sexual problems and an affair going with her wealthy and powerful boss, or the ones with long descriptions of interiors of Beverly Hills houses sandwiched between conversations such as, "The doubt was in my mind—never, oh never, in my heart." I guess she felt life fell somewhere between a Greek tragedy and a rotten novel, but since she had no idea *where*, she kept jumping back and forth between them, stopping only once in a while to look at her daughters and act like a normal person.

She stared at her collection of plays. "I love your father more than any idea written in any of these books," she said to Holly and me as we were putting them into boxes. She looked dramatically off into space and gave an excellent line reading.

"Why?" asked practical Holly. I mean, we loved our father because he was our father, had been reasonably nice to us, and loved us because we were his kind, but actually we weren't alone in our theory that he was a crashing bore. I guess Holly thought Mother was being slightly hasty when she threw aside all the plays of Chekhov for him.

"*Because*," she said loudly to make sure my father was listening, "he loved me enough to give up something important for me, and no one else had ever loved me enough even to spend the day with me after he had spent the night. That's why."

"Huh?" came from both of us.

"Sex lured me as much as fame," she laughed. We stared at her. "Please laugh," she said softly. "*Laugh!!*" she screamed. "What I said was funny!" She looked at us and then said softly, "Didn't you think it was funny?"

"Uh, yes," I said.

"You aren't laughing!" she yelled.

"On the inside," Holly said.

My mother laughed, hugged Holly, and stroked her hair. "I love your father," she whispered, "because he was the only person—the only one out of all those thousands of people who came to the theatre—who looked at me the way I wanted to be looked at."

"*We* think you're a great human being," I said, trying to lighten things up a bit, but she was already lighting a cigarette and was off again on how education really screws people up.

My father was wrapping plates in newspapers and listening to the entire conversation. Because Mother was like that, it didn't surprise any of us.

After my mother died, things were a little less colorful, but then my father's ex-wife Janet was a little less colorful than Mother. When my father's mistress Linda came down from Oregon because she missed the loving my father blessed her with, things livened up a bit. Then Janet's aged mother Ruth came because she missed Janet, and we all lived happily ever after until one day when I was sixteen, my father looked at me really hard.

I was running in from jogging. I wasn't a health nut or anything, but there was this guy who must have been at *least* eighteen (maybe even twenty) who used to jog along the wall that separated Pacific Avenue from the Presidio. Because I knew I couldn't have his love (this is sounding like Mother), I would have to "grab a few scraps of happiness" from jogging around the park with him and becoming healthy.

Anyway, I had come rushing into the house, and my father was reading exams in the library. He was teaching public speaking. When he lived in Oregon, he had been teaching theatre. I guess his first love was theatre. Mother used to describe him as a sad man because he "was smart enough to realize he was nothing." I had said that that didn't sound like a brilliant realization, and Mother said that it was a lot more than most failures realized.

Mother had heard there was an opening for a professor in the speech department at San Francisco State. Because he thought it might help her to move to San Francisco, he gave up teaching theatre, took retirement and the new job, and moved into my mother's childhood home on Pacific Avenue. He thought he had finally done the right thing to please her. He didn't dislike San Francisco State; he liked the house; he liked San Francisco. So we stayed on after the death. He had no real memories about the place because we hadn't even finished the moving in when Mother decided to get dramatic and do the suicide act.

Although my father didn't like teaching speech, he had all my mother's money; he had Linda to sleep with, Janet for cooking and company, and Holly and me as an excuse for why he wasn't writing great books and articles on the theatre. So, as I said, we lived happily ever after until that day in 1972 when I came in from jogging, caught my foot on the stairs, and said, "Oh fuck it!"

I heard my father laughing in the library. Since I had probably sprained my ankle, I didn't think things were all that funny, but because I knew that at sixteen you were supposed to have control over your emotions, I didn't cry.

We had lived in reasonable harmony until my father came to the door of the library; looked at me at the foot of the stairs; said, "Annie, you are so very much like your mother"; went back into the library; picked up his pen; looked over at me in my gray U.C.B. T-shirt; put his pen down; put his head in his hands; and cried.

HASTINGS, HEARTE & DANIELS

118 AVENUE OF THE AMERICAS

NEW YORK, NY 10013

May 6, 1974

Anne Sarah Foster
430 Pacific Avenue
San Francisco, CA 94133

Dear Ms. Foster:
RE: Enclosed Manuscript
    Thank you for sending us your short story.
Unfortunately, it does not fill our publishing
needs at this time.

                          Sincerely yours,
                          THE EDITORS

---

                          430 Pacific Avenue
                          San Francisco, CA 94133

                          May 10, 1974

Martin Goldsmith
Senior Editor
HASTINGS, HEARTE & DANIELS
118 Avenue of the Americas
NYC, N.Y. 10013

Dear Mr. Goldsmith:
RE: Form letter you sent me when I asked you
    not to send a form letter.

I am writing in response to your letter
that doesn't even deserve a response.

One. I addressed my first letter to <u>Martin
Goldsmith</u> personally, and the response was
signed with a rubber stamp, "The Editors."
(Shit!) I am assuming you didn't receive it,
or you would have answered it; so I am enclos-
ing my great short story again. Since I don't
take the boot in the ass lying down, you're
going to keep hearing from me until you pick
up a pen instead of a rubber stamp.

Two. Your "Editors" commented that my
short story "didn't fill your publishing needs
at this time." What do you mean, "Does not fill
your needs at this time"? <u>My short story is
universal</u>! <u>America needs it</u>!

Three. Would it interest you at all to
know that my mother really <u>did</u> kill herself?
That will add some tragic realism if you want
to add that in a footnote.

Thank you for the time I hope you will
spend answering this.

Sincerely yours,
Anne Sarah Foster

P.S. It's not really <u>that</u> bad, considering I
knocked it out in about half an hour.

HASTINGS, HEARTE & DANIELS

118 AVENUE OF THE AMERICAS
NEW YORK, NY 10013

June 12, 1974

Anne Sarah Foster
430 Pacific Avenue
San Francisco, CA 94133

Dear Ms. Foster:
Because I wanted to read your manuscript
personally before commenting on it, I have not
been able to respond to your letter of May 10
until now.
You have a very interesting style of writing, but I would suggest you send your story
to an agent, as our publishing firm publishes
books, not individual short stories.
I wish you the best of luck.

Sincerely,
Martin Goldsmith
Senior Editor

MG/ht

430 Pacific Avenue
San Francisco, CA 94133

June 15, 1974

Martin Goldsmith
Senior Editor
HASTINGS, HEARTE & DANIELS
118 Avenue of the Americas
NYC, N.Y. 10013

Dear Mr. Goldsmith,
Thank you for responding to me in person
even though it took a whole month to read a
crummy, short, twenty-page manuscript.
Since you don't handle short stories, but
were the only publisher who had the courtesy
to respond to me "personally," I have decided
to do you a big favor and expand this into the
"Great American Novel," and give you guys first
crack at it.
It will have some recurring themes, so in
case it becomes famous, English teachers will
be able to find something in it to teach; it
will have something for everyone in it: sex,
violence, insanity, love, death, S & M, recipes
—you name it, I'll add it.
Enclosed is Chapter 2.

Sincerely yours,
Anne Sarah Foster

P.S. Also, when you sign your letters "sincerely yours," I am going to assume you
are (sincere, that is).

I was born because my mother didn't want to work. It wasn't that she didn't try. Since jobs where she would make fifty thousand dollars a year and work for about two hours a day at something that wouldn't put too much strain on her brain were hard to find, she had a baby and was stuck for life.

After three years of training to be an actress and two years of living in New York *being* an actress, after deciding to "give it all up" for my father, she took a fifty-five-dollar-a-month apartment in Portland and waited for my father to get around to giving Janet the axe. Since dropping the bombshell after twenty years isn't the easiest thing for someone to do, my father said he would have to "see how things went." Being slightly liberated, Mother didn't want him to "keep her" (although this didn't bother her a bit after they were married), so she decided she had better get some form of employment. She wasn't surprised to find that actresses *never* got paid in Portland, and acting wasn't even counted as "job experience."

The idea of me was conceived on a bench outside of the Oregon Medical Insurance Society in 1954. It was noon hour, and my father (still in the process of "seeing how things went") was meeting my mother for lunch. He found out she had just up and quit her job in this "den of psychological tortures" (her description). Since she'd only been working there two hours, it didn't really alter her pattern of living.

The lady from the employment agency, who wore a lot of gold rings and dialed the phone with a jeweled telephone dialer, had sent Mother over to the Oregon Medical Insurance Society with a smile. Miss Sims was positive she was going to get her commission *this* time because the Oregon Medical Insurance Society was a "worthwhile" organization, and not one that (in Mother's words) tried to screw over the public. Because Mother didn't know that *all* insurance companies screw over the public, she thought it was a company that helped people by paying for their hospitalization. Shit!

My mother was a college graduate (she had decided not to mention acting—an instant boot out the door, she had discovered from other employment agencies). She mentioned her three years at Portland City University because all the Miss Simses of the world feel comfortable with people who have never ventured more than 100 miles from home. But the Miss Simses of the world are not at all glad to see college graduates even if they *are* from the area: college graduates always want more money, and you just can't send them to a tire company to be an invoice clerk because they somehow have acquired a set of ideals. Liberal arts grads are worthless . . . give them each a good high school grad with a year of business school, and all the Miss Simses of the world come up with an instant commission.

Mother was the worst of them. She typed seventy-five words a minute (with thousands of errors, but, in her words, typing errors were unimportant in the whole scheme of things). In appearance she was the type that companies want, but in reality she was of the type who are incapable of company loyalty. Miss Sims saw her commission just out of her reach about three times every day when a job came in that would be "just perfect" for an attractive college graduate with "the smarts" (employment agency lingo that Mother picked up later when referring to herself) who could type seventy-five words a minute (Miss Sims decided not to tell my mother's theory about errors).

My mother. In those days, I guess because she was young, she really attempted to be idealistic. She didn't want to be a typist for a company that recorded "Muzak" because she once worked in a department store and *hated* Muzak and actually felt that if she refused to type for them, it somehow, in her twisted mind, would save other department store workers from having to listen to it. Miss Sims just couldn't see what a dislike for the music they *played* on the Muzak had to do with why my mother didn't want to work for a company that recorded it. It wasn't as if there were no "future" in the job. She told Mother that if she were mechanically inclined, it could lead to a larger salary and perhaps to the actual dubbing of the music sound.

"I don't give a rusty fuck about the future," Mother had wanted to say. Not knowing how true it was, she kept the act clean and said she'd give the Oregan Medical Insurance Society a try, but "never, oh *never*, a company that records Muzak!"

"Suit yourself," said Miss Sims, discouraged as usual by Kate.

Mother's first day at the Oregon Medical Insurance Society started at 8:45, and naturally Mother had been out late the night before with some Italian who had stopped her in the middle of the downtown shopping area and told her she was the most beautiful girl he had ever seen. Mother had a certain style that made people notice her. She always said it was a combination of her abilities as an actress and her natural beauty, to which my father responded that it was probably just her deft use of cosmetics. Anyway, flattery would get you everywhere with Mother, so she spent the evening with the Italian (who was a ring sizer at Zales Jewelers), listening to how beautiful she was and wondering how she was going to get out of sleeping with him. Because my father was still living with Janet at the time, Mother had evenings free. She figured you couldn't tell foreigners you were a lesbian because they aren't put off by that, so she finally told him that her husband was dead. Mother cried real tears (not for her mythical dead husband, but for her need to *make up* one). Naturally she wasn't jumping to go at 8:45 the next morning. Anyway, she said, she hated the way all girls on their first day "on the job" look cheery and bright.

Mother was to be a claims representative. This simply meant that she would have to spend three months memorizing all the different aspects of this huge medical insurance company, and then be the person called by all 400,000 people the insurance company serviced, when they had questions about their policies. Mother recalled she had never known anyone who *didn't* have a question concerning their payments from a medical insurance company.

She met her boss: a management trainee who would probably do less work than she ever would and already got paid three times as much. "Jerry" told her that the company was "really open" and that everyone used first names. When Jerry told her three times in the first half hour that "communication was the main trouble with this world today," Mother wanted to vomit. Although Mother thought that was a trite and insipid remark, how could she disagree? She detested motherfuckers like Jerry.

Two hours later she was sitting on the bench.

"I quit!" she said when my father came around the stone fountain.

"You quit?" My father had a distinctive laugh. "Why?"

"I want to have your child," she said almost as well as she would have said it for her Yale auditions.

That, she said, was the day I was conceived. The actual conception took place sometime after their marriage six months later.

Janet, who had never had children of her own, folded the newspaper with the notice, "Born: to Dr. and Mrs. Matthew Foster, a girl, Anne Sarah."

In Janet's place, Mother would have ripped up the notice and sent a crisp and tacky congratulations card. Janet just felt sad because a child was the one thing *she* had wanted to give him.

HASTINGS, HEARTE & DANIELS

118 AVENUE OF THE AMERICAS

NEW YORK, NY 10013

June 25, 1974

Anne Sarah Foster
430 Pacific Avenue
San Francisco, CA 94133

Dear Ms. Foster:

    If I am to continue reading your novel, I would suggest you send me an outline of your book.

    I would also be very much interested to see how exactly you are going to show me that your book is "universal."

Yours,
Martin Goldsmith
Senior Editor

MG/ht

430 Pacific Avenue
San Francisco, CA 94133

June 30, 1974

Martin Goldsmith
Senior Editor
HASTINGS, HEARTE & DANIELS
118 Avenue of the Americas
NYC, N.Y. 10013

Dear Martin (if I may call you Martin),
Of course my book is Universal! It touches
childhood, death, infertility, job dissatisfaction, women's liberation, suicide,hate/love
relationships, maternal love, irony, sincerity,
and insanity. And those were just the first two
chapters!
Enclosed is Chapter 3. I have decided it
would be artistic to write in flashback. You
see, it makes all the stuff about my mother
touching. Because you know from the beginning
that she knocks herself off, everything she
does becomes more significant. God, look what
that did for Love Story! Who the hell would
have cared if Ali McGraw threw snow at Ryan
O'Neal unless you knew she was going to die
. . . young. Also, American lit teachers like
flashbacks—straight narrative is nowhere in
the classroom.
The reason I am going into all this stuff
that happened before I was born is that I've
decided on a title. It will be called Heritage
(I mean, if I'm writing a story about my family, Heritage is the best fucking title I can
think of). I realize that Heritage is the name
of a furniture company, but then there is a

book called <u>Atlas Shrugged</u> and there is also an "Atlas" moving company and an "Atlas" tire company, so I don't think <u>Heritage</u> will cause any special problems.

<u>Heritage</u> is also a really good kind of title to have on your coffee table—you know, like <u>Exodus</u> or <u>The Source</u>—big letters. Since most best sellers are only purchased to spend time on a coffee table, I'll try to make it pretty long too—people like their friends to think they read long, hard books like <u>Hawaii.</u> If I were to call it <u>The Sex Hex</u>, <u>Roger's Rammer</u>, or <u>Box Lunch</u>, it might sell, but, you know, people wouldn't want it sitting right out there for everyone to see. That way, it would ultimately lose out in sales. People don't buy books like <u>Liquid Lips</u> for their aunts for Christmas either. <u>Heritage</u> is best. When it comes out in paperback, you can always put a dirty picture on the cover for those <u>Stewardesses in Cages</u> creeps.

This is destined for the best seller charts!

Sincerely yours,
Anne Sarah Foster

P.S. Key to reading it: take note of the sentence in the next chapter where Mother says a pervert is a "deviant from the norm." That is one of my recurring themes.

P.P.S. You may call me Annie.

chapter 3

My mother met my father six years before they were married. He was forty-six years old, looked fifty-six, had just been rejected from the drama department faculty at his alma mater, the University of Wisconsin, and was directing a production of *Uncle Vanya* that even before tryouts had become a campus joke.

Because he claimed to base his life on his desires rather than his fears, Mother had given him a bad time from the beginning. "You couldn't have *desired* to take over the drama department at *Portland City*," she would say. "And," she would laugh, "you also fear I'll leave you."

"Katie," he had said while emptying her ashtray for her, "I believe one could turn it around and say our marriage is based on my *desire* for *you*." He walked up behind her chair and put his hands on her breasts.

She didn't acknowledge this at all, which was much worse for my father than if she had just removed his hands. She inhaled her cigarette smoke deeply before she spoke. Then she said, "You really believe you want what you've got, don't you?" My father said nothing. "It just seems odd to me," she continued, "that you would *desire* to be a lousy director, a professor at a third-rate college who doesn't write anything, and a father of two little girls who might turn out like your wife."

"Kate, don't . . . " he said softly.

"I'm sorry," she said, reaching for his hand, "but I'm just sick of hearing shit."

"So am I," he said.

She smiled. "Leave me, then," she said. "You threw your greatest love out the window once before, and I came back." Mother laughed and got up. "Try it," she hissed. "You could get lucky—I might come back again." She paused and then said, "But not fucking likely!"

Later, after she died, my father said to Janet that the trouble with Mother was that fear was the controlling force in her life or some garbage like that. Janet asked him if it had ever occurred to him that Mother was simply crazy, and they both laughed.

My father was born in Pekin, Illinois, in 1903. His family lived on a farm about twenty miles outside Pekin, and of course we grew up reeking with guilt because we never had to shovel horseshit. His parents (whom I had never met) looked exactly like the couple in the painting "American Gothic" (Mother's description—she had never met them either).

Since his abilities as a farmer were zero, his life on the farm was a total flop. ("He was even a real loser at *that*," Mother would say. "If fate points its finger at you and says, 'el-blot-o,' just *giving up* has more dignity than floundering through life." I would say I didn't think giving up made *anyone* look like hot shit, and Mother would say, "I'd rather be dead than boring.") My father left home at seventeen, "leaving behind a void that was [and I *quote* him] definitely forgettable."

"Didn't you mean 'instantly filled'?" Mother asked him when he was telling his life story for the hundredth time.

Looking uncomfortable, he had just gone on.

His eloquent comments to Holly and me often consisted of your usual parent-had-it-worse-than-you statements like, "I spent twelve years getting up at four in the morning, milking six cows, and shoveling shit on a farm, and I don't want any of it slung around here!"

"If you didn't want shit slung," I asked him, "how come you married Mother?" He stared at me a minute, and then slapped me across the mouth.

Since he talked a lot about his grandmother, and because she was the only relative whose picture he kept, I figured she must have been the only one he gave a rat's ass about. In the picture, she and his grandpa were standing on the main street of town, and the streets were flooded. In response to Holly's question regarding the condition of the streets, he simply said, "The streets of that hole were *always* flooded."

Mother was generally sarcastic about the farm bit, but once —defending him (probably after a roll in the sack)—she said, "There have been lots of great people who came out of the Midwest."

"Name two," Holly said.

"Well," she said after a long moment of thought, "Johnny Carson is from Nebraska . . . and Scott Fitzgerald . . . he's from the Midwest too."

One of the more intriguing things about the great days in old Pekin, Illinois, was that my father went to a one-room school. Because Mother used to read those books to us about kids in a prairie town who had to study one thing while the kids from other grades went up front to recite, his most re-quested memory was his schooling. Mother always said this system allowed the child to develop at his own speed, so he wouldn't become a victim of the American educational system, which only fucks up gifted children (i.e., herself? i.e., us? She never exactly said). What she didn't realize was that if *anyone* was a victim of the American educational system, it was my father.

Because he was always encouraging us to become scholars, reading became one hell of a chore. I mean, I'm sorry, but at eight years old, who the hell wants to read *The Secret Sharer* when under your bed is a comic book with a sea monster on the cover holding two skin divers in a bottle? Mother was a secret comic book reader too. Of course, she claimed to be the kind of scholar that pissed off pure scholars because she could grasp out of the air what they had spent lifetimes studying. My father used this as an example of the shit that was slung around Lake Oswego.

His education really came from reading the complete works of Shakespeare, Milton, Jane Austen, etc. (literature biggies: Mother's expression) when he finished his assigned studies in that romanticized one-room schoolhouse. Mother called him accidentally self-educated. She said that if they had had comic books or pornography lying around the place instead of Shakespeare, he would have read those and become a pervert. Holly once asked what a pervert was, and she said it was a deviant from the norm.

"So," she said one day when I was eight, "you made it all the way to Portland, Oregon. Hot shit." She was cutting out a picture of herself from the movie page of the paper (lovingly called by Portland's community theatre addicts, "The Theatre Page"). "A shit community theatre production of *A Doll's House*, all to be here with you, my love," she commented loudly, goosing my father as he brought her her coffee. Doing his usual thing, my father was fixing breakfast for us (Mother never ate breakfast because her great dream was to be fifteen pounds underweight, so she could eat anything she wanted without feeling guilty). She sat curled up on the sofa in her bikini underpants with the morning paper and a pile of scrapbooks. "Community theatre sucks!" she said in her most professional stage voice. She glanced at me and then at six-year-old Holly and said, "But I was *great!*"

"You were okay," said my father from the stove. "No better, no worse. Just okay."

"So you consider yourself a better critic than Walter Kerr who called me—if you recall—'one of the finest young American actresses'?" she asked.

My father put the previous night's glasses in the dishwasher. "Yes, as a matter of fact, I do," he said.

"Well, then why don't you send *The Times* your great resume and ask for a job?" she chided.

"Because," he said nervously, "I am a *teacher* and not a critic."

"That's every professor's excuse for not doing anything—he's a motherfucking good *teacher*," she laughed. "Who are you impressing? A bunch of little nerds who don't read their assignments? A good *teacher*, Christ Almighty!"

"And I suppose your excuse for not fixing breakfast is that you are an actress, not a wife?" he asked slowly.

"We all need an excuse for everything," she said shortly.

When he was angry, my father had a way of rolling his eyes so you knew he was about to let holy hell break loose. Holly and I buried our heads in the comics. "You're a loser," she said calmly.

She looked at him very hard with those wide eyes, Holly looked at him with loganberry jam smeared on her chin, and I reread the back of the *Meet the Beatles* album. Mother made a wide, expansive gesture and said, "Ahh, the Happy Lake Oswego Family at Breakfast!"

She walked toward my father and ran her hand slowly down his back, and he touched her cheek with his gray beard, set down the egg turner, and buried his face in her naked breasts.

"Excuses," she said.

"I wish we didn't have to live with excuses all the time," I mumbled, finishing the *Meet the Beatles* album and starting on the *Camelot* album.

"Then *do* something, Annie," she said. "Look at this . . . sick woman, sicker man loving this woman only because she's sick, and two kids sitting there, eating fucking pancakes, and wishing there were no excuses. *Use it*, Annie, and you won't have to answer to anyone."

"Huh?" I asked.

"That's what they used to say to us in acting classes," she said. "If you had a cold, they'd say 'use it,' and you'd play Lady Macbeth with a cold."

"I don't get it."

"It means you take something that's a disadvantage—like living with a crazy mother—and turn it into an advantage."

"How can I do that?"

"That's up to you," she said. "Ahh, *I* really knew how to 'use it.' Once I played Isadora Duncan with a broken arm. You've got to figure out your own ways to use things, Annie . . . God . . . God . . . I wish *I* knew how to use *this* . . . "

"That was very deep and very moving," my father said, "and I honestly can't believe there was ever a time when I wondered why Yale accepted you. You have quite a talent for the drama, Kate." He poured Holly some more milk and said, "Isadora Duncan with a *broken arm?* You played *what?* Sure, Kate, sure."

"I did! You know, graceful and fluid in a cast . . . "

"What's the name of the play she's in, Kate?"

"It doesn't matter," she said. "You just burned the fucking eggs." She tossed her hair, stepped over the editorial section of the paper, and resumed her position curled up on the sofa. "Katie McNeil," she read out loud with a newsman's detached clarity, "wife of Dr. Matthew Foster, Professor of Drama at Portland City University, and former Broadway actress, is appearing through the courtesy of Actors' Equity in Portland Civic Theatre's production of *A Doll's House.*"

My father started some new eggs. "Stupid fucking hick town," she shouted. Leaving the breakfast preparations unfinished, my father started to storm into the study. We all knew the shit was about to hit the fan.

"I love you, my darling . . . love of my life," my mother said softly. This time she was not accused of having a good line reading. My father turned around, walked to her, put his arms around her, and kissed her neck. He took her hand and gently led her to the bedroom and shut the door.

"I wasn't hungry anyway," Holly said to me. "But it makes me awfully sad."

"*Use it,*" I said sarcastically.

HASTINGS, HEARTE & DANIELS

118 AVENUE OF THE AMERICAS

NEW YORK, NY 10013

July 5, 1974

Anne Sarah Foster
430 Pacific Avenue
San Francisco, CA 94133

Dear Annie,
Thank you for your letter. Where's the
outline I asked for? Because I read many things
every week, and it is hard to remember from
chapter to chapter, I simply can't take the
time to read each small fragment as you happen
to finish it—especially with your "artistic"
flashback style. How about 100 pages at a time?
I see you have left your name intact in
the story. Are the other names changed? How
much of this story is really true?

Yours,
Martin Goldsmith
Senior Editor

MG/ht

430 Pacific Avenue
San Francisco, CA 94133

July 8, 1974

Martin Goldsmith
Senior Editor
HASTINGS, HEARTE & DANIELS
118 Avenue of the Americas
NYC, N.Y. 10013

Dear Martin,

When you are dealing with an "artist," you don't ask this artist to produce like a machine. I have my own way of writing, which doesn't include an outline. Maybe James Joyce used an outline for Ulysses, but I bet he just did a lot of crossing out.

If you can't follow my story one chapter at a time, there must be something radically wrong with your power of concentration. How the hell did you make senior editor anyway?

In answer to your question about how much of this shit is true, it is partly fictional.

Enclosed is Chapter 4. If you are getting bored, I'll add more sex and violence, but I don't really think Americans mind being bored too much—they buy Norman Mailer all the time. If people are a bit bored, they think they're reading something above them.

Love,
Annie

P.S. If you read this as if you are reading Nabokov or Jacqueline Susann or any other "serious writer," it will start looking a lot better. Also, if you do send me one of those "we regret to inform you" letters, I hope you really do regret it.

chapter 4

If you think my relationship with my parents was sick-o, you should have heard my father talk about his. He made us all (including my mother, amazingly enough) feel sorry for him because his parents were such ass holes. Mother once said he was trying to point out, in an indirect way, that *we* could do a hell of a lot worse. She said he felt vaguely guilty about the fact that we—his own flesh and blood—were only peripheral details in his life story.

He told us about one time when he had a bad case of scarlet fever for three weeks and was in bed the whole time. His mother just brought in food at mealtimes, and his father never once stuck his head in the door to see how he was. Since he didn't visit either Holly or me in the hospital when we had our tonsils out, we just shook our heads with amazement when he got into his "fucked childhood" stories.

Our paternal grandmother had only seen my father once since he was seventeen. This was the time my mother—still an undergraduate having a hot and heavy affair with him—convinced him that after he finished a convention in Chicago, he should go downstate to Pekin to see the folks because he hadn't seen them in some thirty years. My mother (with her usual great sense of the drama) had thought it would be sort of like a combination of an Arthur Miller and a Eugene O'Neill play: the reunion of a family after thirty years of silent hostility. Of course, real life is always more boring than imagined scenes, so upon arriving in Pekin, my father walked out into the yard where his mother was talking to a farmhand. After thirty fucking years, she just glanced up and said with great disgust in her voice, "That there is my son." I guess my father didn't consider this too great a welcome after thirty years, so he left that very day, and that was the last time he saw her. He had completely missed seeing his father.

He returned to Oregon and squeezed a little sympathy out of Mother by telling her about this emotional experience of visiting his long lost parents. She sat up in bed, looked at him, and said, "How come *you* turned out so nice?" (God! Mother could be a hypocrite, but then when feeling sexy, *everyone* is susceptible to saying things they don't mean.)

"I was loved by women like you," he said.

She laughed, lit a cigarette, and said, "Don't you ever worry that your screwed-up childhood will have some horrendous effect on you in future years?"

"Don't you?" he said.

"It already has, Foster," she said. "I'm here in bed with you, aren't I?"

"Well, maybe that's the terrible effect *my* childhood had on me," he said.

Because bedtime stories about "big bad bears" and fairy princesses get pretty boring after the age of three, my father did manage to entertain us with stories about his mother. One story was about the day Will Rogers died. My father had already left home, but his younger brother had reported to him that his mother heard the news on the old radio, started screaming, smashed the radio, ripped up all the old clippings about Will Rogers she had secretly saved under the mattress, set fire to the mattress, and sat there moaning. According to our Uncle Hugh, she used to punish her cats by hanging them out the upstairs window in a bag, had the locks changed every three months because she believed the neighbors were trying to kill her, mashed up the garbage can with an axe because she believed the same neighbors were secretly putting their extra garbage in it, hid behind the neighbors' bushes and leaped out in the dark with a flash camera as they were putting out *their* garbage cans, and was reported to have hit her husband over the head with her false leg.

My Uncle Hugh left Pekin and moved to Nebraska right after the episode where his mother insisted that all three of them wear the cheesecloth gas masks she had made; she believed that those neighbors were now trying to kill them all with poison gasses. My mother always commented over her shoulder that being Grandma Foster's neighbors must have been pretty interesting.

Uncle Hugh went to Nebraska and worked as a hired hand on some other shit-hole farm. The last we heard from him was 1966—just before Mother died—when he wrote us a cheerful letter from the county jail, saying he had hit some guy so hard that the numbers bounced off his watch. After Mother died, my father had too many other things on his mind to try to track him down. His mother and father were both killed in a fire of mysterious origin, but because his mother was notorious for setting fire to things, everyone figured that their house was the final straw.

When my father had left home, armed with his high school diploma and his birth certificate, he took a train to Chicago, worked as a dishwasher, and waited out the month until he was eighteen. Then he joined the army.

Later, during the anti-Vietnam/Kent State days, my father would tell me that I simply couldn't be anti-military, because to some, like himself, the military life was an escape, a promise of a future, and a "desire personified rather than a crushing hand smashing life and obliterating freedom" (my father's eloquence probably should be followed with a [sic]). He said he thought killing was wrong, but he just couldn't be anti-military.

Through some intensified language program, the army taught him Japanese and sent him to Honolulu, no doubt as an interpreter. As I said, he was a crashing bore and didn't even use

that experience like Robert Altman did when he made *M.A.S.H.*
He didn't even have any good army stories except about the
time he almost died of food poisoning (if you like stories about
people throwing up), about how the coffee tasted like a "liquid
afterbirth," about the time he had a prostitute (not even any
"hot sex"—they ended up just *talking* and then having a "warm
personal friendship"—shit!), and about how, with some of
the other jerks, he had impersonated an officer over the phone
so they could go into town for a party. He was out just at the
beginning of the Great Depression.

When he came back from "overseas" (he always referred to
Honolulu as "overseas," as if he had been stationed in New
Guinea or something), he got a scholarship and went to college in the Midwest. He followed his heart in two ways. One:
he studied theatre instead of something useful, and Two: he
met and married Janet.

In retelling the story to us of how my father got mixed up
in his fated first marriage, Mother would dramatically tell
the part about their meeting. (Shit, she was an out-of-work
actress and had to practice on *someone*.) "These are the facts,"
she'd say with a look designed to indicate that it pained her
very much to tell this, but we knew she loved to. "These are
the facts. While carrying an old flat from one side of an empty
stage to the other, your father looked up and saw Porky Pig
in her prime!

"Now," she would say, gesturing with her hands, flipping
her wrists, and letting her long fingers follow, "now, I must
sidetrack away from all those facts and get into some feelings.
Feelings are, in fact, what do concern me. Facts are crap, because if you believe the facts, you can't understand the feelings." She inhaled her cigarette and blew the smoke out of
her nose and continued. "Janet was two round breasts, felt
through two sweaters, a slip, and a 38D support bra; she was
a few white inches of flesh above a stocking; she was fast
breathing and 'no, no, not any more—not that high'; she was
all round—round breasts, round ass, round face, round curves

—hot breath, hot promises, and those few fucking inches of white skin he was allowed to touch."

"And you?" I asked.

"I came along when Janet was 37, and her steamy college promises had been delivered as 15 years of occasional missionary position sex, and the breathing had been only to say 'no, no, no' and not to indicate desire. Christ! I had cool gray eyes; I was slim, delicate, ironic, passionate, young, a self-proclaimed multi-orgasmic woman; and I *delivered!* God, did I *deliver!* My heavy breathing was ecstasy—not promise. My breasts and thighs were *his,* and he buried his heart in my passion!"

Because I'd seen *Gone with the Wind* and *An Affair to Remember,* I knew about passion, even at eight. But I'd seen my father *live* with his passionate, young wife, and I just couldn't *imagine* good fucking was worth putting yourself through sheer hell.

She shook her hair. "I was young," she said softly, "when he was a slightly portly man of forty-six, afraid of his failing sexuality. I was what he needed right then—in 1948 . . . later, maybe not."

The truth (without Mother's additions and distortions) was that my father met and married Janet. She was not slim, cool, ironic, or passionate. Janet—I found out later after she came to live with us—must have been warm, loving, short, and curvy. She had sparkly brown eyes, did real cute things like push my father into snow banks, and, I'm sure from observing her behavior thirty years later, told him he could do everything he couldn't do, made him laugh, and let him cry. Their relationship—from what I pieced together from observing her and from stories here and there—was probably not much different from the one they had years later. She took care of him; they were occasional and not too passionate lovers. She was probably a very good wife. But she was not my mother. . . .

After their marriage in 1933 ("A quiet simple affair in the college chapel, how fucking sweet": my mother's comment) he became a civilian in charge of military education in California, a sinecure that lasted through most of World War II. Out of his usual respect for his wives, my father immediately instigated an affair with his secretary. While he was banging away, Janet and all her undelivered sexual promises washed his shorts, mopped the bathroom, and tried to get pregnant.

After giving the secretary the boot because she threatened to "tell," he of course took up with another woman, and they would drive out to the desert in a DeSoto, make passionate love, and drink Napa Valley wine. Maybe she was strong and left him; maybe she wanted to do his dishes and wash his shorts too; who knows, but he left her for another . . . and another . . . and another. . . .

My mother said he spent a few more years fucking over the public by working for the military, but since he had always thought of himself as an intellectual, he continually talked about "going back to school."

"God," said my mother, "all that fucking around . . . makes you sick, doesn't it?"

"He fucked around with you," I said, "and you thought *that* was okay."

"What?"

"You were his lover. That didn't make you sick."

"Darling," she said, raising her sunglasses and looking me directly in the eye, "I wasn't just a lover . . . I was the love of his *life!*"

I guess she expected the music to swell at this point, but when we just sat there staring at her, she said, "Life is so boring compared to *Troilus and Cressida.*"

"God," I said, "and I have a good seventy years left to go."

"Use it," she laughed. "Write your own parts."

HASTINGS, HEARTE & DANIELS

118 AVENUE OF THE AMERICAS

NEW YORK, NY 10013

July 15, 1974

Anne Sarah Foster
430 Pacific Avenue
San Francisco, CA 94133

Dear Annie,

    I can assure you that if I ever send you
a "we regret to inform you" letter, I <u>will</u>
regret it. I must admit I enjoy our correspondence.

    I do think, however, you had better add
that violence you were talking about. You'll
need to grab the readers pretty soon, or
they're going to give this the "deep six."
Although America does buy Norman Mailer, you
must not assume that people enjoy being bored.

    Your writing seems to take on the charac-
teristics of someone very young one moment, and
then it takes on the next moment the tone of
someone who has lived a long time. How old are
you anyway?

<u>Sincerely</u> yours,
Martin

P.S. Are you pretty?

July 18, 1974

Martin Goldsmith
Senior Editor
HASTINGS, HEARTE & DANIELS
118 Avenue of the Americas
NYC, N.Y. 10013

Dear Martin,

Okay, enclosed is the violence. I'm sorry
I waited so long before adding it, but as you
recall, you were pretty slow about reading my
terrific Chapter 1.

Would it be better if I were really young,
and a genius and all, or would it be better
if I were old and seeing things through young
eyes with all the insight that years of living
and suffering have given me? I could be which-
ever you think would go over better.

For your biographical note on the book
jacket: I was born in 1956 (not unlike the
Anne Sarah in the story, although she is fictional), my mother killed herself when I was
ten years old, and I am a writer who is using
tragedy for personal gain just like all the
fucking businessmen, politicians, and yellow
journalists in the world.

I am pretty—you know, long legs and all,
and I do want to be famous like Grace Metalious
and Scott Fitzgerald. I'm five feet eight,
weigh 117 lbs., and have a noble soul.

Sincerely yours,
Annie

P.S. What's this "deep six" bit? Were you in
the navy? My father was going to give us
"the deep six" all the time too.

chapter 5

My mother died in September of 1966, two days before the San Francisco public schools opened. When I mentioned to Holly that the one good thing to come out of this was we got to miss an entire week of school, she stared at me for a moment, and then pointed out that if I were to say such a thing to Dad, our bodies would probably be placed in the morgue next to Mother's. Of course she was just joking, for all that time, in spite of all my father's bad qualities, we actually didn't think he was capable of killing.

Because we saw murder all the time on TV, it wasn't real. Mother's classmates from Yale got murdered all the time on crime shows, and then showed up the next week on a soap or something. Death wasn't final; it was show biz!

The morning Mother did the suicide bit started off like any other morning. This meant we all got up not knowing what to expect from Mother and hoping for the best. I remember looking around my room and seeing the sun come in through the skylight. I climbed up on a footstool and looked through the window at the rose garden below, and I manufactured a whole network of spider webs with dew drops on them between the rose bushes. My mother was the kind of romantic who made me *want* to see them, but the kind of cynic who would say I was stupid for inventing them. Because Mother knew her realities were distorted, it disturbed her.

On the other side of The Birdbath, I heard Holly's radio playing "No Milk Today My Love Has Gone Away." Since I always thought that song reminded me of a Christmas carol, I remembered it didn't snow in San Francisco. Life would be really different without snow.

The night before, Holly had said my father was pissed off about moving here, but I didn't really believe it at the time because if you could have a skylight, a butler's pantry, and a real library with a ladder and all, well, it was worth leaving what Mother called "the armpit of academia"—Portland City University.

When Mother said that either theatre screws up people or screwed-up people like the theatre, I thought my father was rather fortunate to get out of all that shit, be able to go to the office, teach speech, and come home without worrying about rehearsals or taking the chance of "getting screwed up." Besides, he was in his early sixties anyway, so what did it matter?

I heard Holly get up. She walked through The Birdbath and leaned groggily against my door. "Early to bed, early to rise/ Makes a man healthy and wealthy and wise," she said.

"Don't be full of clichés, Holly," I said.

"Mother *always* talks in clichés," she groaned, stretching. She picked up my hairbrush and started to work on the night's tangles.

"*She* doesn't think so," I said.

Poor Mother, all her life she probably thought she was being so original, when you could read any second-rate play and find most of her dialogue—slightly laundered—but there just the same.

"Do you think Actors' Rep will take her?" I asked.

"They already have," she said. "It's just a question of money."

"She used to act for free in Oregon."

"There wasn't any money," she said. "I guess you were supposed to get off on the clapping. She always said she did it under the name of art."

"Shit, I know that," I sighed, "but Mother's not an artist."

"I know that; you know that; Dad knows that; even Mother, I think, knows it, but she says the world is easily fooled."

"When did she say that?" I asked.

"Remember," Holly said, "when we were in New York last year, and her old agent got her on a talk show even though she was a 'has been'?"

"Yeah, but, Holly, she really believes she's an artist . . . I *think*."

"Sure she does, but you know Mother, she had to let the folks out there in television land know she was putting something over on them."

"I don't get it," I said.

"Neither do I," she sighed.

Holly brushed her teeth. Since you just have to brush them again after breakfast, I never really saw the necessity of brushing them *before* breakfast. I put on a robe and went downstairs to the floor below. I noticed Mother in her bedroom sitting cross-legged in front of a full-length mirror. Because I knew she had been up late the night before, I decided it was best not to be pushy and say, "Good morning." She saw my reflection in the mirror.

"You hungry?" she asked—a strange question from her.

"Daddy and I went out walking last night and bought a coffee cake."

She was wearing a large, brown T-shirt and stared at me for a moment—her eyes wide.

"It's sort of a caramel nut kind," I said. "Fresh. You should go off your diet today 'cause Daddy says there's this kind of disease you can get where you can't eat *anything*, and you throw up all the time, and they have to feed you through a tube."

"A tube?" she laughed. "That sounds delicious!"

"Really, Mother," I said. She just stretched her arms high over her head and hummed "See What Tomorrow Brings."

"*You're not listening to me, Mother!*" I yelled. When she hummed like that, she was kind of scary.

"I am, darling," she said. "If I don't eat, they'll have to feed me out of a tube."

"You're pretty, Mother," I said.

"You don't have to flatter me," she snapped, "by saying I'm pretty, because I'm *beautiful!* You're beautiful, we are all beautiful, and this is a beautiful . . . uh . . . tea rose morning!"

"A tea rose morning?"

"You must learn to think in images, Annie."

"But that's a crappy image."

She pushed my hair out of my eyes. "You're your Mother's daughter," she said.

"But I'd *never* use a shit-o image like that."

"Listen," she sighed, "go eat your fucking coffee cake, tell that lazy sister of yours to get up, tell that father of yours to go somewhere so I won't have to look at his face, tell the world they aren't ready for me, and for God's sake, Annie, don't *ever* tell me my images are crappy again!"

When she sat down again, she crossed her legs, looked up at me, and was silent for what seemed like three minutes. She stared at me without blinking for such a long time that my eyes began to water in sympathy. Silence. You can't just walk away from someone who is staring at you so hard. She suddenly screamed so loud it startled me. "*Get the hell out of here, you little bitch!*" As I backed away, she crawled after me, grabbed my legs, and jerked so hard I fell on top of her. She buried her head in my lap and said very softly, "I'm so very sorry, Annie."

I looked up and noticed Holly standing behind me. She bent over and stroked Mother's hair. Mother looked up at us and smiled. Because a smile was the last thing we expected, it was kind of scary, but then, Mother was like that.

"Oh," she said, stretching her arms, "oh, the adventures I've lived and the people I've known. . . . Had I the patience to write them all down. Oh, had I the eloquence to do them justice. Annie, you could . . . you could because," she laughed, "you don't use crappy images, do you? Oh, if I could communicate what they meant to me. . . . And they *did* mean something to me. . . . "

"Who?" asked Holly.

"Who? You ask who, Holly?" We were both sorry she had asked that question. Mother thought for a while and then said, "All the people who gave me the excuse for suffering. God, suffering is much, *much* better than boredom!"

"What about when you make *other* people suffer because you're just bored?"

"I do *not* like to suffer!" she snapped. "Oh," she continued as if she hadn't been interrupted, "it is just like how I could never communicate to people that I'm really worth so much, much more than one would ever guess. It's just that I don't know how to *tell* them this."

"You could publish *The Diary of a Former Actress* or something," I suggested.

"*Former?*"

"Well, I mean, former . . . uh . . . Broadway," I said. I was getting hungry, and since it was Mother's habit to go through an entire *scene* rather than just one speech, I tried to end it by saying, "We like you. You're good."

"Or just once," she continued as if she hadn't heard me, "or just once could I have someone not tell me to be quiet when I cried." Grabbing my legs again and putting her head in my lap, she said, "Hold me, Annie, hold me . . . and I promise I'll make you laugh when it's over. I promise I'll listen when it's over. When it's over, I promise not to dig my fingernails into my breasts; or not starve myself; or not laugh at other people's failings or agree with those I despise. You don't have to love me to want this to stop. You just have to be human!"

"I love you, Mother," I said, now knowing exactly how to respond to this eloquence. For once, Holly was more at a loss than I was. She said nothing.

"Be quiet," Mother whispered. "Let me finish. I was just getting to the good part." Mother spoke in a rational, almost instructional tone of voice. "When your pain and your passion are all you've got that mean anything to you (besides your old letters, old loves, old scrapbooks, and your old hat with the lilacs on it), and your life is absent of passion, you tend to hang on to your pain . . . uh . . . just because that's all you've got left . . . uh, without it you're *nothing!*"

She got up and walked as dramatically as one can when all one is wearing is a brown Portland City University T-shirt, went over to the door of her room, turned around, and said cheerfully, "Scram. Your coffee cake is on. I can smell the bloody thing!"

As he took the coffee cake out of the oven, my father asked us what Kate was carrying on about upstairs.

"Usual stuff," said Holly.

"I guess," I added, "she just wants to believe that all the regular, normal stuff she feels—that everyone else feels too—is sort of holy."

"Where'd you get that, hon?" Daddy asked.

"Oh, she said it once."

"For someone who is as sucked in by herself as your mother is," he said, "she at least has an objective view of the situation."

"Maybe that's what screwed her up," said Holly, with her mouth full.

"Oh, your mother isn't screwed up," he said. "She just thinks it would make her a more distinctive person if she were."

"*That* sounds kind of screwed up to me," I said.

"Oh, we're all a little flaky at times," he said. "Listen, I've got to go over to campus. You girls draw straws for the dishes. I've got to run."

He gave us each a quick kiss.

"Aren't you going to brush your teeth?" Holly asked (I'm sure someday she'll be a dentist!).

"I'll get a mint downstairs in the library. I'm in a hurry."

"Shall I take some of this up to Mother?" Holly asked me.

"Naa . . . " I said. "She's on another damned diet. You wash, and I'll dry."

Now, I'm aware of the melodramatic fact that one tends to speak of a dead person in terms that are overly favorable or at least sentimental, so that's why I've made an attempt to be totally objective about Mother. Before she actually died, I don't think it occurred to either Holly or me to really decide whether or not we loved her. She was crazy, yeah, but until she kicked off, she was just as we had always known her: sometimes she was okay, and sometimes not. But that's the way it is with everybody, I guess. Poor Mother. She wanted so very much to be "different."

Because I was more like her than Holly, we got along better. Our favorite song was Judy Garland singing "Happiness is a Thing Called Joe." I mean, in spite of all our attempts to appear cynical, both of us loved to cry at shit movies. We'd sit and weep (while my father chuckled) at things like when Ralph Richardson—in *Dr. Zhivago*—says, "The Tzar's been shot." We would also cry *every time* in *Gone with the Wind* at the really dramatic part where Scarlett stuffs a turnip in her mouth and says, "I'll never be hungry again," and at the part where they are all looking at the casualty list and the band starts playing "Dixie" and everyone joins in even though they are still crying over all the dead people on the casualty list.

Mother was never religious, never a Christian, and she never even believed in Jesus (it probably had something to do with all the times *her* mother told her to "put her faith in Jesus Christ and things would be better"—I mean, that would have been enough to even turn off Thomas à Becket), but she went right ahead and sobbed in *Ben Hur* when Jesus stumbled under the cross and Charlton Heston tried to help him and the Roman soldiers pushed Chuck away. You see, Mother was always caught up in the drama of everything rather than the reality. The difference between Mother and me was that I loved all that dog crap too, but I do know it's the theatricality that I love. Until she killed herself, we thought that "deep down" Mother knew it too. *Knowing* you're full of shit can save your life.

My father kept saying that if he had gone upstairs that morning to brush his teeth, he might have been able to stop her, and Holly keeps saying we should have been more patient and taken her the coffee cake. Uncle Hollistor says Mother was determined to destroy herself—"After all, she went back to your father"—and she would have done it one way or another, so no one should blame himself.

That morning, in September of 1966, while Holly and I were doing the breakfast dishes, my mother shot herself with a gun my father had bought in Hawaii for decoration and self-defense.

When we heard the shot, I asked what it was, and Holly said casually that Mother had probably shot herself. Since it wasn't Mother's nature to set off explosives, and since it did sound as if the noise had come from upstairs, we both decided we had better investigate the situation. As I started to open Mother's bedroom door, I was stopped by a note attached to the doorknob. It read, "Holly and Annie. Do not open the door. I am dead. Love, Mother."

When you're ten, or any age for that matter, do you *believe* a note like that? The first thing I saw when I opened the door was a bloody ashtray, then blood on the carpet. Although I think I stared at the room for a full minute, I remember nothing else about what I saw. I don't know whether or not it was selective amnesia or just that I didn't need to look further. I remember Holly screaming, and I remember slamming the bedroom door and shaking her. "When I said she'd shot herself," she cried, "I was only kidding . . . I was only kidding!" As I shook her, she started crying—not for Mother yet, but out of shock. I didn't know any San Francisco telephone numbers or anyone in San Francisco to call. I really don't know how long it was before I went to the hall extension of the phone and calmly told the operator that my mother had shot herself.

Leaning against the wall, I took several deep breaths. Holly stood still and watched me. "What would Mother say now?" I asked. Holly didn't answer. "You know what she'd say, Holly?" The tears were starting to come to me. "She'd say, 'Use it, Annie, use it.'"

When the police finally reached my father at school, his initial reaction was panic. Later, he expressed almost entirely hate and bitterness. All he could say was, "How could she do that to two little girls?" I lay on my bed all that afternoon trying to figure out why, and Holly sat silently in her room, and my father efficiently went about taking care of things.

Because Mother had always said suicide notes were cheap ways to get sympathy, she left only a Last Will and Testament. I don't know whether or not she typed it out that morning, but it read:

I, Mary Kate McNeil Foster, being of sound body and sound enough mind to make out a will, do hereby bequeath to . . .

My daughters Annie and Holly, my amethyst necklace, my love and apologies, and the knowledge that I died with clean hair whilst sober as the three of us once had that discussion about suicide victims (for we *are* victims, you know) who wander around for days before the event with greasy hair and chain-smoke all the time.

To my best friend Hollistor Kent I leave the "Letters-to-ruin-people's-lives-with" that he gave me last Christmas, and I give him my permission to mail any of them out he likes. Also I leave my love and apologies, my underlined copy of *Peyton Place*, and since this is too dramatic to waste, my permission to write a play about the death of Kate.

To old Janet Foster, I leave her goddamned ex-husband.

To all the men who have had me (in every sense of the word "had"), I leave nothing and no apologies.

To my husband and love of my life, Matthew Foster, I leave my glass bird because it belongs with all the Easter eggs I made for him.

> Who really died, we'll never know.
> Perhaps someday we all will go.
> One death kills two and often more:
> That's what suicides are for!

P.S. If it could be arranged, I'd like to have Marlon Brando at my funeral.

I don't think my father would have ever let me read it, but in the confusion of that afternoon, I found the typed sheet next to my mother's door. My father read it. He didn't cry or anything like that. He just stood there for a long time. Finally, he said, "She was crazy; she was mad; she was awful. And her poem wasn't even original."

118 AVENUE OF THE AMERICAS

NEW YORK, NY 10013

July 23, 1974

Anne Sarah Foster
430 Pacific Avenue
San Francisco, CA 94133

Dear Annie,
        Because this chapter really held my atten-
tion, I now believe I will be able to interest
our editorial board in your work. Of course,
I was waiting for the suicide, and now that
you've given it to us, I do hope your book
hasn't peaked at Chapter 5.
        I think it is wonderful you are young.
Looking at old themes, young eyes often see new
shapes—new forms.
        I hope you will notice the "sincerely"
before the "yours" this time.

                        Sincerely yours,
                        Martin

430 Pacific Avenue
San Francisco, CA 94133

July 31, 1974

Martin Goldsmith
Senior Editor
HASTINGS, HEARTE & DANIELS
118 Avenue of the Americas
NYC, N.Y. 10013

Dear Martin,
God, I like that—"new forms." I hadn't
really thought about it that way. Since I was
trying to write a purely commercial property
designed to make people think they're reading
literature, I was amazed when you seemed to
really like what I'd written.
As my mother dreamed of losing so much
weight she could eat anything she wanted to
without feeling guilty, I must admit I dream of
writing something so important that no one will
blame me if I don't write another thing. You
know: a "one book novelist" like Harper Lee,
who's probably sitting around in Alabama col-
lecting her royalty checks. When you're in a
play and it's over, well, that's it, but when
you've written something "important," well, you
can read it over and over again for life.

Love,
Annie

P.S. Do you really think it is good?

chapter 6

"Your father," my mother said, "needed mistresses. With the exception of me, they probably never knew that under that good lay there was a very unoriginal man." This was two summers before she died. While Holly and I were fighting the heat in the country club pool, Mother tanned her body and read a script Uncle Hollistor had sent her. She always picked odd occasions to fill us in on the past. When I was eight, the past didn't interest me in the least. I don't think the past interests anyone who really doesn't have any—maybe that's why the future didn't interest Mother: something must have told her she didn't have any.

Mother turned over on her stomach and turned completely around so her chin was resting on the edge of the pool. "Never love a businessman, Annie," she said.

"But Daddy isn't a businessman," I said.

"No, honey," she answered. "He's a businessman at heart who somehow got an 'artist complex.' "

"Aren't you really a wife at heart who somehow got an artist complex?" I asked.

"I was an artist who wanted to be loved. Is that so fucking hard for you to understand!" she yelled and put her hand on my head and pushed me in under the water. Because I thought she was just teasing me, I didn't panic until I realized she wasn't going to let go. When I finally fought my way to the surface, she was laughing.

Holly looked disturbed. "It seems like it would be a lot easier," she said, "if we all were just what we are."

She was suddenly really pissed off. "*Listen, you ass!*" she screamed. "If that's the way you feel about it, you guys were designed to play with dolls, respect your elders, and be seen and not heard, so shut your ass!" We treaded water, she threw down Hollistor's script and picked up *The Group*. She turned her back to us.

"I'm sorry, Mommy...."

She was crying. "Annie, Holly, you know if I had wanted to be what I was, I never would have been an actress, and if your father wanted to be what *he* was, he would have been a branch credit manager and never married me."

"And me?" I asked.

"While you're still young . . . a child, pretend to be what you're not. It's still just called play . . . yes, play. Play before you're too old."

I didn't understand. "You're not old, Mommy."

She cried for a moment, and then started to laugh. "I'm too old for ruffles, too old for youth fare, the kiddie menu, Cheerios, chocolate sodas, Juliet, plans, dreams...."

"You're *thirty-four*, Mother!"

"I know. I know."

On the other side of the coin, my father was always giving us the business about going to graduate school so we could make a "substantial contribution to society."

"Did *you* make a substantial contribution to society?" Holly asked him once.

"I became a college professor," he said with the same tone of voice you would expect someone to use when saying, "I invented the wheel."

"Mother says that college professors are mainly responsible for the deterioration of society."

My father chuckled. "If I hadn't become a college professor, I never would have met your mother," he laughed. "And," he continued, "I never would have married her, and she would still be at large in the world spreading her nasty rumors about college professors beyond the confines of our family."

We all giggled but were hushed up by the sight of Mother standing in the doorway with an awful expression on her face. "Your 'substantial contribution to society,'" she said icily, "is one-fourth of a book on 'The Function of the Maid in Greek Tragedy,' which nobody gives a rusty fuck about anyway!"

"Kate . . ." he said so evenly it scared us.

"Watch it," she laughed, "or I'll spread the awful truth about college professors." She grinned at us and then whispered, "Watch it."

Besides being responsible for the deterioration of society, according to Mother, another ugly truth about college professors was that they were "fucking underpaid." She was always bitching about money. Holly and I both agreed that it would be pretty horrible to depend on some man for money.

"Your father," said my mother, "makes less than an automobile factory worker. Shit! And he gets *credit* for it because he nobly teaches other suckers to do the same thing."

Holly looked at her. She was driving along McAdam Avenue, which ran along the Willamette River into downtown. Since she rarely watched the road when she drove, we sort of wondered each time we reached a destination how we had got there alive.

"But you *said*," Holly exclaimed, "that you could never love a businessman, and they're the only ones who make any money nowadays."

"Actresses do."

"I read somewhere," I said, "that only five percent of all working actors make over five thousand dollars a year!"

"*I* made over five thousand dollars in summer stock and doing commercials while I was still a *student!*" she shouted.

Mother wore several gold bracelets that clinked together while she lifted her cigarette to her mouth; then, with cigarette in hand, she adjusted her sunglasses, said "Fuck," as a light ahead turned red, and shifted the car back into neutral with a terrific metallic sound of clanking bracelets.

"Choices," she said out of the blue.

"Choices?"

The light changed, and Mother went through the whole process of taking a drag from her cigarette, shifting the car, and adjusting her sunglasses and bracelets.

"I chose that fuck-o."

"How come you call him a fuck-o if you love him . . . you always say how much you love him," I asked.

"Listen, little child, have you in your short and very under-lived life ever heard of the word *because?*"

"*Because* he was an el-fuck-o you loved him?"

"*Because because because because!*" she screamed.

She drove the car off the road so quickly that for a moment I saw my life pass before my eyes, the car going right off the bank into the river, and our bodies tagged for identification in the morgue. She stopped it with a jerk, got out, and started walking very quickly down McAdam Avenue toward downtown.

"Mommy, where are you going?"

She didn't answer, but walked out into the traffic, ignored the cars that barely missed her, kept walking on the wrong side of the road, and disappeared around the bend.

"Where do you suppose she went?"

"Hell if I know," Holly said.

After what seemed like about half an hour later, Mother's tear-streaked face appeared at the window of the car. She tapped on it, and Holly rolled it down. She shoved a box of doughnuts in, looking over her shoulder all the time as if she were passing an illegal narcotics shipment to us, and said, "I thought you little farts might be hungry."

"Thanks," Holly said, "we were."

118 AVENUE OF THE AMERICAS

NEW YORK, NY 10013

August 4, 1974

Anne Sarah Foster
430 Pacific Avenue
San Francisco, CA 94133

Dear Annie,
    I believe you have too much ambition to
become a "one book author." Also, HASTINGS,
HEARTE & DANIELS isn't always pleased to invest
in a "one book author."
    Because I think I like you, I'd really
like to help you channel some of this ambition
into a serious effort. I feel this chapter to
be unfocused and insufficiently related to the
previous chapter. Perhaps the book itself
requires a clearer focus. Think about an outline. When I see more clearly where this manuscript might be going, I can help guide you in
making it a more marketable book.

                                    Best,
                                    Martin

```
                              430 Pacific Avenue
                              San Francisco, CA 94133

                              August 7, 1974

Martin Goldsmith
Senior Editor
HASTINGS, HEARTE & DANIELS
118 Avenue of the Americas
NYC, N.Y. 10013

Dear Martin,
     You're fucked. As far as I'm concerned,
your job is to make sure my spelling and punc-
tuation are right before you shove this off to
the printers. Save the literary criticism for
the critics.

                              All my love, anyway,
                              Annie

P.S. Do you have any pull toward getting this
     into the Book-of-the-Month Club?
```

chapter 7

If my mother's stories about my father's first wife, Janet, were to be believed, she wasn't really hot stuff in the sexual department.

Well, after she came to live with us, I really could believe it. Since she was the type who always wore beige doubleknit pantsuits that were a tad bit too short, I'm sure that all her life she was out of style—not that it mattered, but. . . . And I don't think Mother called her "Porky Pig" for nothing; she *did* look like Porky Pig—round-faced, cheerful. She was kind of the Julia Child type—the kind of person you'd really like to know, but couldn't see yourself passionately kissing in a round red bed. Because, according to Mother, my father was the champagne, roses, and steamy sex type, I can kind of see why he was always fucking around.

"Mistakes," Mother used to say, "ahh . . . mistakes."

My mother's mother, who was a palm reader, a reincarnation believer, and a handwriting analyst, once studied my father's handwriting and came to the conclusion that he had one of the strongest sexual drives she had ever seen come across on paper. Supposedly, when the tails of your "g's" and "p's" are long and reach through the line below, you have a strong sexual drive.

"He did," Mother would say. Sex education for us was in the form of a romance colored by Mother's memory and imagination. "Ah, when I was twenty," she said. "Summer . . .

Brown from the sun, I smelled like fresh cut grass. I would lie in the sun on the grass, dive into the water, come up and see him—standing under a tree in a three-piece suit—watching my body move. And I'd pretend not to see him. I'd stretch and dive again and again, and finally lie on the grass . . . wet. He'd come over then, kiss my neck, my hair, my eyes, and we'd walk across campus to his office, and I'd leave wet footprints all the way up the stairs. When the door was locked, he'd kiss my breasts, my back, my legs, my cunt—fuck me all over the floor. And I'd be wet from the pool, wet from him, shaking with joy—he did give me joy, you know. He loved every part of me: my eyes, my hands, my hair, my youth . . . That's what it is . . . all the audiences in the world couldn't love me like that . . . wet, sweating, smiling. . . . "

"I'm not going to let that happen to me," I said.

She laughed. "When I was a kid, I thought intercourse . . . screwing, whatever, sounded gross too."

"No, I don't think it sounds gross. I'd like to screw Gregory Peck, maybe."

"Then it will happen to you . . . I can see it now, Annie and Gregory Peck . . . his deep voice, her long legs. . . . "

"No, I don't mean sex—I mean romance."

"*Romance?*"

"It seems a whole lot of people have given up a whole lot of things for it. I'm not."

"Then you'll have to write your own roles, Annie, because sex runs the world."

"You're full of shit, Mother," I said, and she slapped me across the face.

While we were on our way to the Oregon coast for what Mother called one of those "grotesque family-type vacations," Holly and I sat on an air mattress in the back of our station wagon, eating "Sweet Tarts" and listening to Mother talk about sex. My father's pipe smoke was making us both sick because it was blowing back, but we knew not to interrupt Mother.

"You never loved any of your mistresses," she said to him.

"I loved you," he said.

"*I* was different—I mean any of your fuckettes."

"Kate, I can really think of a thousand better things to talk about."

"Well, then say something articulate that doesn't have to do with the lovely Oregon scenery or our fucking *future!*" she snapped.

"Talk about whatever you want to, Kate," he said. "I find it very hard to be articulate under pressure."

She laughed. "You never loved any of your mistresses because you really loved Janet a lot, didn't you?" she chided.

Holly whispered that Mother was probably feeling guilty again about busting up his first marriage. When she was feeling guilty, she always started in on how much Janet had meant to him. We knew she was just trying to come off as a generous person.

My father sighed. Obviously conversations about his past sex life either bothered or bored him. There was a long silence, and then very uncharacteristically he said, "I did love one."

"*Ah HA!*" yelled Mother, and then a little too eagerly asked, "Whom?"

"Oh, she was a girl named Shawna in one of my productions in Wisconsin."

"*Shawna!*" laughed Mother. "God, her parents had dog puke taste—that's worse than Gladys!"

My father continued. "Her father—even if he did have bad taste—was a very famous heart surgeon."

"So," said Mother sarcastically, "if sexy Shawna broke someone's heart, he could fix it up right away!"

"He wasn't able to fix mine."

"Did you love her as much as you loved me?"

"No—I never loved anyone as much as I loved you."

"Watch that past tense," warned Mother. "Did you love her more than Porky Pig?"

"*Janet,*" my father corrected. "No, I didn't. Does that please you?"

"It doesn't surprise me." She was silent for a while, looking at the motel billboards as we approached the coast. "Deep down," she said, "I think you don't love anybody."

My father didn't answer.

"You're *supposed* to say," she said angrily, "I love *you*, Katie!"

"I love you, Katie," he said sadly.

For the next couple of weeks, Mother pestered my father with thousands of questions about Shawna, whom Mother kept referring to as the "number one fuckette." The only info she could squeeze out of him was that Shawna was afraid her mother was going to kill herself, so when my father took her home, she'd make him wait in the car while she went in to see if her mother were still alive. "You just get off on sickies," Mother said. "Ahh . . . fuck her!"

When Shawna married a medical student, my father lost contact with her. "Well," my father would say, "her father was a doctor, and it is said that women always look for their father when they marry."

"Ah . . . what is love?" Mother asked in a tone of voice that was halfway between sarcasm and sadness.

"Love, my beauty," said my father, "is being able to stand someone day in and day out." He took a sip of beer and turned another page of *Life* magazine.

"Well, I guess I must be just a passion," Mother said. "You can't stand me, can you?" she asked in a teasing voice.

Ignoring me, my father got up, went to her, and started unzipping her dress. I figured it was time for me to go to bed.

118 AVENUE OF THE AMERICAS

NEW YORK, NY 10013

August 14, 1974

Anne Sarah Foster
430 Pacific Avenue
San Francisco, CA 94133

Dear Annie,

First: my job involves a little more than correcting spelling and punctuation before I send the book to the printers. Since I've yet to decide whether or not HASTINGS, HEARTE & DANIELS will even have its editorial board look at <u>Heritage</u>, I would suggest you be less obviously arrogant until the contract is signed. Because I believe you have talent, because I admire your clean and direct technique, and because I like you, I've taken on the rather bothersome task of reading one chapter at a time whenever you happen to finish it. We must respect each other, or this will never work.

Second: Are your recent chapters short because you like to write letters to me, because the book <u>did</u> peak with the suicide, or because short chapters are becoming your style?

Best,
Martin

430 Pacific Avenue
San Francisco, CA 94133

August 17, 1974

Martin Goldsmith
Senior Editor
HASTINGS, HEARTE & DANIELS
118 Avenue of the Americas
NYC, N.Y. 10013

Dear Martin,
 I am now on my knees: You are a <u>wonderful</u>
editor—so perceptive. Because you understand
my artistic temperament so well, I have nothing
but the <u>highest</u> respect for you. (Is that
better?)
 Now: Have you ever read Kurt Vonnegut?
Have you ever heard anyone complain about <u>his</u>
short chapters? If you want me to move away
from my "clean, direct technique," the chapters
could be longer, but that might be more boring
than <u>The Tin Drum</u>. Look, if this is only 300
pages long, you can <u>still</u> sell it for $10.95.

Peace,
Annie

P.S. Have <u>you</u> ever written anything?

chapter **8**

After receiving his belated Ph.D. from the University of Wisconsin, my father had hoped to teach there. No way. His dissertation was on "The History of the Traveler Curtain" (I swear), and I guess the faculty at Wisconsin didn't think the students would be enriched with his vast knowledge of this subject. Because his course work was only "workmanlike," his job recommendations from the faculty weren't exactly glowing. He had only two job offers from all the places he applied, and if you can believe it, the *better* job was at Portland City University.

"The drama department there was a mess," my father would say. "The kids barely looked up from their card game in the student lounge to glance at me." He paused for a moment and said, "But Oregon was a beautiful state. . . . "

"Oh," Mother would say in this often-repeated conversation, "so you stay on and on and on here because Oregon is a *beautiful state!*"

"I did not say that was my reason for *staying;* I just said it was a beautiful state."

"*Christ!*" she would say. "I suppose if you had taken the job in South Dakota, you would say *it* was a 'beautiful state'?"

"You're acting as if I were making excuses."

"Aren't you?" She shook her long hair. "Everything else you do is justified with an excuse. My excuse was I loved you, and yours—Jesus!—is that Oregon is a fucking beautiful state!"

My father said nothing.

Mother laughed. "I guess there *is* no excuse for staying on and on and on."

"I like it."

"Sure you do. It's easy, you run things, the students are so jack shit they don't know you're only an expert on traveler curtains, and you would have a very difficult time finding a job anywhere else."

For a minute, my father was silent. "Do you suppose he'll hit her?" Holly whispered to me.

My father chuckled. "Well, Kate, *you* not only went to school there, but, my brilliant one, you stayed there and graduated."

"*That,*" she said, stroking his face, "was because the love of my life was there."

Portland actually was a nice little city. Although Oregon was "nowhere for theatre," it was into ecology, outlawed pop top cans, and elected Senator Morse. It was built on a river and unlike L.A. or Omaha, if you didn't venture too far away from the old sections, you could call it "not offensive to good taste." Mother called it a "Shit Hole" and Holly always pointed out to her that she had a way of turning *any* place she happened to be into a shit hole. "*Life's* what is so shitty for you," she said. "Not Portland."

"Ah . . . life," Mother had articulately answered.

In 1948, my father began his uneventful career at Portland City University. Although he didn't remember the first time he saw Mother, of course Mother remembered it very well. Like me, my mother was blessed (cursed?) with an unusual memory for details. My father often said that Mother's head was so stuffed with details that the general picture was distorted. We tended to agree with him.

During registration week of my mother's sophomore year, she saw my father for the first time. She had walked over to the theatre to see who was hanging around, and my father was hurrying down the stairs from his office to go over to the gymnasium to continue registering all those jerks who probably thought if you majored in drama at Portland City University, you'd become a big star like Diana Lynn. Shit.

My mother was standing in the foyer of the theatre, examining the new pictures of the previous year's productions to see if there were any good ones of her, and ignoring some guy who had walked over there with her. As he told her how he felt "intensely about the process of turning a dead page into living action," Mother yawned, looked up the stairs, and saw my father. Mother said something tacky to us like, "I saw the sun rise in his eyes," but we'd seen pictures of my father taken in 1948—slightly paunchy, gray hair, evil looking—so we *knew* he just didn't have the kind of eyes the sun rose in. Warren Beatty, yes—my father, no.

Mother had laughed her throaty laugh. "You must be the new theatre history man who knows all about traveler curtains," she said (rumors spread fast in drama departments). At that time in her life she looked like Candice Bergen, was less bony, less calculating, less bitter, and from what my father reports, much kinder.

"Uh, yes," he said without even breaking his stride. Because this was his first teaching job after all those years of working for the military and plowing his way through graduate school, he really wanted to show how professional he was. A professional doesn't even stop for a beauty.

Since she knew he was going to be casting *Uncle Vanya* soon, Mother figured she had better say *something* so he'd remember her. She moved quickly toward him, took his bearded chin in her gloved hands, and kissed him lightly on the cheek. "I'm Katie McNeil," she said, "and I'm talented!"

My father did stop then, gave his wonderful laugh, and took her hand. "My God, you're beautiful—and talented too, well, well, well," he chuckled. "I'm happy to know you, Katie McNeil."

He resumed his walk toward the door and went out whistling.

"God, I like his mouth and laugh," she said to the boy beside her.

"I heard he's a real creep," said the boy.

"Yeah," she laughed, "so did I."

Poor Father: he had just met the woman who was going to royally screw up his life, and he had said he was "happy to know her." Shit. Poor Mother: he didn't even remember that wonderful scene.

The first time he remembers seeing her, she was sitting in the student lounge under the *Oedipus Rex* poster, wearing a hat over one eye.

"You know," he said with a laugh one evening at dinner, "when I came for an interview at Portland City, there was a pair of dirty tennis shoes under the coffee table in that lounge, and when I accepted the appointment in the fall, those goddamned shoes were still there."

"Well, what does that signify?" Mother asked.

"Does something always have to signify something, Katie?" he asked, "or may I just tell my daughters an amusing story?"

"Well, I think the whole thing is disgusting," she said, "the way that whole department had gone down the tube." She paused and smiled at him. "What was even more disgusting was the way you let it *stay* that way."

"I picked up the shoes," he said lightly.

"Ah, yes, dear, yes," she said. "You *did* pick up the shoes, didn't you?"

My father shook his head and said to us, "I remember your mother and your Uncle Hollistor . . . she was so pretty . . . 'such a waste,' I thought . . . I didn't know how well she hid talent and ambition. They'd sit there, you know, with their feet up on the radiator and talk about *musicals.* I was trying to teach baroque scenery, and they would talk about *South Pacific.*"

"Not *South Pacific,*" Mother interrupted. "I was only interested in the ones with the obligatory 'Latin American' scene."

Stirring her wine with a fork, she shook her head at my father. "Tell them the rest of the story," she said. "Tell them what you said to me."

"Your mother," he said, "was drinking a cup of the department's coffee. . . . "

"No, no, I'll tell it!" she interrupted. "You don't tell stories well—it is so important to tell stories the right way—you know, the sounds, the smells, the dirt. . . . " She leaned forward and said, "That coffee tasted like something someone had thrown up, and Hollistor and I were saying how much we liked lots of confetti and pink fans in musicals, and your father was planning a jack shit season of real interesting plays for us like *Friar Bacon and Friar Bungay*."

"Musicals don't belong in academic theatre," my father put in.

"*Academic theatre!*" she laughed. "You're trying to call *Portland City University* academic theatre!" My father cleared his throat. "*None* of us," she hissed, "including you, my love, belonged in academic theatre. At least Hollistor and I weren't being pretentious about things." She waited for my father to answer, and when she saw she had beaten him at that one, she said, "Anyway, we were right at the net stockings, when our lively chat was suddenly disrupted by your father storming down the stairs yelling, 'Whose car is that parked out in front of the theatre!' " She laughed and went on. "He sounded like Hitler—he really did. 'Well,' I said, 'it's mine. Don't you remember me? I'm the one who's talented!' " Pouring herself another glass of wine, she went on. "And he really thundered —I mean, like the building shook—'*Talented or not, it gives you no right whatsoever to park your car in front of the building where it says no parking!*' And I said, 'Cool it, Foster. Don't pop your cookies, I'll move it.' "

She laughed very hard, stopped, and waited for us to join her. Because our father had a fork in his hand, we just managed a lame smile. "You know what that man told me?" she asked. Since she was shaking in a weird way, we didn't answer.

"He told me," she said, choking on her wine and laughing, "that I'd get a lot further in life if I didn't sass him back. Did you hear *that*? I'd get a lot further in life—further in *life*—if I didn't sass him back! He actually said 'sass'!"

"What did you say?" I asked.

She put her face in her hands and whispered, "I didn't say anything . . . you see, I was in love with him."

HASTINGS, HEARTE & DANIELS

118 AVENUE OF THE AMERICAS
NEW YORK; NY 10013

August 21, 1974

Anne Sarah Foster
430 Pacific Avenue
San Francisco, CA 94133

Dear Annie,

Well, since you ask, I have written two full-length novels. Although I managed to avoid the draft, I have been very interested in the role of the individual man in the military machine. My novels are both about navy life—mostly taken from my brother's letters. He was killed in World War II.

I tell you this because I want to let you know that although I may seem hard-boiled, I do know what writers go through. Also, I too considered my novels very good, and they are yet unpublished.

You have a writer's spirit, Annie. I'd
like to see you finish this.
Can you give me a hint as to how this is
going to end?

Best,
Martin

----

430 Pacific Avenue
San Francisco, CA 94133

August 28, 1974

Martin Goldsmith
Senior Editor
HASTINGS, HEARTE & DANIELS
118 Avenue of the Americas
NYC, N.Y. 10013

Dearest Martin,
If I were to tell you the ending, I'd be
able to see into the future. My grandmother—
on my mother's side—claimed she could, but I'm
sorry, that gift just isn't running through my
DNA. Besides, you wouldn't want me to spoil
the suspense, would you? I want to give you the
true pleasure of experiencing my story while
it unfolds, just as a reader would. If you know
what happens, how the hell are you supposed to
have a fresh approach to it?
Let me give you some weekly entertainment,
okay?
How did you avoid the draft and not get
in the navy? Were you deformed in your childhood or something? Were you a foreign correspondent? Why the hell don't you just snip all

that red tape there at old HASTINGS, HEARTE &
DANIELS and get your crappy war novels
published?

What do you look like anyway? If you
aren't deformed, do you wear polyester leisure
suits or anything jerk-o like that? Are you
real New York hip, or one of those Harvard
English majors who couldn't bear the thought of
teaching?

I'm curious about you. Do you really
believe in me?

Love,
Annie

chapter 9

During the summer of 1949, when Kate, my mother, was nineteen, she came to what she later called "the fork in her life" and decided her affair with Matt Foster, my father, had to stop. She had several choices. One: she could leave Oregon without a word, go back home to San Francisco, and make him beg her to come back. Two: she could put all her energies into "making it big" and show him he was only a stepping-stone on her pathway to fame. Three: she could ask him to give Janet the boot in the ass, marry her, and live happily ever after. I guess because all the movies in 1949 ended with someone getting married and living Happily Ever After, she had been brainwashed into believing that rot.

My father called at nine in the morning. She was asleep in her fifty-five-dollar-a-month apartment with the antique bed. Because it was Monday, she hadn't got fresh flowers for the table yet. Since Matt, my father, couldn't come over on weekends, she never bothered to fix up the place until Monday. His weekends were filled with interesting things like taking Janet to the hairdresser, going to the grocery store, and picking up cleaning. Although those are the things that make marriages so tedious, Kate longed to share them with Matt. She'd never been in a goddamned grocery store with him, and somehow romanticized it. She always imagined the two of them in the produce or wine section but never thought about having to buy toilet paper or toothpaste. Because she found it hard to enjoy a minute of her life that wasn't spent with him, Kate couldn't imagine he'd ever enjoy a minute of his life that was not spent with her. When he had a nice weekend on the Oregon coast with Janet, she was livid.

Since it was summer, there were no classes. Grandmother and Grandfather had suggested that Kate come home to San Francisco during the summer and decide what she wanted to do with her life. Because her mother was a little crackers and hard to get along with, and because Matt was in Portland, she decided to stay in Oregon. When Kate didn't do exactly what the old bat wanted, she didn't get any money from home, so Kate uncharacteristically said she would go to work.

She got a job in a tavern. While hoping that sometime during the summer her "right direction" would hit her, she wiped tables and fucked Matt Foster (but not at the same time, of course).

The past spring, she had been accepted at Yale Drama School. She didn't really want to go there; her ambitions were self-destructive: she wanted to "give it all up" for my father. Kate was a reasonably talented actress who had the belief that anything to which she set her mind would eventually come her way. Because my father often said he didn't think she was much good, she didn't tell him she had auditioned for Yale; she didn't want him to discourage her.

The regional auditions for Yale were held in San Francisco, and Kate took the Southern Pacific to Oakland and got a bus to San Francisco. She sat next to a dull, average-looking man who struck up a conversation with her. Since Kate rarely told strangers the truth, she decided to speak in a British accent to spice up the journey, and naturally he asked her where she was from. She explained that she was from Australia and was taking a trip down to Mexico City because her husband had been murdered in Vancouver, B.C., and she needed to forget. He mumbled he was sorry to hear that and said he was going to San Francisco to assist with the auditions for Yale Drama

School. "Perhaps then," said Kate in her most American voice, "you would care to walk with me to 450 Geary Street. I believe we are going to the same place."

"Figures," he said.

Even though it was late February, it was warm, and Kate looked good considering that she had just spent fourteen hours in a train. As she sat in Union Square feeding the pigeons with the unfinished half of the coffee roll her friend on the bus had bought her, she went over her audition piece.

At two o'clock she walked down Geary Street and up five flights of stairs in the building across from the Geary Theatre (the ancient elevator didn't seem to be working that day), and sat around with all the other people trying to look casually theatrical.

She really couldn't hear much of what was going on in the other room, but she did hear that everyone before her had to sing "Happy Birthday," so the judges could get an idea of voice quality, she guessed. When she was called, she went in, looked the three judges right in the eye, was disappointed that her bus friend wasn't there, did her audition piece, and stood around with her teeth in her mouth. "Thank you, Miss McNeil," said the oldest one of the three.

"Uh . . . you're welcome."

"That will be all, Miss McNeil."

"Oh." She awkwardly picked up her coat.

"Are you waiting for something, Miss McNeil?"

"Oh, no . . . ah . . . well, ah . . . I thought you might want me to sing 'Happy Birthday,' but it's no big deal."

"Oh, that won't be necessary."

At that point Katie decided she didn't want to be an actress anyway. She walked down four of the five flights of stairs. The stairs went down in such a way that one could look down from the top all the way to the street floor. When she was just about to reach the bottom stair, one of the three judges called down to her. "Miss McNeil!"

Kate looked up four floors.

"We have decided we couldn't let you go all the way to Mexico City without hearing you sing 'Happy Birthday.' "

Kate practically ran all the way up the stairs trying to decide whether or not she should be pissed off or pleased that her bus friend must have related the story about her dead husband, belted out "Happy Birthday" in a way that would have made Pearl Bailey worry, shook hands all around, picked up her coat, and made a grand exit, the way Mother always did so beautifully.

Six weeks later, she was accepted at Yale. Her first move was to rush down to the theatre at Portland City University, pick the lock (she and Hollistor had devised an easy way of breaking in, so they could play the piano in the middle of the night), and place her letter of acceptance on the wall that held all her pictures and reviews. After backing up and looking at it with satisfaction, she realized that it wasn't a very smart move as far as Matt Foster, my father, was concerned. She figured it was just the kind of excuse he needed to keep on with his boring, comfortable life with Janet and send her off to cold New Haven. No, better stick around for the summer and make him need her.

Because my father didn't relish the prospect of finding a new mistress, he was delighted that Kate was planning to stay for the summer. Since he was getting old and was not as attractive as he had once been, beautiful blondes who looked like Candice Bergen, were interesting company and good pieces of ass, *and* came equipped with father complexes weren't running around all over the place. My mother spent the spring finishing up credits so she could graduate a year early, lying out in the sun around the campus pool, and thinking about the man she loved and how to persuade him she was not replaceable.

I can't imagine blowing a chance to go to Yale Drama School for a man, but unlike Mother I don't live for passionate moments. Because I appreciate them, though, I am like her.

When classes finished, Mother—with her useless B.A.—made an attempt to get a job as a secretary. Since she made too many mistakes typing, her effort didn't work out. Finally, she got a job in this tavern that had a loud Jimmy Rushing-type jazz band. I remember later when my father used to accuse her of always having had an easy life, she would say, "Have you ever *ever* carried five million pounds of beer glasses for eight hours? I did . . . for *you!*" Mother tended to exaggerate.

Actually, the tavern was called "The Ole Water Hole" and was decorated with a Western motif. There were these little sections of the huge room called "The Dance Hall," "The Saloon," "The Jail," etc., all filled with tables. They had mezzanines all around the top that held pool tables and were fine for dropping pool balls over the railings on the cocktail waitresses when the customers above desired service. When Mother would tell us that the whole place was full of professional hookers as well as girls who just fucked without having to have a "relationship," her eyes would light up.

The guys who came in "The Ole Water Hole" were either servicemen in town who heard that this tavern was a "swinging place" or guys looking for the hookers. Because the management charged a cover charge and watered the drinks, they made pots of money in spite of the people they hired. Their first idea was to hire girls who were over five feet nine inches tall, so you could see their noses over the Western bar. Since Mother was tall, they took her even though she spilled things. When they discovered their pay and hours didn't attract all that many leggy, tall girls, they relented and hired *anybody*— including the head bar girl, who was an admitted prostitute and used the place as a front for lining up johns, and the bartender, who couldn't go back to Iowa because he was wanted for embezzling ten thousand dollars from an insurance company. Mother said it made Dickens' sweatshops look like I. Magnin. After being there only one month, she discovered she had been there longer than anybody, including the owners. That's what a swell place it was to work in.

While she was there, Uncle Hollistor was in Chicago getting his master's degree. He sent her a postcard with this dead man on it, lying in the middle of the desert surrounded by cows' skulls, being eaten by vultures. On the back was printed, "End of the Trail." Did she want to go to Yale? She told herself yes every time she emptied a tray of heavy beer glasses into the dishwasher, but then the next day my father would go to the basement apartment and bring her champagne. "I would have fresh flowers," she told us. "He would come down the stairs, and I'd open the door before he could knock . . . I'd kiss him before he could speak, and it would be all kisses and tears. As he unbuttoned my blouse, he'd sigh at the sight of my breasts, lean over and kiss my back . . . the sucking, the flowers, and so much, much more . . . screwing me on the floor, fucking me on the bed . . . I'd come and come and come . . . laugh and cry . . . mostly laugh; I made him laugh. As much as sex, he needed laughter, romance, secrecy—so did I . . . so did I."

As the summer sun slanted over the bed, Mother really would believe she wanted to be a wife. He would hold her, tell her she was beautiful, and it was all so clandestine, all so exciting, and all so forbidden. She must have been the last of the romantics. Shit, everyone knows that when you're married, sex is just roll-over-in-the-morning-and-get-on-with-your-day. But Mother believed differently; that was her mistake.

She felt dizzy all summer. My father would drive her up over the Washington border, they'd eat seafood along the Columbia River, and they'd drive way up through the woods. They would park, spread out a blanket, and drink wine into the late afternoon. At five, they would head home because Janet would be home from the Bureau of City Records and Mother would have to get ready for her "descent into hell" (work at "The Ole Water Hole").

Every summer I can remember, Mother would watch the sun slant through the trees and be reminded of the summer of 1949. "During that summer," she would say, "I loved! And when you love the way I did, you really do know what all those goddamned birds and poets feel." Once I made the mistake of asking her exactly what birds and poets really did feel, and she told me I obviously had never been in love or flown. O, my mother the madwoman!

Al was Mother's boss at "The Ole Water Hole." Since he was one of those shady, backgroundless, cigar-smoking, right-out-of-the-movies tavern owners, Mother was fascinated by him. "I bet," she said, "for five thousand dollars he could have found a hired assassin for me."

"Why didn't you have him knock off Janet as she walked out of the Bureau of City Records?" I laughed.

"Don't joke about that, Annie," she said. "I do have *some* scruples!"

Mother claims that working at "The Ole Water Hole" was the only job she could get, but we believed she actually liked working with all those criminals and whores and all. When the bartender who couldn't go back to Iowa because he was wanted for embezzlement was off, Al would sometimes let Mother work behind the bar. Because this was better than running around the place with "nine million pounds" of beer glasses, Mother liked it. Men were surprised to see a girl behind the bar, so she got tipped without her actually having to carry anything; she could steal beer nuts and pepperoni, and help herself to Coke or beer without looking like a company pilferer.

Since Al was the hardest man she had ever tried to talk to, Mother would come in early and pick up an extra couple of bucks making sandwiches and try to grill him about Portland's criminal element, which she was *sure* Al was linked to. Making sandwiches was relatively easy work, and if she spent an hour with the pastrami, she could go home early. Al used to sit in the little Western office and stare at her. She *knew* he wasn't staring at her because of her erotic body since Al had made it clear, when he condescended to keep her on, that he was doing her a big favor because she wasn't cute enough. "I'm a tit man," he had said, "but I suppose if you had tits, you'd want to make more money and go work a classier joint."

"Lord no!" said Kate. "If you don't want to keep me, just say so."

"You'll do—just not my type, like I said."

Later, after she got to know him, Mother asked him what type of a girl he really did like, and all he said was, "The kind who screws and shuts up."

Al would watch her while she made the sandwiches. Because he wasn't doing figuring or anything, Mother would *assume* he would want to start up a conversation. Being a very verbal person, she found it hard to imagine someone *not* wanting to start up a conversation. She would begin by being banal (I mean we all resort to banality once in a while—even Mother) and would say something about the weather. Al would say nothing. She would say something about business. Al would say nothing. "Shit," she would say to us, "I knew I was *never* going to get all the details on the underworld activities!"

"But you didn't *know* he was a criminal," I said.

"I knew," Mother stated with authority.

One Saturday night, when all three hundred tables were packed, people were squashed in between, the band was playing at an incredible level, and her tray was heavy, Al came up behind her and asked, "How are you doing, Kate?" Mother pointed out that to ask such a stupid question that night would kind of be like asking the meat packers in *The Jungle* how they were doing after that poor slob fell into the boiling lard. Then she said, "I am an artist, and I do not belong here!"

"You're not an artist," he stated. "You're just lazy."

Mother followed him into the office. "Now that you're talking to me, could I ask you a question?"

"What?"

"Uh . . . " She paused. If he really *was* involved with the Mafia, she thought, if I asked him anything, I just might end up on his list—he might think I was with the F.B.I. or something. "Uh . . . is it ever okay, under extreme circumstances," she asked, "to tell a customer to fuck off?"

"What circumstances?"

"When people throw pool balls over the balconies and aim for my head."

Without a word, Al walked over to the space between the rows of tables that was directly under the railing of the balcony. He looked up, looked down, walked over to Kate, and said, "Yes."

At 3:30 A.M., Katie was wiping off the tables and enjoying the silence of the place, and Al was leaning against a pillar, drinking a beer. As Kate passed by him, he asked her if she could give him a ride home. Kate hesitated. Al looked at her very hard and said, "Don't worry, kid, it has nothing to do with screwing. I told you I'm a tit man, and you're not my type."

"Well, okay, then."

On the way over the bridge to the east side of town, Al asked her what all this "artist bullshit" was.

"It's my excuse for why I can't type, hustle drinks, or play championship volleyball. It's because I'm so artistic."

"You paint?"

"No," she laughed. "I'm an actress."

"Hell, kid, you'll never make it in Hollywood. You have to have tits."

"God, you're tit happy," she said. "Katharine Hepburn, Lauren Bacall . . . shit, there are billions of small-breasted stars. Besides, I have no intention of being a film actress. I may go to Yale next year and study it as an *art*."

"An *art*? What is this shit!"

"I've been accepted to Yale University, and I'm trying to decide whether or not I should go. It isn't just a pipe dream— I've been *accepted*, you know . . . And besides, I *do* have other options. I may get married."

"Listen, Kate," he said after a long silence. "I don't know what all this artist shit and all this Yale shit is all about, but

I get the feeling you might give up a good thing for some guy."

"He's not just 'some guy,' he's the love of my life," she said quietly.

"Look, I don't know anything about this jerk—maybe he's the best you ever had—but whoever the bastard is, you're going to hate the bastard for taking you away from something."

"He's not taking me away, I'm making the choice."

"In a couple of years, you'll turn it around in your mind. Hell, I don't care." He gave her some directions to his house and then said, "You never leave somethin' good for someone, or you can't help hating them later when you start missing it."

"You're full of shit," said Kate. "I could never hate him. I said he was the *love of my life!*"

"Movies," said Al. "They always say that in the movies." They drove on. "You know," he said after a while, "first time I married I was thinking of traveling to Singapore . . . you know, working my way over on a freighter or something. I know that's not like Yale, but that's what I wanted to do. But I got married . . . yeah, married this woman and started working in her father's tavern in L.A. Well, that was a long time ago, and look where I am. If you go, you may wind up alone, but at least you'll be alone doing what you wanted to do all along." He sighed. "You're a good kid—foul-mouthed— but okay."

"Thanks for the advice," she said as they drove up to his apartment building, "but you just don't know . . . you don't know. . . . "

He shrugged. "Maybe I don't—who knows?"

"Al?"

"Huh?"

"Are you really connected to the Mafia?"

He kissed her over the eyebrow. "Give 'em hell, Lady," he said and got out.

The next night Kate asked where he was, and the bartender who couldn't go back to Iowa said he wasn't coming in that night. She never saw him again because she heard he had sold his interest in the tavern (as every owner did after a couple of weeks) and was somewhere in Seattle.

There was this man who came to "The Ole Water Hole" every night and sat up on one of the mezzanines and paid Mother two dollars to take a drink to some guy on the dance floor below, and every night he sat up there and watched them. He would always have Mother tell the guy that the drink was from some girl whom he would spot at random. Every night it was a different pair, and every night he got an intensified pleasure out of watching the drama below. After the tavern closed, Mother would go every night to the same twenty-four-hour coffee shop—where all the fags hung out after the bars closed. She would amuse the drag queens and the others with her stories about the goddamned man who liked to sit up on the mezzanine and play God. As she sipped her coffee and ate the shitty pumpkin pie, she hoped that my father would call her in the morning. She was planning to ignore what everyone else had said, what Al had said, and her own instincts. Was she afraid of failure or success? "I was just twenty years old and in love," she said.

After my father dropped Janet off at the Bureau of City Records, he called Katie from a pay phone. "If you bring champagne," she said, "I'll fix a crab salad for lunch."

She thought again about what Al said, wrote him off as a self-appointed philosopher, and decided to have a stab at the marriage bit.

Since she had never mentioned marriage to my father, she was a tad bit apprehensive about what he might say. Before she went headlong into the cold of New Haven and professional competition, she wanted to make bloody sure he had no intentions.

While she waited for him to arrive, she put green onions in the salad. She had shaved her legs and, although it was

90 degrees, had put on a slip because he liked to take a long time undressing her. Shit, I wonder how many mistresses are so stupid to think things are going to be the same after they become wives. What wife would put on a goddamned slip in 90-degree weather? When Mother told her romantic stories, all I could see was Mother sitting around in a slip eating crab salad, not figuring on the picture of our family sitting around the dinner table yelling at each other and eating lamb chops in Lake Oswego. Mother really thought she could accomplish the unreal: make their marriage into one long erotic luncheon. I'm sure "true love" distorts people's thoughts, and good sex does something to the minds of even the best of us. Poor Mother.

She heard my father's car drive up. He had the wine under his arm and made love to her before lunch. "We have something to drink to," she said as he poured the champagne.

"Something to drink to?" he asked, putting on his shirt.

Kate had put on her slip and walked casually across the room to the table, picked up her glass, tilted her head, looked up at him, and smiled the mischievous smile he lived for.

"You going to tell me?" he asked.

"I've been accepted to Yale," she stated, raised her glass, and clinked it so hard against his that the wine spilled.

"You're joking," he said, and then after a pause, "I didn't know you'd auditioned."

"I didn't want you to tell me I didn't have 'a chance in hell,' " she snapped.

He stroked her hair and said nothing for a while, and then said, "Well, you'll be going in September."

"I have no other choice, Matt."

"That's the first time you've said my first name—you've always called me 'Foster' before."

She laughed. "Everyone changes some when they are dashed on the rocks of reality."

He laughed. "Well, I guess congratulations are in order."

He kissed her. "You're going to be a very fine actress some-day, Kate."

"Yeah . . . maybe," she said halfheartedly.

"You'll get seen at Yale, and besides, the people there know people who can get you work."

"*Acting* work?"

"Yes, acting work, you wise ass."

"I hope so," she said flatly.

"You don't seem too excited."

"I wish you *weren't* so excited," she said, getting slightly tearful in the way Mother did so beautifully.

"I'm happy for you, Katie. You must really *have* something to have interested them."

"I love you," she said softly. My father ate his salad.

After a very long silence she said, "Do you think about death?"

"All the time," he said. Another long silence.

"Do you love me?" she asked.

"What do you think?" he answered.

"I don't know, dammit!" she yelled. "You come over here, kiss me, fuck me, and *say* you love me a hundred times, but are you just going to sit back there and say you are *happy* for me?" There was another long silence. I guess my father really didn't know what to answer. He really didn't know what she expected.

"You're *happy* for me!!!" she screamed. There was still an-other long silence. "The day I am to lose the love of my life, you say you're *happy* for me? You know I won't come back. Shit, Foster, don't you know if you let me go now, you'll lose me?" My father was quiet for a while. "I won't come back," she said, "and you won't see me again!"

"Kate," he said finally, "you're a beautiful girl who's just been accepted to one of the best schools in the country, and you are acting like a victim. Didn't you ever think of *me* as a victim of your seduction?"

"Don't accuse me of feeling sorry for myself, if you're going to do the same thing . . . Jesus! . . . Screw you! You didn't have to say you loved me . . . and you *did* . . . many, many times. You didn't have to fuck me up!"

"You can blame me for a lot of things, Kate," he said, "but you can't blame me for fucking you up. That's been there for a long, long time."

"Shit," she said. There was another silence. Finally, Kate got up, poured herself some more wine, and said cheerfully, "Hollistor wrote me today from Chicago."

"Huh?"

"Oh, Foster, I was trying to be on the lighter side, as they say at the end of the six o'clock news when they tell you some screwed, cute story about some family who was on a picnic, and their fucking dog followed them five miles to the park, and they turned around and he was eating a hotdog or something. They always say, 'and now on the lighter side' so you'll know that they are finished talking about starvation in China or our great America, or corruption in some system we were brought up to believe in . . . anyway, I am trying . . . trying very, very hard to be on 'the lighter side'!"

My father was quiet. He stroked his beard. "Well," he said after pouring some more champagne and finishing his salad, "what did our friend Hollistor have to say about the big, wonderful world of graduate school?"

"Well," said Kate, settling down with her wine—when she was telling a story, she was at her best—"they did *The Glass Menagerie*, and Hollistor was the stage manager." She took a bite and spoke with her mouth half full. "He had this great story about how a bat got onstage, and during one of Amanda's real dramatic speeches, this bat was making nose dives at the audience, who were screaming with laughter. Poor Amanda didn't know what was going on, and when she came offstage to change her costume, she was really upset that the audience was roaring with laughter, so Hollistor just said, 'Oh, it's just one of those Saturday night audiences, they'll laugh at anything!' So Amanda went onstage, saw the bat, and forgot her lines. Meanwhile, everyone backstage was soon becoming a bat expert. Someone on the lighting crew brought out a bee-bee gun and twenty bee-bees later still hadn't caught the bat. Then Hollistor had this great idea that during intermission they would turn off all the lights in the hall, and the bat would fly toward the light on the stage, and they would catch him. Then the director said no, they would turn off the lights on the *stage* and leave the lights on in the hall, so the bat would fly there. I guess no one thought that bats can't see."

My father was slightly amused. "I thought bats *could* see," he said. "They are nocturnal and see *better* at night."

"That doesn't matter," she said. "I think someone played around with the sound system and screwed up the bat's radar with the sound, if that's possible, and the bat fell out in the hall and someone accidentally stepped on its head."

"That's very interesting," said my father as if he were bored.

"I have this *theory*," said Kate loudly.

"Oh, uh . . . what's that, darling?" he asked dutifully and almost sadly.

"Two people live and breathe the same situation for a long time, and one person thinks one thing about it, and the other person sees it entirely differently."

"What *are* you talking about?"

There was a long silence. Mother wanted so very much to say that she loved him, and had he ever thought of marrying her? She wanted to say that she didn't want to go to Yale, but she didn't want to take the chance of being rejected, so she said nothing.

Since my father really didn't know how he could live if she left him, he wanted to tell her to stay there forever in her basement apartment, working at night as a cocktail waitress, and being there in the afternoons for him. My father wasn't stupid. He couldn't leave Janet. Because they had so many shared experiences, had been part of each other for a very long time, they needed to finish life together. He loved Janet, and he couldn't just throw away twenty years. He also knew he could not ask Kate to give up her whole life, and a chance to go to Yale, for a few afternoons a week. If he did ask her, he knew she probably would, and he couldn't take that responsibility. He knew her well enough to know she would hate him for it in a couple of years.

"To Yale!" he said lifting his glass.

She wanted to grab him and beg him to ask her to stay. She wanted to "give it all up" for him right then. But Kate wasn't stupid either. She lifted her glass and decided to wait until she really *had* something to give up.

"To love," she said.

"To you," said my father.

HASTINGS, HEARTE & DANIELS

118 AVENUE OF THE AMERICAS
NEW YORK, NY 10013

Sept. 2, 1974

Anne Sarah Foster
430 Pacific Avenue
San Francisco, CA 94133

Dear Annie,

You really do have one hell of a nerve.

With your love for grotesque details about the past, you will be interested to know that I was not drafted because of an incident which occurred when I was seventeen. All through my childhood, I was bored stiff with church and

always imagined myself standing up and screaming in the middle of the silent prayer. These
purely hypothetical thoughts kept me entertained during countless services. One day, when
I was seventeen, I found myself actually doing
that. I was taken to the nearest hospital,
sedated, and never forced to attend services
again. Because I had a record of psychological
disturbance, I was not drafted. Do you find
this more or less colorful than if I had been
a foreign correspondent?

I am not a Harvard English major who
didn't want to teach; I'm a <u>Princeton</u> English
major who didn't want to teach. I would never
consider wearing a leisure suit, and you interest me. Is <u>Heritage</u> a true story, or did you
make the whole thing up?

Also, the reasons I haven't attempted
publication of my two novels about World War II
navy life are that they weren't very good and
that just being a senior editor in a publishing
house does not give one the power to "snip red
tape" in order to publish crap. Remember that
when you're writing, okay, Annie?

Best,
Martin

430 Pacific Avenue
San Francisco, CA 94133

Sept. 7, 1974

Martin Goldsmith
Senior Editor
HASTINGS, HEARTE & DANIELS
118 Avenue of the Americas
NYC, N.Y. 10013

Dear Martin,
    In this next chapter, I'm going into my
mother's background, because if you're writing
a book called Heritage, everyone expects to
hear about it. This book is about insanity in a
family, and everyone knows that people go
bananas because of something that happened
during their childhood. In case this book is
ever adopted, like David and Lisa, by Psychol-
ogy 101 classes, I want to make sure they have
a whole hell of a lot of childhood shit on both
the narrator's parents (I mean, where would
The Three Faces of Eve be without the revela-
tion that she had been made to kiss her grandmother's corpse in her goddamned childhood?).
    Besides perversion, I've decided to use
flying as another recurring theme. Flying is
one of your more popular recurring themes in
literature. Both Aristophanes and Alfred Hitch-
cock use The Birds as a title. Erica Jong was
afraid to fly, Jonathan Livingston Seagull
found the meaning of life through flying, Anton
Chekhov symbolized destruction of youth and
freedom (or something like that) by shooting a
sea gull, Antoine de Saint Exupéry found something spiritual on his night flight, and Jean

Anouilh somehow even got Joan of Arc confused with a lark.

You will notice in earlier parts of this book that I have subtly introduced this recurring theme. In the very first chapter and also the suicide chapter, the bathroom with the birds on the wall plays an important part, and you recall in the last chapter Mother says she finally "knew what birds and poets felt like," and when I asked her what they did feel, she said I had obviously never been in love or flown.

I will try to carry this theme all the way through the book. Maybe then it can pass as "structured fiction" rather than just commercial crap. What do you think?

I promise to try not to lose perspective on this . . .

Love,
Annie

P.S. In addition to asking how you dressed, I asked what you <u>looked like</u>. Am I dealing with Quasimodo or something?

chapter 10

My mother was born in Berkeley, California, in 1930. Her father was a renowned physics professor who almost won a Nobel Prize and was always secretly disappointed that none of his four daughters enjoyed his great love for the p-3 orbitals. His dissertation *title* was a page and a half long and about some aspect of physics that never was clear to me. In order to be a physics genius, you just have to wipe out life. You can't "almost win a Nobel Prize" and still get into movies, skiing, or being aware of what is happening to your family around you. Besides reading the periodicals in his field, my grandfather's entire exposure to the outside world was *The Wall Street Journal*, and I'm sorry, but if you see the world only through the eyes of *The Wall Street Journal*, you might as well realize you'll never understand beauty, poetry, Mickey Spillane, and all the other things that really matter. Of course my *own* father was a sort of sociological phenomenon too: by *1970*, he had *never heard* of "Supercalifragilisticexpialidocious" or (I'm not kidding) "Doe a Deer a Female Deer." Believe me, there *are* people like that! He even skipped the "People" section in *Time!*

After my maternal grandmother had been committed to the California State Hospital in 1960, my grandfather used to make occasional pilgrimages up to Oregon to see how Katie was doing with her "failure husband" and her extremely precocious daughters. Since I preferred to be called "intelligent" rather than precocious, he often rubbed me the wrong way. He didn't see too well then, and he would listen to talking books on interesting things like "The Orbits of Electrons" and feed us Life Savers before dinner. Once he confessed to us that Katie was his favorite daughter. Holly asked him why the hell he picked her, and he said it was because she was most like his wife.

"But Grandmother went bananas!" Holly had said.

In his first accurate comment to us about life around him, my grandfather said, "But your mother *is* bananas." We were so used to Mother's odd ways, we just assumed he was making a good joke.

Actually, before she killed herself, I didn't think Mother was any crazier than her other sisters. They were loony in a more conventional, acceptable, American way.

Allison, the oldest sister, is now into "jags" and sells real estate, goes to health spas, has face lifts, is into stereos, tax shelters, hanging pans in the kitchen, getting a tan, and microwave ovens. She's always having terrible problems: i.e., she can't find a color TV that fits the space their black-and-white was built into in the kitchen. She's hopeless.

Caroline was always sorry she wasn't born black or Jewish. She was a card-carrying Communist party member, wore jeans when you still had to buy them in the "men's work clothes" section of Montgomery Ward, and smoked dope in 1939. (I'm serious, I've heard it a thousand times—as if it were worth a medal of honor—that Caroline "smoked dope in 1939." Shit.) She had an illegitimate child the year after Mother died. Today, she's a potter in Sausalito who started taking credit cards in 1971 and rips off the tourists. She somehow explains it by saying she sells "tasteful" pieces instead of thermometers in sea shells.

Ramona . . . well, Ramona married this jerk, jock, Air Force captain (Mother always called him "Air Force One"), who couldn't wait to go out and shoot the North Koreans and then the Commies in Vietnam. She's "into Art" and takes token art courses at Occidental College, belongs to the "Beautify Pasadena" organization (Mother always wondered why she didn't just go the whole hog and belong to the "Beautify Emeryville" organization), and plays tennis in designer tennis dresses.

It really wasn't that Mother was crazier than any of them—she just couldn't decide on a life-style, so she became an actress, hoping to experience everything. Her mistake was giving it up. If Allison, Caroline, or Mona had suddenly been set in a life-style that wasn't conducive to their natures, they'd probably have bumped themselves off too.

Before marrying my grandfather, my grandmother had been married twice. The first had ended in divorce, which in those days, was frowned upon. Her second marriage—to a real, sure enough "import-export" dealer—ended when he suffered a heart attack on a ship between Bali and Java. After a brief period of mourning (I think about two weeks), she met my grandfather at the Berkeley Faculty Club, found out from someone that he "really might win a Nobel Prize someday," got her claws into him, and started our family.

In addition to her two previous marriages, she had been around the world with an actor, was the daughter of a U.S. ambassador, had spent every holiday abroad, had danced one long waltz with the President of the United States, owned a camel (purchased in Egypt on one of her round-the-world trips and donated to the S.F. zoo), had majored in astronomy at Smith College, and had once been presented to the King of England.

"Your grandmother was a lady," my grandfather said to us. "I know it is hard to believe it now, but she was a *great* lady."

"Perhaps," said Mother over her shoulder, "the remembrance of someone is often more colorful or beautiful than the person actually was."

"Perhaps it is," he said.

Mother poured herself another drink, lit a cigarette, and said to me, "*You* see her, Annie, as a few bones in a bed at the State Hospital, spewing out nonsense—ah, but in her *prime*—well, she could have been an actress if she had wanted to, but in those days . . . Christ, just like *today* . . . women started to feel guilty if they turned thirty and were still running all over the world. Sad, isn't it? She ended up at 430 Pacific Avenue with four brats!"

"And eight servants," my grandfather added.

In addition to her colorful globe-trotting, grandmother had been the 1920s version of a Jesus freak. She really believed in the Devil and once (to my mother's great amusement) actually had suggested exorcism to rid Kate of her morbid desire to watch deformed people on the street.

She still sits in the State Hospital and mumbles to herself about how if Kate had only put her trust in the Lord Jesus Christ, she wouldn't have done such a horrible thing to the family. "As she pricks her fingers with stolen needles from the occupational therapy room," Mother would say, "and marks the sign of the cross in her own blood on table napkins, she still believes her lot is better than being dead."

Now, in the hospital, she has to be watched because she sometimes sneaks into the baths and holds people under the water. Until the nurses heard her saying, "I baptize thee in the name of the Father, the Son, and the Holy Ghost," they thought she had developed a definite homicidal tendency.

When we were little, Holly and I used to refer to her as "The Holy Ghost," until my grandfather told us that if we did that anymore, the real Holy Ghost would get us someday.

Because the State Hospital smelled like snot and because the other patients were always saying weird things to us, visiting her was not one of my greatest childhood memories. She'd hold my hand and say, "All that's left of Katie, God rest her soul. If only she'd left *no one* behind, we'd be through with her . . . we'd be free."

"Look to your ancestors," she'd say from her bed, "and you will see yourself."

"All right, Grandmother," I said in my best bedside manner.

"Look to Jesus," she said, "and you will find yourself."

"Okay, okay," I said.

HASTINGS, HEARTE & DANIELS

118 AVENUE OF THE AMERICAS

NEW YORK, NY 10013

Sept. 12, 1974

Anne Sarah Foster
430 Pacific Avenue
San Francisco, CA 94133

Dear Annie,
    After reading Chapter 10 on Monday, I see
your "fictional" family is making quite an
impression on your "fictional" heroine. Because
this is written in the first person, is this
perhaps—now note that I say "perhaps"—about
you? I hope the title <u>Heritage</u> doesn't indicate
your narrator is going to commit suicide as her
mother did, because you've created a character
I want to see live. I do. I like her, and you
as well.
    In answer to your question regarding my
looks: as you would put it, in soul I am tall,
dark, and handsome, but in real life I have the
spirit of Hugh Hefner and the looks of a young
Marcus Welby.
    Ship me the next swell chapter as soon as
you've finished it.

Best,
Martin

P.S. Isn't a patient baptizing other mental
     patients in a bathtub a bit much?

430 Pacific Avenue
San Francisco, CA 94133

Sept. 15, 1974

Martin Goldsmith
Senior Editor
HASTINGS, HEARTE & DANIELS
118 Avenue of the Americas
NYC, N.Y. 10013

My Dear Martin,
    I do not think the baptizing scene is "a
bit much." First of all, the fictional character of the grandmother is—I'll admit it—
loosely based on my own grandmother. I will
have to admit she didn't really drown people
by attempting to baptize them. Actually, she
would sit up late at night when all the television stations had gone off, watch the test
patterns, and be convinced that she had commu-
nicated with the Virgin Mary. When she got
bored with the Virgin, she would switch chan-
nels and try for the saints. Now that's true!
The reason I didn't use it in the book is
because something similar happens in Group
Portrait with Lady, so I figure a lot of people
see religious figures in television patterns,
and I didn't want to be accused of getting
ideas from Heinrich Boll either. Since it is
much easier to believe drowning someone in a
bathtub than communicating with the Virgin,
trust me, it isn't "a bit much."
    Enclosed is the next chapter. Again you
will notice how I move the story in and out of
time like they do in Two for the Road.

In rereading the first part, I discovered that "Christmas" is also a recurring image. I'll push it because it goes with all the religion stuff. Also, if you want me to come down heavier on the "flying" theme, I can always have Mother as a child feed the sea gulls in San Francisco Bay and find truth or something . . .

All my love,
Annie

P.S. WARNING: I'll say or do <u>anything</u> to get famous !

HASTINGS, HEARTE & DANIELS

118 AVENUE OF THE AMERICAS

NEW YORK, NY 10013

Sept. 17, 1974

Dear Annie,
    I <u>know</u> I like you.

Love,
Martin

                              430 Pacific Avenue
                              San Francisco, CA 94133

                              Sept. 19, 1974

Dear Martin,
        You have very good taste. Go back to work.
You have a chapter to read.

                              All my love,
                              Annie

My mother spent her childhood and adolescence in the house where she died. I always felt it was kind of like going for your birth control pills to the same doctor who delivered you —sort of makes you feel you haven't been anywhere.

"Things would have been different," my mother often said to my father when we were little, "if my babies could have had my childhood . . . ferry boats, sea gulls, the nickel merry-go-round in Golden Gate Park . . . Instead of being brought up in this shit hole, they could have *lived!*"

"The way you live?" my father asked. "Crying in the night, castrating your husband, living in the past?"

"I live in the past because I have no future!" she snapped.

"They do," he answered.

"Memories are much more beautiful than reality," she said.

"Couldn't anticipation be beautiful too?"

"Fuck you!"

"Fuck you too, Katie."

My mother came over and kissed him. "Things would have been different if we hadn't *had* children."

"Yes," said my father softly. "I would have left you."

"No, you wouldn't have!" she said cheerfully. Then she laughed a weird kind of laugh. "If you had, the Holy Ghost would have come and struck you down!"

"You are *mad*, woman," my father laughed.

"Mad for you, you fucking bastard," she said delicately.

When questioned during their middle and late years, neither my grandfather nor my grandmother could pinpoint the exact day when my mother stopped being a "joy to the heart" and started being bitter, gloomy, and in general weird. My grandmother said she had *never* been a joy to the heart, and my grandfather said it started about the time she learned to talk in sentences and they knew how her mind worked.

"Katie did it all to us," Grandmother now mumbles whenever we visit her.

"Tell us what she *did!*" I would say.

"Did you know, Annie . . . " Grandmother said once very softly and confidentially so the other patients couldn't hear, "did you know, Annie, that I can communicate with the dead?"

"Even Mother?" I asked. "Or does she still not communicate with you even though she *is* dead?"

Grandmother fooled around with her hands for a minute and then said, "I can communicate with *all* dead souls."

"Well, what does Mother have to say today?" I asked, ignoring the look from Holly that told me I had said the wrong thing.

She pressed her hands to her temples. "Katie isn't *saying* anything," she said very definitely. There was a long silence and then she started to chuckle. "Katie is laughing . . . " she whispered.

"What's she laughing at, Grandmother?"

"She's laughing, Annie . . . " Grandmother paused and carefully stacked up the two-year-old magazines they kept around the place. "Katie is laughing . . . because . . . because . . . she is going . . . to get us all where she is now."

"Dead?" I asked.

"No," she said. "In Hell. Crazy and in Hell."

My grandparents claimed Mother had had a "normal childhood" and was raised in a "normal environment." (Was my grandmother any more capable of creating a normal environment for her daughters than my mother was for us thirty years later? I doubt it.)

Every day, my mother was driven to school by Grand-mother's chauffeur. In her red coat with the hood, she played by herself during recess, masturbated by shimmying up the pole on the swings, and dreamed of stage lights and other truths. Of course she was taken to the ballet, the opera, and the theatre, and—as all those ass hole actors do—found something there that was missing in her real life.

She organized the neighborhood theatrical productions and since my grandmother didn't know the nature of the bizarre and morbid comedies my mother produced, it pleased her. For a kid's plays, Kate's were quite professional. She directed the other children in dramas consisting mainly of stories about psychopathic killers who butchered maidens (costumed from a trunk containing all Grandmother's evening dresses from the grand old days) or particularly graphic rape dramas. From the cleaning woman, she found out all about what happens when one is raped and thought it made for good dramatic material.

Because she was no longer holding her baby sister over open gas jets, everyone thought she was doing very well. School bored her, she liked the flavor of pure salt, she drank vinegar and pretended it was wine, and she spent lots of afternoons just lying in bed staring out the window at the other house across the alley.

Since Grandfather worried about her continual crying fits, he tried to cheer her up by taking her to ride the cable cars (maybe that's where she got that professor fetish/father complex thing), and Grandmother kept saying that if she would learn to love the Lord Jesus, life would be brighter. She told Mother thousands of times that Mother should be grateful that she wasn't a spastic or a pauper. "Just think! What if you'd been born a *Negro*?" Grandmother asked her once.

"I wouldn't have to be so goddamned grateful!" she yelled, and Grandmother washed her mouth out with soap and put her to bed. She cried the entire night, and finally about five in the morning, Grandfather came in and asked her why she was still crying.

"Because I wish I were dead!" she sobbed.

She spent many afternoons wandering around the neighborhood, bouncing a tennis ball. The teenage boys who played basketball over in the park called her the weirdo, and every time she walked by, they would start slowly bouncing their basketball around and around with imitations of Katie's odd and blank look on their faces. As she would hold her head high, she would run her tongue through the space where her baby teeth had fallen out. She invented stories where she was grown-up and beautiful, and when the Russian dancers came to town, she put on her red rainboots and her bathrobe and high kicked all over the living room. On the days when the rugs were taken back for the hardwood floors to be cleaned, she would skate around on the slippery surface in her stocking feet and pretend she was a famous ice skater. Since the news was full of World War II, the rest of her games consisted of things connected with combat: mostly saving her dolls from attack, or being the only beautiful female nurse in a jungle camp.

"The only truth I knew," she said to me when I was a little girl, "was that someday I was going to turn into a bird and just fly off and leave them laughing."

"Why don't you ever leave *us* laughing?" I asked her.

"Obviously, Annie, because we don't have the same sense of humor."

"You know," Grandfather once said, "I often blamed Katie's mother—your grandmother. She saw things that weren't there and refused to see things that were put in front of her eyes."

"How do you mean?" I asked.

"Well, she didn't see there were sometimes moments when Katie showed a spark of genius or a hint of kindness."

"Huh?"

"Well, Annie, I think she sort of talked your mother into the idea she was crazy."

"I still don't get it."

"Oh, your mother . . . to her, being crazy sounded so much more interesting than being normal."

When he said that, poor Grandfather didn't know the extent to which Mother's theatricals would go.

HASTINGS, HEARTE & DANIELS

118 AVENUE OF THE AMERICAS
NEW YORK, NY 10013

Sept. 23, 1974

Dear Annie,

    I'm delighted that you informed me of your new recurring image. I shall watch with eager anticipation for any references (obscure or not) to birds, flying, and Christmas. Since you said perversion is also a recurring theme, I think you should explore it more than flying, as we both know dirty books sell better.

    I may be on a business trip to the West Coast sometime later this fall. Maybe we could meet. I mean, I would like to see you very much. As I've said, you interest me.

    Are you sure your mother died when you were only ten years old?

                         Very best,
                         Martin

430 Pacific Avenue
San Francisco, CA 94133

Sept. 27, 1974

Dearest Martin,
       I said earlier that this novel would be
long, so that readers' friends who saw the book
on their coffee tables would think they read
long, hard books like War and Peace. At first
I had assumed that two of my typed pages
equaled one printed page. Yesterday, as a
purely scientific experiment (not, of course,
trying to get out of writing), I checked out
exactly how much type equals how much print.
I discovered that one of my typed pages equals
about 4/5 of a printed page of Malone Dies.
Now, I realize that Malone Dies is a very short
novel, but we do have a similar subject matter,
and if Beckett can't keep readers for more than
one hundred and twenty-five pages, I might have
trouble keeping them for six or seven hundred.
I figure that twice as long as Malone Dies
would be about right.
       Second: yes, my mother did kill herself
when I was ten years old. How else could you
explain why I'm so fucked up? But don't worry,
I am going to be the only one in my goddamned
family who defies her heritage and uses it!
The fictional Anne Sarah is more fucked up than
I am. Because my mother tended to talk a lot, I
know all those details about her past. But we
are so different: She was an actress who spoke
"other people's words," and I am a writer
creating my own! She tried to write (every
motherfucker thinks they "have a book in
them"), but I'm really writing! She was crazy

as a bedbug, and I am so normal I'll probably disappoint you when you visit here. She wanted to die, and I want to live and make a million dollars off my swell best seller.

Love,
Annie

P.S. Yes, yes, do come! You interest me . . . in more ways than one.

chapter 12

During the ten years of my life that my mother was alive, I pieced together several things about her life between the psychotic kid stage and the time she met my father.

I found out that during her seventh grade year she spent a lot of time picking her nose and eating the contents. When she screamed at me loudly once for scratching mine, I uncovered the secret.

"Big deal," I said. "A finger up the nose isn't going to ruin my life." I couldn't understand why she was getting so hysterical.

"Annie," she said, holding a butcher knife over my finger, "if you *touch* your nose one more time, I'm going to cut your finger off!"

Because I'd known Mother long enough to know she really wasn't going to do it, I just said, "What's the big deal?"

"People will ostracize you for that sort of thing, my dear," she said. "They will banish you from society!"

This was getting a little dramatic for me, so I decided to just say, "Okay," and leave her alone, but good old Mother *had* to finish the story. As I've said before, she loved stories.

"Let me tell you, Annie," she said.

"*Must* you?" I really wanted to get outside, and Mother's tales could go on forever.

"It will be very short," she whispered, "I promise."

"Uh . . . okay."

"When I was twelve, the boys in my class teased me so much about my nose picking that I didn't want to go to school. They ran away from me . . . laughing . . . every time . . . and I mean *every time* I came near them. One day—this is the good part, Annie—one day they cornered me in the schoolyard, stripped me naked, and stuffed mud up my nose!"

"Are you making this up, Mother?" I asked.

"Does it matter?" she asked. She started to walk out the door, stopped, and turned around. "Things that happen to you in your childhood can affect you in later life."

"Is that what made you nuts?"

"That's what made me stop picking my nose!" she snapped.

Uncle Hollistor told me years after she was dead and gone that Mother had lost her virginity at thirteen. Since everyone in her class hated her (probably because she picked her nose so goddamned much), she regarded it as a kindness and not perversion when her science teacher made a sexual overture toward her.

"In the name of science?" I asked.

"You're far too cynical, Annie," he said.

Shit. Her fucking science teacher! A professor fetish! Christ!

From a few dusty trophies still saved in the attic, I also know she was a high school speech champion, and from a series of notebooks that she wrote short stories that usually didn't have any action in them but were about people sitting in one place and all the things going on in their heads.

Later, I showed them to my father, and he said Mother had wanted to be a writer for a brief period.

"Was she a *good* writer?" I asked him.

"You read the stories, honey, what do you think?"

"She was full of crap," I said.

He didn't say anything, so I figured I was bothering him. Just as I was about to walk out of the study he said, "She was a better writer than she was an actress."

"But she was 'one of the finest young American actresses'!" I said.

"It's easier to dazzle with a performance than with a short story," he answered.

"How come?"

"Because," he said, "you can go back and look at a short story and see what was actually there. With a performance you just rely on your memory."

"Huh?"

"Performances just end in a burst of applause, but writing can be read over and over again. If it's good, then each time something new can be discovered." He sighed and then said, "Your mother could dazzle people, but when it came to words on a page, she had to play by the same rules as everyone else."

"Did she dazzle you?" I asked.

"No," he said sadly. "At the time we met, I just wanted to be dazzled by something." He sat there and looked really beaten.

"She *saved* her stories," I said, "so she must have *thought* they were good."

"She saved *everything*," he said sadly. "She liked memories."

HASTINGS, HEARTE & DANIELS

118 AVENUE OF THE AMERICAS

NEW YORK, NY 10013

Sept. 30, 1974

Dear Annie,
    Since I don't exactly know when I'll be able to get away to the West Coast, I can't tell you my time of arrival yet. I will let you know as soon as HASTINGS, HEARTE & DANIELS lets me know.

Although your writing is very interesting,
I think we should be objective: maybe you could
add that sex and violence you were talking
about.

Also, a question: is your mother's loss
of virginity at thirteen part of your recurring
perversion theme, or did she really?

Is there a reason why, except for a brief
mention, you've completely ignored World
War II?

Best,
Martin

---

430 Pacific Avenue
San Francisco, CA 94133

October 3, 1974

Dearest Martin,
God, it's a good thing you weren't James
Joyce's editor! You really have trouble following the pieces of an intricate puzzle that fall
together before your eyes. I've already put in
the sex and violence: A mother shooting herself
while her daughters are in the house doesn't
count as violence? A mother telling her daughters she was "fucked all over the floor"
doesn't count as sex? Come on, Martin! If
you've read the works of Sigmund Freud or
Jacqueline Susann, you will recall that they
both think that sex is the controlling force
in our lives. Besides being a sexual power
play, this book shows what people will or won't
do in the name of sex: Mother used it to

destroy herself, and I may, my dear, use it to
get what I want!

Also, in the next chapter, I point out
recurring patterns from one person to another.
I have indicated by my title that when one is
related by birth, one follows a pattern, but
sex can also create a pattern. From sex comes
birth . . . Get it? (!)

Whether or not the loss of my mother's
virginity at thirteen was true or not (or perverted or not) isn't important. The reason it
took so long for Vladimir Nabokov to be discovered as someone other than a Cherry Tart
freak is because ass holes like you considered
him a pervert because he wrote about a
thirteen-year-old girl having sex! Those Blow
the Man Down writers really fuck things up for
us artists!

World War II is not glossed over because
I don't want to do any research on it. This
book is about human emotions and not about
historical facts! Just because your brother
was killed in the goddamned war and because you
write unsalable books about the navy does not
mean that everyone is lining up to read books
about World War II. Maybe there is a reason
publishers didn't snap up those epics about
navy life. Okay, maybe From Here to Eternity
was a gigantic best seller, but the biggest
best seller of all time was The Valley of the
Dolls, so there's room for a bit of everything.
Look, I didn't even go to see Patton, and when
Arthur Miller made only two small references to
World War II in Death of a Salesman, no one
gave him a hard time about it. Besides, my
mother was in high school during the war; they
had money so it didn't affect them; my father
was already out of the service; and my mother

had the good taste not to fall for soldiers.
If you want to read about World War II, go to
<u>The World Book</u>!
Would it make you feel better if later on
I make my narrator a Vietnam war protester?

Love,
Annie

P.S. I will leave it up to you as to whether or
not I am putting you on.

chapter 13

In the first years of my parents' marriage, I'm pretty sure my father didn't fuck around—maybe a little when my mother was pregnant, but he was really bananas about her. As I've said before, he *did* have a weakness for women and clandestine sex, so sometime after Holly was born, he took up with Linda, who would be yet another cause of his undoing. After Mother died, Linda came down to California to live with us. She had been a half-assed choreographer in Portland, and when Mother found out about her (I even think it was in some ass hole way like lipstick on the collar. Shit.), she just laughed and said she didn't know there was such a thing as a professional choreographer in Portland. "More of them than professional actresses," my father said.

Actually, Linda had come from New York. Even though her father was some big time Broadway director, *he* hadn't even been able to squeeze out any work for her, so she said she had "had it with the city" and came to the West Coast to live the simple life. She ended up doing free-lance choreography for various community theatres and colleges in the area and teaching dance on the side. I don't think my father ever really loved her. I mean, she was nice enough, but she wasn't all that interesting.

"I like women who don't have ceilings," my father said once.

"Linda's got a very low one," Mother commented.

"Yes," my father paused profoundly, "limited . . . Linda's limited."

"But knows three hundred exotic positions?" laughed Mother.

"I don't know what you're talking about," lied my father.

We figured my father took to her because she adored him so much. I mean, who can resist being an object of worship? I can remember at nine sitting in the student lounge of the theatre and watching Linda watch my father. She would just sit there and stare at him the way the people in the Museum of Modern Art stare at cube-shaped nudes descending a staircase. While watching him talking to his colleagues about anything from "next year's season" to "theatre theory," "theatrical commitment," or any of the other bullshit theatre professors talk about, she would have this look on her face as if she were watching Michelangelo at work on the Sistine Chapel. Even at the tender age of nine, I could see her resenting Holly and me, or anyone, for that matter, who knew my father better than she did.

Old Kate got a lot of perverted enjoyment out of walking into the theatre as "the wife" and seeing everyone pretend they didn't "know" about Linda. "It was just like that when I was bouncing the springs with him," Mother said. "Porky Pig would walk in and everyone would be so kind to her because she didn't 'know.' God! People are such jerks." I guess it was as hard for Linda as it had probably been hard for Mother when he was married to Janet, to take second place. I would sit there and watch Linda watching him, and think that was probably just the way Mother had been fifteen years earlier, and maybe even Janet twenty years before that. The one thing Holly and I really couldn't understand was why he was worth all that emotional energy from three reasonably intelligent women, but when sex is involved . . . well. . . . My father *must* have been a terrific lay, because I'm sorry, he just wasn't gorgeous or charming. "What *is* it?" I asked Mother. She thought for a very long time, and then said, "He liked my stories, Annie, he liked my stories."

"Do you think Linda is in love with him?" Holly asked her.

"Of course," Mother said, "but it will wear off . . . it did with me, and in the meantime, I am thoroughly enjoying the fact that she is every bit as jealous of me as I was of Porky . . . only, unlike me, she doesn't have a chance."

"Maybe that's what Porky . . . uh . . . Janet said then," I put in.

"Oh, no," Mother said lightly, "Janet was *just* his wife. I was beautiful, and I was the love of his life!"

"You say that a lot."

"To keep reminding myself," she said.

Before she started tossing the salad with my father, Linda had been married for a short time to my Uncle Hollistor. He married her sometime after he went to graduate school in Chicago and returned to Oregon to write, and sometime before he became a "great American playwright." Because Linda wasn't even pretty, Mother was amazed when Hollistor called her at Yale and told her he was tying the knot. "At least I thought you'd have the good taste to marry someone with fewer acne scars," she had laughed.

Linda was slightly heavy, always pretended to be interested in what everyone else had to say, was a pretty good dancer, and spent a good deal of time in the bar of the Mallory Hotel (with all the other Oregon theatre failures), drinking and (as Hollistor put it) waiting for Elia Kazan or Josh Logan to call. Hollistor would say, "I can sympathize with a theatre failure in *New York*—you know, the 'for every light on Broadway there's a broken heart' bit—but if you're even *in* Oregon, you are saying you are a failure right from the start."

When Hollistor was still a student at Portland City University, Linda had done some choreography for them and liked Hollistor. She met my father at that time too, but he was so wrapped up in my mother, he didn't notice her then. She was always amused by Hollistor's black humor, and Hollistor was impressed by the fact that her father (who had since disowned her for "using his name" without his permission to get work) was a "major New York director."

Fresh with his useless MFA in drama, Hollistor came back to Oregon to write plays. Waiting around for some high school to do another production of *Oklahoma!*, Linda would sit with Hollistor in the Mallory and drink whisky sours on the rocks. ("How *could* you!" Mother would say. "I can excuse Linda because we're all a little perverted, but *whisky sours on the rocks!* Shit!") They'd talk about the good old days before my father came to Portland City, go back to Linda's apartment and listen to records of old Broadway musicals, go to bed together, and talk about Hollistor's writing.

When Linda got pregnant, Hollistor "made an honest woman of her" in 1953. When Linda suffered a miscarriage, also in 1953, Hollistor filed for divorce and Linda didn't contest it because, as she said, "Who wants to be married to someone who doesn't want to be married to you?" Simple. Even Mother said that was sort of a bastardly thing for him to do, but he pointed out that he married her because she was pregnant, and the condition no longer existed. Of course, now it is easy to get an abortion (if you can afford it), but then, abortions were done in Chinatown, up dark stairs like in *Love with the Proper Stranger*, and a single mother—well, that was out of the question. Hollistor said that everyone had to be a bastard at least once in his life, and since he had been so good and married her, he deserved a chance to be a bastard. Mother said he was fucked.

My mother always said you should never marry unless you were *really* in love (she loved the word "really" and used it with great emphasis to make any point whatsoever). Hollistor told me *never* to marry for love because all someone has to do is say "Good morning" to you in the wrong way and you're shot for the whole day; if you don't care very much, it doesn't bother you. I would tend to believe Hollistor because he's alive, Mother is dead, and they were *both* screwed up to begin with.

I do know that Mother was "in love" and she had a jack shit marriage. Of course Hollistor has never been in love and *he* had a lousy marriage, so you can see why I plan to never marry.

Sometimes I think about marriage, and I believe that the man I marry will look like Paul Newman, and I won't have any problems because I am different. He won't love other women because I'm so fucking special! And I won't hate him because we will both smile over our orange juice and kiss over our martinis and never shop in the household cleaning section of the supermarket. Then I think again and realize I am an idiot! Everyone thinks he's special. Mother's mistake was thinking she was too special, that she could sit back and let love bring her happiness. Love should be gravy; you have to work for meat and potatoes.

HASTINGS, HEARTE & DANIELS

118 AVENUE OF THE AMERICAS

NEW YORK, NY 10013

October 8, 1974

Dear Annie,
     Don't think for a minute you're putting me on. If anything, you're putting yourself on. From my knowledge of critics or even housewife readers, they will find a lot more in what you write than what you put in.

I will be in San Francisco next Friday,
October 18. I'm so looking forward to meeting
you. I'll phone shortly after I arrive.

Warmest regards,
Martin

---

430 Pacific Avenue
San Francisco, CA 94133

Oct. 11, 1974

Dearest Martin,
What do you <u>mean</u> housewives and critics
will find more in <u>Heritage</u> than is really in
it? Christ, the thing is so full of fucking
symbolism, it would take at least a semester
for an English class to figure it all out! Do
you think I should really knock them over the
head with it, so they'll know I meant it all
to be there?
All through the next chapter, I have patterns that are carried out from one generation
to the next (i.e., "Hollistor found me amusing
in the same sort of way he found Mother
amusing").
I also have references to people "playing
God." As you recall, my grandmother was very
hung up on religion, so even though we are a
bunch of atheists, religion is part of her
heritage, so it probably affects us in some
way. I refer to God and Otto Preminger as being
the same thing to undercut my meaning with
humor. I don't want it to end up like <u>The Night</u>
<u>of the Iguana</u> where they are real serious and
significantly cut the iguana loose and talk

about playing God. I realize that Tennessee Williams is a really great writer and all, but The Night of the Iguana didn't provide too many laughs, and we all sure could use a few laughs now.

Also, in this next chapter I have a rather long description of a card game. If it seems a little boring when I explain the rules, just remember that Vladimir Nabokov in Ada goes into a long description of a game of Scrabble! Now everyone already knows how to play Scrabble, so I thought at least I'd invent a game and then use it as a device to show how people always want to find ways to play God. Now, I think this game is kind of original, so if you want to figure out some way to patent, market, and sell it, or even make a deal with Parker Brothers, I would be willing to talk terms.

I also say that "sex screws up everything," and I hope you realize that that is a really universal statement. You must realize how many of your potential readers and even English professors will be able to identify with it. Sex does screw things up, you know.

I'm really looking forward to meeting you too. Even though you don't see exactly what I'm doing with Heritage, you seem to appreciate some of the truly unique things about me.

Let's mix business with pleasure and meet at 6:00 P.M. on Friday the eighteenth in the lobby of the Hyatt Regency Hotel on the Embarcadero. It's so tacky there, the first time I went in, I thought I'd died and gone to Heaven. You will recognize me by a white carnation in my lapel. It will be fake but will look real. You see, everything else in that hotel is real and looks fake. Even the water in the waterfall looks exactly like vinyl. "Most of the reality in our lives and most of the truths told are taken as science fiction." (That's good, I may use it in <u>Heritage</u>!)

I shall show you, my dear, the San Francisco <u>I</u> know and love, which is <u>not</u> "the majestic view as seen from Coit Tower." I will show you a pet store in Cow Hollow where the pigeons fuck in the window!

If you can't make it, I shall jump from the sixteenth floor of the Hyatt Regency and crack my head open on the ice sculpture of President Ford in the lobby!

Love,
Annie

chapter 14

My Uncle Hollistor was a playwright who, early in his career, was constantly getting produced and critically panned off-Broadway. Often, he would get produced in fringe theatres in London, and Mother would say, "If this one is good, maybe it will be transferred to the West End, and he'll have his big break—his *Young Victoria.*" When we were little, it seemed like she were saying that an awful lot about Hollistor. She used to say he was the most talented failure there ever was. Around the time I was four or five, he won the Vernon Rice award for an off-Broadway production that failed at the box office, and then, when I was about six, he won the Pulitzer Prize for his play about Mother, *The American Beauty Arose.* Of course, Mother about popped her cookies, and Uncle Hollistor started making a whole lot of money, was able to sell (unload) all his old stuff, and came to see us in Portland a lot. Both Mother and Hollistor used to lord it over my father that they were the *only* two people from Portland City University who had "made it big," and they had "made it" in spite of the education they received at Portland City and not because of it. Naturally, my father didn't look forward to Hollistor's visits.

Hollistor wasn't really my uncle. Mother had met him in college and they became best friends. Since she never got along with her sisters, she sort of looked at him as a brother. Her sister Allison had moved to Hawaii, where she made a "real killing" in the real estate market, married an insurance man (how boring), and now carries her real estate papers around in a two-hundred-dollar attaché case, owns a Spanish style house, wears caftans while she puts her canned escargots in the shells, has two revolting children, and is always in hock up to her eyes. (Shit! If I spent $5,000 on a free-form gold watch and $90 on each of fifteen different silk blouses, I'd be in hock too.)

Ramona and "Air Force One" hadn't made out much better. Because she had taken all those art courses, Mona got to be a volunteer guide at some jack shit art gallery, had lunch with ladies and talked about *Human Sexual Response*, and was always interested in what little Katie was doing. She and "Air Force One" had even taken a vacation to New York when Kate was performing in *Young Victoria* and said they "didn't understand it." (That's like saying you didn't understand *Anne of the Thousand Days!*)

Mother didn't get along with her younger sister Caroline either. Caroline had stayed in San Francisco and changed with the city. In 1966, the year Mother died, Caroline simply packed a bag and went to Haight Ashbury to meet gentle people. She gave birth to Joy in 1967 and when asked about Joy's father, she always said, "How the hell should I know who he was?" My father later commented that she was a little old for the flower-child thing, and Holly remarked that Mother was a little *young* to die, but things like that happen.

You can imagine why Mother felt the need for a congenial sibling, so she and Hollistor spent the rest of her life closer than friends and happier than lovers, conspiring against the world, her family, and humorless people.

I guess Mother's marriage wasn't too bad until Hollistor won the Pulitzer Prize, began to receive Broadway productions, and started being considered by people (other than himself) a "major American playwright." As Mother read his reviews, I think she really realized she blew it that day in front of the Oregon Medical Insurance Society. When she took that step backward, it was all downhill until she killed herself. Killing yourself is the biggest step backward you can take.

In 1971, Hollistor told Janet and me that Mother probably would have lived longer if she had stayed in New York. I was fifteen at the time, and he was visiting us in San Francisco. Janet, Hollistor, and I were sitting in the second floor living room killing a bottle of Scotch he had brought for me. Even though I wasn't the most attractive fifteen year old in the world, Hollistor found me amusing in the same sort of way he had found Mother amusing. After Janet came back to my father, he had really hit it off with her too. She was just his kind of person. At fifty-eight she earned her living writing romances for adolescent girls with titles like *Springtime Comes to Patti-Lou*. She knocked them out in about a hour and knew they were really dog puke. Of course Hollistor found all this hilarious, and Janet was surprised that she would have so much in common with the best friend of Katie-the-husband-snatcher and ex-husband of Linda-the-husband-fucker. When Katie was an undergrad and Janet was still married to my father, they had sat together and watched the first production of a Hollistor Kent play ever performed. Janet laughed and said, "I thought she was just another student then. Little did I know!"

"Did you like the play?" Hollistor asked.

"Katie told me which parts were funny," she said.

"Katie had a warped sense of humor," he laughed. "How could she have known which parts were funny?"

"I thought she loved your plays," said Janet.

"She did," he said. "*That's* why I said she had a warped sense of humor."

"Oh, Hollistor," I said, helping myself to some more J. W. Black, "the fact that your plays were funny and Mother was warped have nothing to do with each other!"

"To art!" said Hollistor, getting up so we could clink glasses.

"Doesn't it ever bother you to come around here?" Janet asked him, wiping some drops of Scotch off her beige polyester doubleknit pantsuit.

"Doesn't it ever bother you to *live* here?" Hollistor asked her. "Seriously, Janet, how could you *possibly* come back to Matt?"

"You'd probably laugh your head off, Hollistor, if I said I still loved him."

"Yes," said Hollistor, "I sure would!"

"Okay, then," sighed Janet, "let's say *Springtime Comes to Patti-Lou* and *Autumn is a Falling Time* are good for a three-hour work day, and after that you want someone to talk to."

"*Matt?*" asked Hollister as if she had said she beat in her own head with a ball-peen hammer for entertainment.

"Then let's say *Annie*," said Janet, "so you won't laugh at me and think me as strange as the rest of his damned women."

"Fair enough," said Hollistor, putting his arm around me. "I'll say Annie too—that's how *I* can stand coming around here."

"Thanks," I said sarcastically. Then I thought about it and decided I probably *was* the reason Hollistor came around. He had always hated my father, and after Mother died, he never gave him the time of day if he could help it. I smiled. He really *is* coming to see me, I thought. It hadn't occurred to me before.

"You never liked Kate, did you?" he asked Janet.

"Well, I shouldn't be expected to be fond of someone who played around with my husband."

"No, I mean before."

"Oh, she was okay—just very cynical."

"Mother," I said, a little drunk by this time, "is nothing but a bunch of ashes at the bottom of the bay." I put my feet up on the coffee table, and Janet gave me a dirty look. "They're only sneakers," I said. "They won't hurt anything."

"I wasn't talking about the shoes, honey," she said. "I was talking about the constant cynical references you keep making to your mother. She is dead, you know." She sighed. "I just don't want to see you turn into someone like your mother, who will laugh at others' misfortunes."

I glanced at Hollistor, who quickly poured Janet some more Scotch. He had obviously never told Janet about the college musical he and Mother wrote, where my father was the villain and there was an entire production number built around Janet's kidney condition.

"At least you've got Katie pegged," Hollistor said. "You know, she used to go with this basketball player—before Matt came to Portland. This guy took her out in his Chevy and pointed at the dashboard and said very seriously, 'See this, honey? Once someone's pretty little head went right through there.' He was appropriately killed in a car accident, and Katie and I were playing with The Cards and Katie drew the basketball player and started laughing because he was dead and his name was still in The Cards."

"*The Cards?*" asked Janet. Since she'd had as much Scotch as we had, she was beginning to enjoy the conversation.

"Katie and I invented this card game," he said. "You have a bunch of index cards, and on each one is the name of someone you know . . . not just people you know well, but people you think are hysterical. You know—like the lady with the hairy arms who worked in the Portland City University business office who looked as if she were paying you out of her own pocket whenever you cashed a check—just everyone you know in common. Well, we were playing a game with The Cards, and when Kate drew the guy who was dead, she really laughed because we'd forgotten him. That's what Janet means, Annie, when she says your mother laughed at other people's misfortunes."

"Shit, Hollistor," I said, laughing. "Don't be so holier-than-thou. Mother read me that letter you wrote her about this guy who dived off a bridge into two feet of water and was paralyzed for life, and you thought *that* was pretty funny . . . you're as bad—or worse—than she ever was!"

Hollistor roared with laughter and then, trying to be serious, said that that wasn't very funny at all.

By then, Janet and I were both laughing. "How did you play The Cards?" Janet asked.

"It was Kate's idea of being God and Otto Preminger all in one," he said.

"Is there any difference?" Janet laughed, quite drunk by this time. We all guffawed.

"To Kate, there wasn't . . . I don't think," Hollistor said.

"How did you play?"

"It worked like this," he said. "We had *hundreds* of index cards with all the people we knew on them, and we'd shuffle them. Then, you'd draw five cards. One person you'd have to marry and live with for the *rest of your life* with *no* divorce. With one person you'd have to spend a whole month in a fallout shelter with no other human contact and the possibility of immediate death surrounding you. Then, one person you'd have to cast as the lead in your Broadway show that you were staking *all* your money and all your reputation on; the next person you had to look like for the rest of your life with absolutely no plastic surgery; and the last person you had to push off the top of the Georgia Pacific Building."

"Jesus!" giggled Janet.

"Sometimes we'd cast plays," Hollistor continued. "Draw four cards and figure out what show these four people would fit into best; but you couldn't cast the lead—you had to draw at *random* for it. You know, Katie just *loved* to draw at random for things. She always got the janitor in the education department playing Hamlet or something like that. She really thought things like that were funny."

"We've already agreed she had a warped sense of humor," said Janet.

"They both did," I put in. "That's probably why they got along so well together."

"Did you know, Janet," said Hollistor, raising his glass to her, "that I once elected to spend a month in a fallout shelter with you?"

"Not the Broadway play?"

"I mean," he said, "I figured a month of laughing over *Springtime Comes to Patti-Lou* might be kind of fun."

Janet laughed.

"Katie liked to draw out of the deck for who would alter her life in some way in the next week, or who she would sleep with that night—she was really in trouble if she got the Great Dane who always ran around campus—he was on the cards too. She was always hoping for one of the bonus cards. We had people like Marlon Brando, Clark Gable, and Montgomery Clift as bonanza cards, and if she didn't get one, she'd get upset and keep drawing until she did."

"Was that playing fair?"

"Now, Janet," said Hollistor, "did you *ever* know Kate to play fair?"

"I guess not," said Janet and then added, "Was there any way to win this game?"

"Oh, for a while we had a way . . . something about whoever drew the 'best' hand. We generally agreed who were the 'good cards'—except with Matt. Shit, when she would draw him, she'd scream with joy. If I drew him, I'd chalk up an automatic zero for my hand, so we just stopped trying and played for the sport of the thing." He paused and took another sip of Scotch.

"I thought Katie always had to be a winner," said Janet a little bitterly.

"I guess," he sighed, "she figured at this game you couldn't win."

"She won Matt," Janet said simply.

"I don't consider that a prize," he said. "She lost, Janet. She got him and is dead; you lost him and are alive." He shook his head sadly. "You know, Annie, your mother and I were . . . well . . . we were quite a team."

I was surprised by this comment. "She said she never slept with you."

"You don't have to fuck someone to be a team," he said, "no matter what your nympho mother told you."

"You loved her, didn't you," stated Janet.

"Let's say I'll never forget her," said Hollistor.

"Sex seems to screw up everything," I commented from my corner.

"To sex!" said Hollistor, raising his glass.

HASTINGS, HEARTE & DANIELS

118 AVENUE OF THE AMERICAS
NEW YORK, NY 10013

Oct. 21, 1974

My Darling Annie,

I'm writing—partly to tell you how much I enjoyed our two days together in what I think is the most beautiful city in the world, and partly to say some of the many things that were unsaid.

First, let me explain: Because your writing was so worldly wise, I assumed you were too . . . I don't know what else to say.

Because I wanted to say so much more, and because I wanted to know so much more about you, I was disappointed—as well as entertained, I must admit—that all I heard were a bunch of amusing stories about your past.

When we made love, I felt close to you. Did you feel anything for me? Maybe I, like most sex-starved men, was just overcome with a fit of passion, but I don't think it was just the passion—you are a beautiful person. You are so beautiful.

I think I do a much better job at writing
business letters than love letters. I'm sorry.
     Because you have the intelligence and
insight to perhaps make this manuscript sala-
ble, I do hope we can work together so something can come of it. Why not put more of
yourself into the character of the "fictional"
Anne Sarah?
     You are young and eighteen, and I will say
without reservation that you are one of the
most promising eighteen-year-old writers I've
ever met. Maybe you will be the women's
Salinger.
     You have beautiful legs—all the way up.

                              Love,
                              Martin

----

                    430 Pacific Avenue
                    San Francisco, CA 94133

                    Oct. 24, 1974

Dear Martin,
     You're a pretty good lay yourself.
     How am I supposed to know if I have any
deep feeling for you? I only saw you for two
days—besides, I'm part of the generation who
is supposed to get off on balling without a
third act. You would have loved my mother; she
would have told you the sun rose in your eyes.
     You did say we should be honest with each
other. Since you were so honest and told me you
really couldn't make any commitment to Heritage
until you saw the final draft, I'll be honest
with you and tell you you write the worst god-

damned love letters I ever read! "I was overcome with a fit of passion." (!) I mean, <u>really</u>
—would you allow that in a novel? You don't
have to tell me I'm beautiful . . . Probably
<u>everyone</u> looks beautiful from the angles you
saw me—but thanks anyway, it was nice.
     Why don't you come out here again? I
really would like to see you once more. Since
you can always write it off as a "business
expense," you have nothing to lose—and maybe
something to gain.

                        Kisses and all that crap,
                        Annie

P.S. You said I was the "most promising
     eighteen-year-old writer you ever met."
     Shit. How many eighteen-year-old writers
     do you meet?

HASTINGS, HEARTE & DANIELS

118 AVENUE OF THE AMERICAS
NEW YORK, NY 10013

                              October 30, 1974

Dear Annie,
     Because "business expenses" are not only
deductible but often are paid for by HASTINGS,
HEARTE & DANIELS, I'll be on a plane soon.
I do want to see more of the San Francisco you
know and love. I must admit I've been there
many times and have <u>never</u> seen the topless
shoeshine stand. How about in three weeks?

I'm sorry my love letters don't meet your
approval, but since I'm an editor and not a
writer, that might explain why. Either you
don't love me, or you don't write very good
ones either.

Love,
Martin

---

430 Pacific Avenue
San Francisco, CA 94133

November 4, 1974

Dear Martin,
God, I can't wait! I have a million more
things to show you. Did you know that in San
Francisco bars open at 6:00 A.M.? I think
that's just hilarious. What are you going to
do between 4:00 A.M. and 6:00 A.M., huh? (I'm
a laugh a minute, aren't I?)
Otherwise, my life hasn't exactly been
something Lowell Thomas would snatch up to use
on an episode of "High Adventure," but then
writers often write because there is no adventure in their own lives. Well, you did give me
an adventure. . . .
Since you're talking about love now, I'd
like to just think about friendship. I think
we've got that, don't you? If love comes in
time, that's the best we can hope for.
Don't be pissed off at me; I'm still a
kid.

Love,
Annie

P.S. Publish this . . . please. . . .

chapter 15

As I said in Chapter 1, after Mother died, we all lived Happily
Ever After until I tripped on the stairs and reminded my father
of my mother. Until that day, I had never seen my father cry;
I had heard him yell a lot, but even when Mother was around
tormenting him—even when she kicked off—we never saw a
tear.

Because Linda must have heard something going on, she
opened the door by the stairs and peeked out. If she had ever
been pretty, it had faded long before I was born. I always
wondered exactly what Uncle Hollistor had ever seen in her.
Along with her acne scars, she had a wardrobe that made her
look like something Woolworth's went to work on. She also
had greasy hair and chain smoked. She stood there in her tight
black pants with the thighs bulging out, and stared at my
father.

As you can imagine, I didn't know what the hell I should
do. All my mother's screaming, all her odd behavior, and even
discovering her body the day she died didn't fill me with the
same kind of panic I felt when I watched my father cry. He
rolled off his desk chair, put his knees to his chest, rocked
slowly back and forth on the Oriental rug, and he sobbed.
Since Linda didn't seem to be adding all that much to the situation by standing there with her finger up her ass and inhaling
her Kent filter tip, I screamed for Janet.

The first words Linda managed to say were, "Call an ambulance, you ass hole!" and then she dropped her cigarette on the floor by the door, rushed into the library, and tried to hold my father's head in her arms. Because her cigarettes always had Revlon's *Fire and Ice* lipstick all over the ends, the cigarette on the floor was a shocking reminder of the day Mother died and the four cigarettes in the bloody ashtray.

As Linda tried to comfort him, I just sat there like a toad hog, thinking about Kate's cigarettes, and didn't do anything. Finally, I reached for the phone but was stopped by a scream.

I looked up and saw my father leap up and grab my grandmother's alabaster pigeon off the desk. Blotter, pens, and papers from boxes flew all over the floor; Linda screamed at me again to get a fucking ambulance; my father twisted Linda's arm behind her back and hurled her against the desk, and I heard her head crack on the corner. Before my father even got near her, I saw a lot of blood, so I don't know whether or not she was already dead when my father began to bash her head in over and over again with the alabaster pigeon.

HASTINGS, HEARTE & DANIELS

118 AVENUE OF THE AMERICAS

NEW YORK, NY 10013

Nov. 8, 1974

Dear Annie,
     Is this one of your Kurt Vonnegut "short" chapters, or did some pages get lost in the mail?

I'm still working on a time when I can get away.

                              Love,
                              Martin

----

                    430 Pacific Avenue
                    San Francisco, CA 94133

                    November 11, 1974

Dearest Martin,
    Jesus Christ! This chapter is short, but
then, so is life. I just thought I'd hit the
readers over the head with some good, clean,
old-fashioned violence. Besides, Holly was
typing a term paper and needed the typewriter.

                              Love,
                              Annie

HASTINGS, HEARTE & DANIELS
118 AVENUE OF THE AMERICAS
NEW YORK, NY 10013

                              November 14, 1974

Dear Annie,
    Well, well, well, so you were able to mix
violence along with your recurring theme of
birds and flying. Since I imagine alabaster

pigeons are pretty heavy, it is possible someone could crack a skull with one. You're
strange.

I will be in San Francisco next week or
the week after that. Because I want to spend
the entire visit with you, why don't you stay
with me at the hotel? You seem to have inherited the good qualities of your mother and
somehow have eliminated the bad ones. Well, you
know what they say: bad qualities tend to skip
a generation.

Since you were sixteen in the last chapter, I guess it means we will either have more
flashbacks, about two years to go until it
ends, or I'll become a character in it.

Take care, my sweet,

Love,
Martin

---

430 Pacific Avenue
San Francisco, CA 94133

Nov. 19, 1974

Dearest, Daahling, Martin,

God, don't you think it would be a little
too "artsy craftsy" to have my editor a character in my book? Besides, who said it was
autobiographical anyway? What do you want?—
"He took me in his arms in his suite at the
Mark, touched my breasts, licked my cunt, and
made the earth move!"? No, Martin, I know how
to quit while I'm ahead.

But there is one very important sentence
in the next chapter where I say that happiness

is more often remembered than experienced. (Do
you just remember happiness with me, or did you
really experience it?)

I'll see you soon. While you're here, I'll
take you to Alcatraz and show you the actual
cell that Al Capone was kept in. Speaking of
Alcatraz, is love "a prison or a release"? That
was just food for thought from a profound
little girl with "a lot of woman in her."

Love,
Annie

P.S. You're not married, are you? (Speaking of
things that were "unsaid"!)

chapter 16

My mother graduated from high school in 1946. Because she had been an honor student all the way through, and because her parents were loaded, she had the choice of any college in the country.

"Why the *hell* did you choose Portland City University?" my father would ask her.

"Because," she would snap back, "I liked to go camping on the fucking Oregon coast!"

It wasn't until after she died that we found out the real reason. Since Mother was never what one would describe as a "camper," we really did wonder.

"Ahh, heh, heh, heh," Grandfather had said when we asked him. "I thought it would be nice for her to go to Berkeley . . . she could have been close to home . . . maybe we could have helped her." He chuckled. "Heh, heh, heh, that Katie," he said, "she was a wild one. Your grandmother wanted her to go to Smith, and Kate said to her, 'And turn out like you?' Heh, heh, heh, heh. Your grandmother really thought Smith would push Katie in the right direction."

"What the hell did Grandmother think would have been the right goddamned direction for her anyway?" I asked him.

He didn't say anything for a while, and then finally he said, "Annie, you are too much like Katie for your own good. . . ."

"I'm *not!*" I cried, seriously worried.

"Heh, heh, heh," he chuckled. "If you want to change things, you'll just have to rewrite history, I guess. Heh, heh, heh. . . ."

Shit. Mother used to say your future was written in the stars, my father said it was just what you "put in the pot," and now my grandfather was trying to scare me by saying it was all hereditary.

Hollistor told me that since Mother probably knew somewhere inside her, even at sixteen, that there would be no right direction for her, she decided to skip the college crap and fall in love. She had told us dramatically about ceremoniously ripping up her college applications, declaring she would never marry, and embarking on her new career: the femme fatale, moving from one man to another, leaving behind her a "string of broken hearts."

"I don't see what that has to do with why she went to Portland City and screwed up her life," I said to Hollistor.

"She spent the summer after she graduated from high school," he continued, "having a secret and what she called 'real torrid' affair with this faggot philosophy professor at Berkeley, which ended pretty fast when his wife and kids came back from Boston, where they were spending the summer with relatives."

"How could he have a wife and kids if he was a fag?" I interrupted.

"He was a *philosophy professor*," said Hollistor. "They're all a little strange . . . You do know, Annie, there are a whole shitload of strange people out there?"

"*Out there!*" I exclaimed, and then added, "You said it, Hollistor, I didn't."

Hollistor took another bite of pizza and continued. "Well," he said, "she decided then there was nothing else to live for; slashed her wrists; and settled down in a warm bath with a copy of *Emma*. She wrote this great suicide note—really eloquent—and devoted herself, without second thoughts, to the business of dying. Anyway, she was sitting there bleeding in the bathtub and didn't seem to be dying at all. She kept looking at her wet library copy of *Emma* and watched the water get pink. Then," he went on, "she draped her arm over the side of the tub so some of the blood would run over the side and look more grotesque when her body was discovered, and artistically smeared some blood over her face, and tried to concentrate on *Emma*. God, how would you like *Emma* to be the *last* book you ever read?"

"Better than *Pudd'nhead Wilson*."

"Better than *Acting Is Believing!*"

"Better than *The Golden Bowl!*" We both laughed. "Did she die?" I asked.

"Yes," laughed Hollistor, and ate his pizza.

"Come on, what happened?"

"She was lying there in the tub, bleeding away, when—you'll love this part, Annie—just like in the movies, the maid came into the bathroom with a load of towels, screamed, dropped the towels, and hauled Kate out of the tub along with her wet library copy of *Emma*."

"Was it a black maid? They are always black maids who discover the bodies."

"I really don't know," he said.

"So she didn't get to die," I laughed.

"Naa," said Hollistor, "she went to Portland City University, which is about the same thing."

"I don't get it."

"She hadn't applied for admission anywhere on account of the fag philosophy professor, so her father's former roommate was a dean at Portland City—Dean Hanson, a real jerk—and as a favor to your grandfather, he arranged a last-minute admission for her. So the next week—fall of 1946—with her wrists still bandaged and a hat over one eye—Kate left for Portland City University, agreeing to stay one year."

"But she stayed there *three* years!"

"Oh, *everyone* was always talking about transferring. But you know, people tend to stay on and on where they are comfortable."

"How come you and Mother stayed?"

"We were comfortable . . . we were the stars. Shit, of course it isn't all that hard to be a star at Portland City, but . . . well . . . she met your damn father, and I felt I should stay and save her from his awful clutches."

"Were you in love with her?" I asked.

"Let's just say I loved her," he laughed.

Uncle Hollistor told me over and over again that Mother would probably be dead now no matter what course of action she had decided to take back in 1946, or '47, or whenever. He said she was the kind of person who always fought life because she felt it was just a dark shell that sometime she was going to break, then spread her gorgeous wings and fly away like some goddamned bird. Personally, I think she was just nuts and bitter because life hadn't turned out just like she had wanted it to. Fuck, whose life does? Probably, if I had it to do all over again, I would have been born in a nice small town in Ohio, with a mother who baked cookies and made Christmas stockings. At least I would know what to expect from one day to the next. When I told this to Mother, she pushed her hair out of her eyes, laughed, and said, "Then, Annie, you would give up all hope of ever breaking that fucking shell and flying . . . you know most people will never be birds like us . . . you've got to fly over the whole world of goddamned pedestrians."

"You can be weird, Mother," I said.

"Use it, Annie, and soar away," she answered.

Uncle Hollistor said Mother would have died anyway because she always refused to believe that shit about happiness being remembered or anticipated more than experienced. What she believed was that she was being deprived of it.

During her first semester at college, Mother moved out of the dorm. Since her two roommates were both Mormons who didn't even believe in drinking coffee, got up at six every morning, and studied all the time, it didn't surprise Hollistor. He said they were always asking her what she was running away from.

"Naturally," he said, "she didn't last particularly long as their roommate. That dorm was full of all these elementary education majors who put little chipmunks up on the bulletin boards for fall and switched to little bunnies for the spring. We both about puked. God, she almost got kicked out of school . . . drinking with me in the dorm, having the FBI after her for making illegal long distance phone calls, ignoring curfew, screwing fraternity boys—Jesus, how she could have done *that*, I'll never understand . . . but then I always thought your mother had very bad taste in men. Jesus, I loved her then . . . she was the only person I could talk to."

"Why didn't you marry her?" I asked.

"God, Annie, I'm no masochist . . . besides, I told you she had very bad taste in men."

She found a basement apartment in an old house, not too far from campus. If she ate less, she figured, she could live off-campus for what it cost to live on-campus; her parents would never find out; and she would be free to be "a human being at last."

Since the apartment was only fifty-five dollars a month, Mother had to share a bathroom with some man in "the bonding business" and exert herself a bit to make it livable. She painted the drop-leaf table white, made curtains for the windows, and bought a quilt for the antique bed. As it turned out, she rented it again when she returned from Yale to "get" my father—because of all the "passionate memories."

The landlady was an alcoholic named Minny. She used to weave down the stairs, take Mother's chin in her hands and tell her how beautiful she was. "Kate," she would say, "come upstairs and play the piano for me." Because the piano hadn't been tuned since she had started slugging down the old wine, she never noticed that Kate didn't play too well. Minny lived with her husband in one room with all the furniture smashed over to the sides to accommodate this gigantic pool table in the middle of the room. Mother would sit there and play "You Made Me Love You, Mr. Clark Gable," and the landlady would sip red wine and cry about her past when she had been beautiful. Her husband would do trick shots on the pool table. "Poor guy," Mother said, "the balls never went in the pockets. Poor woman: all she had was her past."

"You had to be a real genius to even *find* the apartment," Mother said. "You had to go through a back gate, past two ceramic swans; down some stairs; in a door; down some other stairs; through the basement; around the corner by the washing machine; and around an old bookcase. You know, I bet Anne Frank would still be alive today if her family had hid out there instead of where they did." She smiled. "Oh, the things that went on in that apartment . . . the sex . . . the wine . . . your father."

My father wasn't my mother's first married man at Portland City University. Because married men don't see their mistresses with their hair in rollers or with the flu, Mother found they suited her. Because she was unable to show her good side twenty-four hours a day, she found that seeing someone for two hours put her in a better light. The first one was this guy named Ted Hanson, who she said was a jerk—"Good looking . . . but a jerk." He was a square-jawed, young debate coach. When Mother went with Uncle Hollistor to win the National Debate Championship, she got her claws into him. Although debate interested Mother and Hollistor about as much as computer science interests me, they liked to be "winners" and liked the free trips everywhere. Because Mother thought she'd enjoy being the "other woman" and because the mystique surrounding mistresses intrigued her, she winked back at Ted. "God," she said later, "he was like Kraft Macaroni and Cheese dinner compared with escargots."

"And I was the escargot?" asked my father.

"I *loved* you," she said.

When Mother looked in the mirror and thought her looks were going, she talked about Ted Hanson. She said even though he didn't really have much of a personality or mind of his own, he was damn good looking. "For example," she said, "he would say he really thought *Gentleman's Agreement* was a great and truthful film, and then I would say I thought it was a pile of garbage, and he would say that he really didn't like it that much—a real nerd-o wishy-washy!

"You know," she said loudly, so my father could hear, "he was so spineless, I could get him to say any fucking thing I wanted to hear!" My father was trying to work on his book, "The Function of the Maid in Greek Tragedy," and he didn't want to listen to Mother at all—particularly about how appealing she was to some dumb clod back in 1947. He looked up from the typewriter and said, "Well, Katie, whoever cares least in a relationship controls it, and obviously you cared least in that one. If you don't shut up, *I* will care least in this one, and then I will control it, and . . . " He spoke to her as if she were a little retarded child, "And you wouldn't like that, would you?"

She was wearing a black sweater and moved over to the fireplace and effectively posed herself with one arm on the mantel. Holly and I exchanged glances. "He *desired* me and delighted in me," she said, knowing that my father was typing "Now is the time for all good men to come to the aid of their country" and pretending to be typing something else.

He paused. "*I* desired you and delighted in you," he said softly.

While Holly had the courtesy to sidle out of the room, I watched Mother stretch her arm high over her head and smile at my father. "Ahh," she continued, "blessed is Ted who hadn't enough character to be able to hurt me." She was crying now. Since I never really knew when Mother was just putting it on for another's benefit and when she was really upset, I watched her closely. My father kept on typing "Now is the time for all good men . . . " She spoke very loudly. "Ahh . . . blessed are all the Ted Hansons of the world!" She sunk down to a sitting position and hugged her knees and said very slowly and quietly, "I mean, he did make me feel bright, smart, worthwhile, strong . . . Ahh . . . blessed is me in all my weakness."

My father stood up and slowly applauded. Mother threw a pottery jar at him from the mantel, and I quietly scurried out of the room.

HASTINGS, HEARTE & DANIELS

118 AVENUE OF THE AMERICAS

NEW YORK, NY 10013

November 22, 1974

Dear Annie,
    I believe that most happiness is remembered and not experienced; however, you are one person who <u>forces</u> one to experience it. Because I do remember being very happy when I visited San Francisco, I'm looking forward to it again.
    Since you are someone with a lot of insight, you are probably going to think I'm putting you on when I say I'm in the process of getting a divorce, But I really <u>am</u>. We are separated . . . Believe me, Annie.
    Your novel is getting better—really. Keep

it up and try to have another chapter ready for
me when I get to San Francisco.

> Love you,
> Martin

> 430 Pacific Avenue
> San Francisco, CA 94133

> Nov. 25, 1974

Dear Martin,
    Because I don't groove on the picture of
you "going over my work" while I sit at your
feet and hold your pens like Dora in <u>David
Copperfield</u>, I am <u>not</u> going to "mix business
with pleasure" and give you a chapter while
you're here.
    My novel is "wrenched out of memory that
selective amnesia may have distorted," and it
is much too personal to just hand over in a
manila envelope in some fucking suite at the
Mark.
    You had better not be fucking me while
throwing my chapters in the wastebasket; leading me along and making me think you're going
to publish it just to get some young piece of
unused ass is <u>not</u> professional! Since you
should be here very soon, I'm going to assume
you are (professional, that is).
    Besides, this great best seller is going
to put me through college and maybe even win
the Pulitzer Prize (God, if <u>Harvey</u> can win,
<u>anything</u> can). I'm also going to put in more
dialogue so it can be easily converted into a
screenplay. Hollywood will love it—lots of it

takes place in the thirties, forties, and
fifties, so they can do another costume trip
like in <u>The Way We Were</u>. And don't you <u>dare</u>
tell me I'm being a little premature!

Also, before we hit the rack again, what
is this bullshit about "in the process of getting a divorce"? My God, you must think I'm a
real goddamned moron or something—"in the
process of getting a divorce"! Shit. Look, I
really don't give a rusty fuck if you're married or not—just if you're honest. You know,
"there is such a mystique surrounding mistresses."

Love,
Annie

HASTINGS, HEARTE & DANIELS

118 AVENUE OF THE AMERICAS

NEW YORK, NY 10013

December 26, 1974

Dear Annie,
I hope you had a good Christmas. Jesus, I
know that is the sort of opening sentence
you're probably laughing at, but I had to start
somewhere. I haven't heard from you in over a
month. I know I said it was possible that this
wouldn't be published, but I was only trying
to tell you that it isn't completely my deci-
sion. Because HASTINGS, HEARTE & DANIELS does
have an editorial board who outrank me, I was

only telling you that no matter how much I like Heritage, it is a fact that I can't single-handedly publish it.

Really, I love the way you write, and I'm sorry I upset you. I honestly do think you have potential as a writer, Annie, and I think you are a wonderful person.

Since I enjoyed our time together last month so much, I'd like to do it again after the new year.

> I love you, Annie,
> Martin

P.S. I really was telling the truth about my marriage . . . truly. . . .

---

430 Pacific Avenue
San Francisco, CA 94133

Dec. 29, 1974

Dear Martin,

Since we are being so "honest" with each other (except about your marriage, of course), I guess I should level with you. This novel really is about my life (we can change the names later—when I talk about real people, I write better).

I'm not sure we should see each other—or rather do the "old in and out"—anymore. To be honest, I think our relationship should be professional.

Although I am mature enough to accept rejection, I will probably have to be hospitalized if this isn't published. They say if you "learn something" from writing, you're ahead even if it isn't published. Shit! I "learned something" from observing my crazy mother for ten years. I don't want to have to say, "It made me a better writer," or, "It made me a better person," after my novel is rejected. I don't want to have to kill myself like Sylvia Plath to get the recognition I deserve; and I certainly don't want to be "the women's Salinger"—I would rather have Salinger be _my_ predecessor: you know, like Marlowe was to Shakespeare.

I am going to avoid my mother's pitfalls and live off my royalties instead of dying with the applause. Mother's performance ended in death; my writing will give me immortality!

Love,
Annie

HASTINGS, HEARTE & DANIELS

118 AVENUE OF THE AMERICAS

NEW YORK, NY 10013

Jan. 2, 1975

My Dear Annie,

Since I started off the last letter with "Merry Christmas," I guess I should be consistent and say, "Happy New Year!"

So, now I get "let in on the secret": Heritage is autobiographical—never would have guessed it.

I feel you <u>have</u> followed the role heredity has cast you in more closely than you think: the only reason I read your unsolicited manuscript was because of your sheer nerve. Since your mother got accepted to Yale because of sheer nerve and was a bright woman (as you are) who expected the world to be handed to her, how can you say you aren't like her?

Your mother fell for her professor; and no matter what you say now, you fell for your editor. (Power figures?) Your mother loved what your father represented more than she seemed to love him as a person, and I feel our relationship soured the moment you realized that I alone couldn't publish <u>Heritage</u>. Do you say you didn't love me for what I represented? You sighed, breathed passion, and said you loved me last month with all the feeling your mother would have had. Is this book about your mother, or is it about you?

Best,
Martin

P.S. No playwright named Hollistor Kent ever won the Pulitzer Prize, no actress named Mary Kate McNeil was ever called "one of the finest young American actresses" by Walter Kerr of the <u>Tribune</u>, and no play titled <u>Young Victoria</u> was produced on Broadway in the last thirty years. I looked them up!

430 Pacific Avenue
San Francisco, CA 94133

January 5, 1975

Martin Goldsmith
Senior Editor
HASTINGS, HEARTE & DANIELS
118 Avenue of the Americas
NYC, N.Y. 10013

MARTIN:
     We all know that fiction is much more
interesting than real life, and my name is not
really Anne Sarah Foster either!!! How about
that?

                              Piss on you,
                              Annie

HASTINGS, HEARTE & DANIELS

118 AVENUE OF THE AMERICAS

NEW YORK, NY 10013

Jan. 20, 1975

Dear Annie or whoever you are,
     Who are you really? Hell, why don't you
bring your nameless body over to New York? I'd
put you up at the Algonquin just like Dorothy
Parker. Why don't you answer your phone? Would
you see me if I came to San Francisco?
     Because I really do care what happens to
you, I questioned your reasons for sleeping

with me. But I do think I love you. I don't
want my personal happiness to hinge on whether
or not the editorial board likes this book as
much as I do. You're not being fair to me.
I think I _love_ you, Annie. Don't shut me out
of your life.

Love,
Martin

P.S. There really _is_ a HASTINGS, HEARTE &
DANIELS . . .

---

430 Pacific Avenue
San Francisco, CA 94133

Jan. 23, 1975

Dear Martin,
God, you're stupid! Would you (I mean,
really _would_ you), if you were writing a deep
and highly personal story about yourself, use
your real name? Come on, Martin!
I'll come to New York only to sign contracts. When money changes hands, we'll see
each other again—as "just good friends."
Is it _really_ an editorial board and not
the editor who has the final say?

Yours 'til today,
Annie

P.S. Enclosed is the next chapter. As you will
see, our family has the habit of _not_
acknowledging the existence of those who
fuck us over.

chapter 17

Because time and time again my father, in the six years after Mother pulled the trigger before he went mad, called my mother an "exquisite woman," we figured he had always had the hots for her. When Hollistor told me that *Mother* had instigated the affair with my father, I was awfully surprised.

"She asked *him?*" I asked on the way to the mental hospital to visit my father last year.

"I *told you,*" said Hollistor, "she thought the 'sun rose in his eyes.'"

"Shit," I said.

Neither Holly nor I had inherited Mother's mysterious eyes or unusual beauty, so we always felt a little shortchanged. I had inherited her thin body, but Mother's erotic posture just didn't come with it. What I got stuck with was her unusual memory for detail, which makes me reflect on life too much.

In the fall of 1948, Mother decided to seduce my father. For a month she had been admiring his mouth. She said he had a real sexuality under that paunch (shit, it was just the father complex, I bet). During her marriage, the sex was sure there— just the joy was gone.

In the fall of 1948, Matthew Foster, my father, gave a lecture on "Sex in the Theatre," and Mother sat in the front row and stared at him. Since he didn't notice her at all, I imagine that made him twice as attractive to her as he was before the lecture. She says she was "blinded by the fact that he was talking about sex in public," and he attributed his inattention to her to the fact that he was not used to *speaking* in public. When Mother was sixteen, she told us, she seduced a senatorial candidate who was on a speaking tour of the Bay area by staring at him from the front row. If she could get someone who was almost a senator (he lost), and couldn't get my father, well, there was her challenge. When *I* was sixteen, I couldn't seduce the *garbage* man if I'd sat naked on the garbage can. But, then, that is one of the many differences between me and my mother.

Hollistor, Holly, and I tiptoed down the hall of the private mental hospital to the reception room. "I sure hope I never go crazy," I said, looking around at all the weird-o's.

"Yeah," said Holly. "Mother once said, 'Better dead than crazy.' "

Hollistor laughed. "She got both, didn't she," he said.

My father was sitting in an armchair, thumbing through *Field & Stream*. Since he had never been *near* a field or stream, we figured he must be pretty far gone. "What's new?" I asked him.

He muttered something and shook his head. "On October 6," he said, "Kate told me she loved me . . . more than anything . . . the way I loved her." Because after Mother died, my father had always made a point of indicating that Mother had simply been an unfortunate experience in his life, and because he rarely talked to us on visits to the hospital, we were surprised.

"Was that the day she seduced you?" I asked. Because he hadn't been talking for weeks, we had been told to try to bring him out into conversation regardless of the subject.

"Annie," he said gripping my hand, "would you ever ask a man to make love to you?"

"I don't know. I never *have*."

"Don't, Annie," he said. "It isn't becoming to a lady, and you are going to be a very beautiful lady someday."

Since I thought it was pointless to tell him that when you're eighteen, you're supposed to be in your prime, I just said, "It didn't bother you when Mother did it."

"Your mother was special . . . a special case . . . she did it with class."

"Shit," whispered Hollistor to me.

I shuddered. That place gave me the creeps. It was one of those loony bins for rich people, where they have a polished grand piano instead of an old beat-up upright as they do at the State Hospital. This was one of those places where you pay psychiatric nurses pots of money to arrange bowls of flowers to make the place attractive. I didn't see why he couldn't just be shipped off to the State Hospital where my grandmother was. Since it hadn't bothered Kate to put her mother in a cheap place, I was pissed off at Janet for making us feel real guilty about dumping my father there.

The only other person in the reception room was a middle-aged woman who appeared perfectly normal except that she was crawling around on the floor tracing the floral pattern on the carpet with her finger. "How old are you now, Annie?" my father asked.

"Eighteen."

"Have I been in this damn place two years now?"

"Well, time sure flies when you're having a good time," I said. Holly gave me a sick look, and Hollistor quickly picked up the *Field & Stream*.

"Your mother wasn't more than eighteen herself when she seduced me," he said. "You know . . . when she came into my office that day I thought she was ready to kill me."

I wasn't sure whether he was distorting the story because he was unstable, or whether what he told us was true (because Mother was unstable).

My father continued. "She was very close to some people who were trying to get me fired . . . it was a conspiracy . . . thought I wasn't any good . . . hard to work with . . . troublemaker. . . . And your Uncle Hollistor—she was close to him. He wrote plays then, did you know that, Annie?"

"He writes plays *now, you* know that, Daddy!"

"Your Uncle Hollistor is *not* a playwright!"

"But he. . . . " Holly stopped me with a look; my father was crying.

"He tried to dedicate a production of one of his plays to a professor who *taught*."

"All professors teach, don't they?"

"You don't understand, do you? Hollistor's goddamned dedication read 'To Dr. Russell, who *taught*.' He was some kind of a frigging legend. Everyone kept telling me what an *outstanding* director he was, as if to imply that I was just shit. Your mother . . . always bringing up what *outstanding* productions he did and how the theatre department 'would never be the same,' and all kinds of crap like that."

"Our dear and glorious deceased Mother always tortured people—that was her way," I said.

"Hollistor's dedication read, didn't you get me, 'To Dr. Russell, who *taught*.' Now I just couldn't . . . at that time . . . take any more of that shit. . . . You see, I had a plan . . . a vision for that department. . . . Oh, God. . . . That statement was a direct statement that Dr. Russell *taught,* and I did *not!*"

"I don't think Hollistor really meant it." When Hollistor is standing right there, I mean, what do you say?

"He implied that Dr. Russell was the *only* one who had *taught!* I had no other recourse than to veto the program; he was frigging lucky I didn't veto the entire production!"

He rambled on and on, and then said that on October 6, 1948, Kate stopped him on the stairs that went up to the other level of the campus. She said she wanted to see him in his office.

Because memory plays strange tricks, I wasn't sure if this were all true, but it sounded like Mother. She told him when she could make it, and he was all set to tell her he didn't want any more of her shit slung around the department.

Then my father did something I had never seen him do before: he got sappy, really sappy! He turned his back to us and

159

said that at four o'clock on October 6, Katie walked into his office. She was shaking; she started to speak; it was an attempt to be direct; instead, she was vulnerable. It was an attempt to be cool; instead, she was erotic, and he had never seen anyone so beautiful. "She was slender, almost childlike," he said to the lady who was still tracing the floral pattern on the carpet. Because he couldn't tell any more of this to us, he knelt down and looked her straight in the eyes. "She had gray eyes," he said very loudly to the lady, who ignored him, "and I never realized they were so soft . . . misty . . . she knew how to do that, you know . . . cry on cue . . . but she did it so *well*—so beautifully."

"My God!" Hollistor whispered to me. "He's out of his fucking mind!"

"*Of course* he's out of his fucking mind," I whispered back. "People aren't put in mental hospitals for the *fun* of it!"

My father continued speaking to the lady. "That day," he said, "her heart lay exposed there in those eyes. She was dressed in dark blue . . . tiny lace collar . . . high neck . . . like an old-fashioned schoolteacher . . . erotic."

"Jesus Christ!" whispered Hollistor. "I was just trying to make up for a few differences we had in the past, and I have to listen to this shit!"

Then my father said (and I *quote*), "There was fear and fire and softness and passion in those eyes, and as she spoke and I heard what she had to say, I knew . . . I *knew.*"

She had simply sat there and said she was going to ask him something; because she knew there would be a number of reasons why he might say no, she would understand if he did. She also said she was going to drop his class, so he wouldn't think that grades were a motivation, and (get this) he could *trust* her.

"I'm sure," whispered Hollistor, "the whole population of Portland and perhaps the entire Northwest knew about the 'clandestine affair' as soon as she let out her first orgasmic scream—*trust* her!"

"Then she told me," my father mumbled softly, "I was in love with her, and we were going to have an affair of the heart . . . that's what she said . . . she said I was going to be the love of her life. . . . "

"Maybe we ought to be going," Holly said to me.

"No, we're probably getting to the good part," I whispered.

"Then," said my father, "she said she had wanted the proposition to be businesslike. She said she had rehearsed it, but it hadn't come out as she wanted it to. She said she was a romantic, and that businesslike proposals weren't easy for her. And then she shrugged and said, 'Well, even Marlon Brando's performances don't *always* come out the way he wants them.' Then she kissed me on the mouth and gave me her key."

My father looked at the lady on the floor, and then he looked up at us. "Annie," he said, "I have trouble putting things into words."

"You said it!" Hollistor whispered. Holly hushed him.

"She never did, you know," he continued. "She could always say what she meant. She was logical that day, and she was vulnerable—imagine Kate vulnerable—and I thought she was flaky and untouchable. As she spoke, I really . . . and I mean it . . . knew something about erotic love. Do you understand what I'm saying, Annie?"

I had always thought scenes of grand passion were reserved for *The Umbrellas of Cherbourg*, but according to Mother, she *did* create them in her lifetime. I glanced at Hollistor, who shook his head at me. My father continued without waiting for my answer.

"I *had* to take her. I had known love—I loved Janet. When a man has many mistresses, he knows something about passion, but Annie, suddenly after all those years of loving and lusting, I knew something about loving and lusting at the same time. Maybe it was because she was so young . . . so sure . . . with so much future . . . I don't know." His voice got softer, and he took my wrist and said, "Remember, there are all kinds of strange things that flighty, listless, useless people have underneath the crap. Look at people's eyes, Annie, and maybe they'll let you see it."

He started to sob. Holly touched him, rubbed his hands, and signaled me to call the nurse. Because he was better by the time I returned with her, he said a very polite good-bye to Holly and me, and not a word to Hollistor. It was just as if he weren't there.

HASTINGS, HEARTE & DANIELS

118 AVENUE OF THE AMERICAS

NEW YORK, NY 10013

January 27, 1975

Dear Annie,
    Although you say that grand passion is reserved for <u>The Umbrellas of Cherbourg</u> and only your mother could create it in real life, I think <u>you</u> do. Are you forgetting what happened under the eucalyptus trees in the Berkeley hills, walking across the Golden Gate Bridge, inside the suite at the Mark? Didn't any of that mean anything to you?
    Despite what you think, I was not casual with you—maybe you do think you should "ball without a third act," but with your heritage, I don't believe it. Your mother added a third act to <u>everything</u>.

Please come to New York. I can have a
ticket in the mail as soon as you say.

                              All my love,
                              Martin

P.S. This is very hard for me to say, but I
     gave the completed portion of your "Great
     American Novel" to some of my colleagues.
     They suggested you break the "monotony"
     (their word—not mine) by interjecting
     something between each two chapters—per-
     haps tell the story from someone else's
     point of view—and make it more clear that
     the narrator is learning something.

---

                         430 Pacific Avenue
                         San Francisco, CA 94133

                         Jan. 31, 1975

Dear Martin,
     Good Lord! Who the fuck cares if the nar-
rator "learns something"! I wrote Heritage for
the readers, not for the narrator. If-the
readers "learn something," it's enough—even
important. If Anne Sarah Foster "learns something," we've just got another To Sir With
Love. And how the hell am I supposed to write
it from someone else's point of view! You know,
the trouble with this whole fucking world today
is the absolute fact that no one (not even
Marlon Brando) can see the world from anyone
else's point of view!

Don't pay too much attention to your colleagues (it is true that they only <u>advise</u> the editorial board, isn't it?). Chekhov was also called monotonous! I bet even Evel Knievel has moments of monotony in his life. Think about sexual intercourse—isn't <u>that</u> even a little monotonous: in and out, in and out, sigh, sigh, yes, yes, yes?

<u>True</u> passion, Mr. Studly McNutt, comes from a "meeting of the minds," and ours obviously haven't met!

Best,
Annie

P.S. What is this shit about putting me up at the Algonquin like Dorothy Parker? Your wife still at home?

chapter **18**

Because there isn't just *one* day when someone is normal and the next day he is suddenly walking around crazy, my father must have already been on a downhill slide when he killed Linda. I had toyed with the idea, and still want to come to the conclusion, that if I hadn't fallen down the stairs in my U.C.B. T-shirt, Linda would be alive and my father would be normal. This idea gave me a sort of cross to bear, which I have used as an excuse for why I don't function well with people.

Uncle Hollistor once told me that since I came from a screwed up family, I might well reap the benefits and wander around and do as I pleased because I had been so fucked up by my parents.

"How long is that supposed to last?" I asked him.

"Until you find your calling," he said.

"I already know what it is."

"You do?"

"Yeah, to live, make millions of dollars, and not hurt children the way my mother hurt me."

"How are you going to do that?"

"Well, I haven't figured out how I'm going to make millions of dollars yet, but I won't hurt children because I'm not going to have any. They just vomit and cry, you hate them and then hurt them."

"Well," he said, "since you have that part of it worked out, you'd better work on making a million dollars."

"Plural," I said.

The day I "caused" my father to go bonkers, Holly was out and Uncle Hollistor was in New York writing a comedy about a psychopathic killer. Since Linda was gushing blood and my father was making strange grunting sounds, I was afraid to move because he might rush after me and start hitting me with the damn pigeon. I stood there, backed up against the banister, I guess waiting for Linda to stand up, wipe off the blood, and tell me I was dreaming or watching an episode of "Adam 12." My father set the bloody alabaster pigeon down on the desk and stood there staring at Linda (or what was left of Linda). "Katie, Katie . . . " he said, brushing Linda's matted, bloody hair out of the one eye she had left.

"Do you want me to call an ambulance?" I asked softly.

My father did not respond at first, then said, "For Katie . . . call one for Katie." He touched Linda's bloody cheek, and said, "Kate, wake up, it's all over, Kate." His words turned into moans.

Naturally, you can imagine this freaked me out a little, but I did manage—for the second time in my sixteen years—to pick up the phone and report a violent death.

Since my father wasn't watching me anymore, I edged my way up the stairs. As soon as I reached the top, I ran into the kitchen and saw Janet wheeling her mother Ruth along the ramp that led to the upper level of the rose garden. I didn't exactly have the urge to rush to her, so I waited until she guided the wheelchair into the kitchen before I spoke. I found myself breathing faster. "You're not going to believe this . . . but . . . but . . . I think Daddy has killed Linda." Janet just stood there in her beige doubleknit pantsuit and stared at me. *"For God's sake, Janet, do something!"* I screamed.

At that moment we started to hear the sirens coming down Pacific Avenue. Because I didn't know what else to do, I started sobbing. Ruth was chuckling in her wheelchair. The doorbell ringing frantically set Janet into motion. Without a word, she rushed downstairs; the doorbell kept ringing; and then I heard a strange man's voice. Then Janet screamed at the men to *just* attend to Linda and *not to touch her husband!* I rushed to the top of the stairs, looked down, and saw my father hanging on to Janet (who by then had blood all over her high water, beige pantsuit). Like a little child, he cried for his Katie.

As you can probably imagine, this was rather upsetting for me. I mean, it isn't every day someone sees her father mash in someone's head with an alabaster pigeon. Even though Linda sometimes had made me *want* to vomit, this horrified me so much that I *did*—all over Ruth's hand-knitted, checkered bedroom slippers.

Because Janet rode in the ambulance that carted my father off, I was left in the house alone with Ruth. Now, Ruth never liked *any* of us. Holly once overheard Ruth telling Janet that we were all a bunch of basket cases and that Janet was "out of her cotton picking mind" to come back to my father. Janet had told her that Holly and I were Matt's children, and she had learned to love us almost as much as if we were her own. She had said something retarded about how it was unfortunate that we had had to live through a suicide in the family and how she felt it was her duty and all to help us lead "normal lives" after our "tragic incident." (Normal lives! Shit.) Ruth had just mumbled, "Excuses, excuses." I had pointed out to Holly that, yes, it was unfortunate and awful, but not half as unfortunate as Ruth in a wheelchair, sitting around our house, eating our food, and judging those people who helped her to the bathroom.

Because Ruth wasn't altogether too pleased to have vomit all over her slippers, she started in on what a hell hole this house was. When I tried to explain to her what had happened, Ruth just shook her head and mumbled something about perversion. Then she said, "At least it was Linda . . . never liked her anyway, ha! ha! . . . Linda . . . fat bitch had it coming to her . . . ha! ha! ha!" I decided I had had enough of that, so I went and sat on the window seat in the upstairs living room and watched Pacific Avenue, trying to pretend, as Mother had, that all the cars going by were gondolas.

After about a half hour, I heard Holly arrive. Because it didn't occur to me that she might wonder what all the blood was doing smeared over the entry and library, I was startled when she screamed. I explained once more the whole routine about good old dependable Dad bashing in Linda's head.

"What's going to happen to us?" she asked sensibly. "Are we going to have to go live with Aunt Caroline with her potting and Goodwill clothes?"

"She doesn't buy clothes at the Goodwill anymore," I said; "the nouveau-poor trend is really driving up the price of secondhand clothes. She puts them on her Master Charge at Macy's. Besides, they're not going to send us to a house with leaky plumbing, a bastard kid, and a Hare Krishna guy."

"Allison makes a mint," she said. "Could you stand her? I mean, she lives in Hawaii with palm trees, sun, and 'Lovely Hula Hands.' "

"Holly," I said, "think carefully. Do you really want to fly twenty-five-hundred miles across the Pacific Ocean to end up in an affluent hip house with Aunt Allison fumigating it every time you sneeze?"

No response. We didn't see much of Aunt Allison except on rare occasions when she visited San Francisco in a haze of musky-smelling perfume and clanking gold charm bracelets. Her two children were not what I would call the pride of our family either: they were even more boring than Allison. Bonnie was twenty-one, worked in a bank, lived at home, was engaged to the assistant manager, and already had her silver pattern registered at Liberty House. She had gone to a private girls' school, still subscribed to *Seventeen* magazine, still bought Clearasil, and really looked like one of the fucking Pepsi generation. The year Mother died, she was fifteen, and when she arrived with Allison her conversations with my father always started with something like, "Gee, things must be really hard for you now." Shit.

Her younger brother, Marshall, had been in the Cub Scouts and then in the Boy Scouts, and if he hadn't joined the army after high school, he probably would have been a goddamned Sig Ep Frat boy. As a kid, he beat me up first thing every time he came to visit and told my father that I had a pack of Salem cigarettes under my bed with my comic books . . . and Janet had had the nerve to ask why I didn't like him. To live with Allison would be worse than moving in with "The Brady Bunch"!

The only other possibility was to take the PSA commuter flight down to the land of Taco Bells: L.A., where our Aunt Mona and "Air Force One" lived. Every time she visited, we had to sit for hours and look at pictures in art books. Now, I have nothing against art, and nothing against the Renaissance masters, but we really hated the way Mona got such a cheap thrill out of "exposing" us to them. I'm sure if either of us turn out to be a halfway decent human being, Aunt Mona will take personal credit for it.

She always had the attitude that Mother was totally incompetent and Daddy was an opinionated bore. We had to admit that was sort of accurate, but shit, she sent us "Budding Beauty" cologne long after we had graduated to "Joy," and we always had to be nice to her so we could avoid hearing what a terrible influence our family heritage was on us.

Holly looked at me without a word, and I knew she also felt that waiting on Ruth hand and foot for the rest of our lives would be a step (if only a small step) closer to perfection than one *day* of listening to Aunt Mona talk about her beliefs in Ayn Rand and the individual.

HASTINGS, HEARTE & DANIELS

118 AVENUE OF THE AMERICAS

NEW YORK, NY 10013

Feb. 3, 1975

Dear Annie,

Because I'm not sure you are aware of just how funny <u>Heritage</u> is, I thought I would tell you I regard it as a comic novel. When you said that Janet had blood all over her high water, beige polyester doubleknit pantsuit, were you trying to be funny? I thought that last chapter was a riot—not the material exactly, but the way you presented it.

I really have spent so very little time with you to care about you so much. I guess people of my generation take a first lover more seriously than people of yours do. I do care for you—not just feel responsible.

I only suggested the Algonquin because my apartment isn't in very good shape since my wife left. Because you are a "writer," I thought you'd appreciate the Algonquin. Would you rather the St. Regis?

Please come, as contracts take forever.

I love you,
Martin

430 Pacific Avenue
San Francisco, CA 94133

Feb. 6, 1975

<u>Martin</u>:
Men have died and risked their necks
In theory for love, but really sex;
For sex and love so oft confused
That most people end up being used.

<u>And if you dare tell me that my mother
and I both have a talent for couplets, I will
personally take this novel and the complete
works of Hermann Hesse and ram them up your
ass</u>!

<u>Sincerely</u> yours,
Annie

P.S. I am going to have your child, you fucker.

chapter 19

Once after he married my mother, my father directed *The Three Sisters.* He had suggested that Kate play one of them— I think Masha, the one who taught school, while mother wanted to play Irina and be young again. When she found out he had her in mind for Masha, she just said, "Oh, *The Three Sisters!* God, that's nothing but a boring four acts about not getting to Moscow." She laughed. "I mean," she said, leaning against the kitchen counter, eating her toast from a napkin instead of bothering with a plate, "if you already know at the beginning that they don't ever *get* to Moscow, what's the point?"

"We always think it will be better someplace else," grunted my father.

"Shit. Do any of us," she asked rhetorically, "*ever* get to Moscow?"

"You won't," he said. "Anyway, if you did, what would you have to complain about? If you didn't have anything to complain about, you might have to actually talk."

Holly was about five then and sat on the kitchen stool and listened to Mother go on and on about how she wished she were a really *great* actress like Ellen Terry; about how she wanted to leave Oregon and move kids, husband, and dreams to someplace that "understood her art," about how she wished she looked like Audrey Hepburn, etc. etc. My father ignored her as he finished making breakfast, I didn't know what to say, and Holly licked a spoon, tilted her head, and said, "Don't worry, Mommy, someday you'll get to Moscow."

Mother rushed to Holly and hugged her and said, "Oh, my darling, of course we all will get to Moscow someday!" and we all laughed; Mother hugged my father and put ears on all the pancakes; Daddy did a Viennese waltz with me; and Holly sang "Roll Me Over in the Clover," and we laughed and laughed and laughed.

That was one of the nicest times we could remember about life with our mother the madwoman.

The other time (God, it's pretty horrible when you can only come up with two) was the Christmas before she died—our last in Oregon. Holly and I made her a series of coupons decorated with glitter that were good for things like "one breakfast in bed," "one Tanqueray martini prepared by daughters with scintillating conversation provided by same," "one Jamoca Almond Fudge and Chocolate Brownie double scoop ice cream cone from Baskin-Robbins 31 Flavors," etc. The last coupon was good for "one free trip to Moscow with no stopovers." Mother laughed and hugged us after each coupon, and when she finally opened the last one, she (dramatically as usual) started to cry. "Then I *will* get to Moscow!" she said with the tears just ready to spill.

"First class all the way," said Holly.

Then Mother remembered what Christmas meant to two little girls. She laughed and ran into the bedroom where she had hidden the doll house she had built for us, complete with real towels, pot holders, and canisters—the most domestic thing she had ever done—and a whole family of troll-like doll-animals to live in it. While she was in the bedroom getting it, she made out a coupon for us which said, "one ticket good for entrance to the Kingdom of Heaven where Jesus Christ looks like Peter O'Toole."

That afternoon we all took a walk downtown and Mother talked my father into taking us to see *Lawrence of Arabia.* Mother told us that if *she* had been there, T. E. Lawrence would not have *thought* of being a homosexual. My father said that Lawrence of Arabia didn't look a *bit* like Peter O'Toole, and Holly said that was probably true, but for sure Jesus Christ would. We all laughed and laughed and walked through the Portland Park blocks and sang "The Army Song" from *Threepenny Opera*. When it started to snow, Mother kept trying to bury us alive in it, we stuffed it down each other's collars and other dumb shit kids always do, and even my father tried eating some. Holly looked at Mother with snow all over her eyelashes and asked if this was what Moscow was like. "You know," she said, "with everyone happy where they are and not wishing for something else."

"Well," said Mother, "Moscow is snowy. . . . " We all thought that was very funny, and we laughed and went to an International House of Pancakes and had waffles with all the kinds of medicine-tasting syrup on them.

After my father went crazy, Holly shook her head and said that "no way" could she even consider living with any of our aunts. Since we had assumed that Janet would lose all interest in us as soon as we were no longer connected to our father, she suggested sarcastically that we use the coupon we had given Mother and get the first flight out of S.F. for Moscow. That gave me an idea. "Why not," I said seriously, "empty our savings accounts and get two tickets to New York. We could call Uncle Hollistor after we get there, and then—how can he say no?—we could live with him. He makes a lot of money being a playwright, and he isn't an ass hole, and he *never* talks about how Mother fucked us all up!"

"He'd just send us back," said practical Holly.

"Listen, Holly, can you actually conceive of Hollistor purposely subjecting us to a *lifetime* of coasters, dishcloths, and 'Air Force One'?"

"Not really," she said, "but I don't think it's legal—he isn't a relative or anything." She shook her head again. "It has to be a relative, doesn't it?"

"Legally, yes," I said, "but Holly, oh Holly, morally . . . *never!*"

"You're talking like Mother."

"Uncle Hollistor is the only one who has ever treated us like we should be treated, and he's the only one who won't turn us into nerds or potters in Sausalito!"

"There are worse things. . . . "

"What?"

"Going crazy."

"That's what I *mean!* Shit, Holly, you know we'd go crazy with Allison, having heavy duty conversations about Oriental antiques and the price of 'condos.' "

"Well, we could be potters in Sausalito. . . . "

"Yeah, sure. Have you ever met a normal person who came out of Sausalito? Shit, we'd have to get into T.M., mashed yeast, and heavy duty conversations about 'getting our heads together.' "

"And Mona?" she asked.

"Could you live with 'Air Force One' in Pasadena with their portable, black, fake leather bar and Margaret Keene paintings?"

"I see what you mean," she said.

"Look, I'm sixteen. In two years they can't touch me."

"Well," she said, "I've got four years to go."

"Then you have more to lose by agreeing to become a jerk."

"Well. . . . "

"We can try it. The worst thing that can happen is someone will force us to come back, but face it, Holly, I don't think *anyone* is going to be fighting over us. When we are eighteen, we can come back and live in the house, but now we're goddamned minors and all . . . Shit. Please. . . . "

"Okay."

We had never traveled alone before, but Holly proved to be an expert at travel plans. We visited our branch of the bank and took out the $453.24 we had between us in our savings accounts. Since I remembered being pissed when our father had always made us save our Christmas money and bonds instead of spending it on Barbie Doll clothes, I laughed. Then we took a bus to Geary Street, walked right past our favorite dirty bookstore without even looking in the window, and only paused at the fresh flower stand on the corner by Macy's. "Mother used to always buy flowers here," said Holly. We bought a bunch of daisies and scattered them in Union Square. "These are for her," I said, and then for the first time, we sat together on a bench and cried for her. To make ourselves feel better, we went into Blum's and ordered double hot fudge sundaes, and then went to the United Airlines office at the corner of Union Square and purchased two tickets to Kennedy airport. When we gave our correct names, we expected a lot of hassle because of our age and all, but they just took our cash, smiled, and that was it. Shit, they make it so goddamned easy for you, no *wonder* there are so many runaways—as long as they've got the cash, they don't give a rusty fuck.

"Shouldn't we tell someone?" asked Holly.

"No," I said. "We won't tell *anyone* until we're already there."

As she was packing, Holly came through The Birdbath to my room. "This is crazy, Annie," she said. "Someone or something will screw up. This is a really insane idea."

"Our whole family is insane, Holly," I said with conviction. "Let's 'use it.'"

Feb. 10, 1975

Dear Annie,
    Your last letter came as quite a shock to
me. I'm sorry, I assumed you had taken the
necessary precautions. If this information you
casually threw out to me is true, I would
appreciate a letter from you explaining the
situation and what you think should be done
about it.
    If it will help, I will send you some
money.
    Since you and your mother both sometimes
have distorted reality, I'm going to ask if you
are really pregnant. First, I learn you are not
really Anne Sarah Foster, and then you are
pregnant—what am I to believe?
    I tried to call you again. Why did you
disconnect your phone? If you indeed <u>are</u> going
to have my child, I deserve more than a P.S.

                              Best,
                              Martin

                              430 Pacific Avenue
                              San Francisco, CA 94133

                              Feb. 13, 1975

Dear Martin,
     Of course I'm going to have your child.
Although I may be stupid enough to get pregnant, I do know enough not to scare the hell
out of you before knowing for sure.
     Publish my book and feed your child.
(Ha! ha!)

                              Piss on you,
                              Annie

P.S. I'm really not stupid. Don't hate me. . . .

chapter 20

My mother went to Yale Drama School from the fall of 1949 through the spring of 1952 and got her MFA with the highest honors in acting. Even though she went there just to "show my father," she stayed because it was the first situation she had been in that really challenged her. At that time in her life, she loved challenges; it's too bad that life and the day-to-day things killed the spirit that was once inside her.

God, Kate actually had to *work,* and that left little time for her usual introspection, longing, or fucking around. Sometimes she dated other actors or technical people connected with the school, but since her heart was still in Portland, Oregon, with a paunchy jerk, the dates were few and for the most part platonic. My father received literally hundreds of letters from her. Through this correspondence, describing her three years in detail, he watched her grow up. During Christmas holidays she would stop by Portland on her way home to San Francisco and make love to my father on his living room floor while Janet worked at the Bureau of City Records. He'd always laugh and say, "I thought you were never coming back. You said I'd never see you again if I 'let' you go to Yale."

"I *meant* it wouldn't be the same," she snapped. "Besides, I'm weak."

During her last year, she announced that a Broadway director had seen her act at Yale and was planning to give her a small role in his show the following November. "Is it a good role?" my father asked her.

"Well, it's not too big," she said. "I die before the first act ends—you know, get cancer and just go . . . but everyone in the play is really torn up about it, so they *talk* about me all the way through. First, the family is torn apart because they fight over this land I owned, then my mother goes crazy because her daughter died of cancer, then my father takes another woman because my mother is crazy and no fun to be with anymore, and then she dies and her Doberman pinscher kills my father because he was such a son of a bitch, and every one is *still* talking about my cancer and how none of this would have happened if I hadn't died, so even though I only have one scene, the audience *can't* forget me!"

"Is he a good director?" my father asked.

"A *good* director wouldn't pick this play," she said; "he's a director of hits. The best thing is that the play he's doing next—it's practically a one-woman show—is called *Young Victoria*, and if I do a real good job of dying in this one, then maybe. . . . "

My father kissed her. "You're strange, Katie," he said. "And beautiful."

"God," she laughed. "I wish you were a reviewer."

My father once commented, after Mother had "given it all up," that it would have been good for her if she had had to go and starve and work her way up like most actors do. He said their whole marriage would have been different because she wouldn't have *left* a career, she would have come back to him out of desperation.

"Would you have married her then?" I overheard Linda ask.

"Probably not," he said. "I would have comforted her and encouraged her to go back and keep trying."

"Why the hell didn't you just tell her to go back and cash in on her success? Hell, even *I* remember *Young Victoria*. It was a big hit. Elia Kazan thought she was brilliant and wanted her to do a play for him. She had them all in her hand, and instead, she came here and screwed up everything for the little people who never had anything to begin with. Why didn't you send her back, Matt?" Linda whined.

"I couldn't," he said. "You see, I loved her very much."

"She was self-destructive."

"Oh, she was," he said sadly, "but she loved me too . . . I think . . . I know."

"You're a pervert, Matt."

"Kate tells me we both come from a long line of them."

Linda didn't answer for a moment, and then she said, "There's no escape for your children. Either they are at home being exposed to her, or they're in school realizing their mommy doesn't bake cookies and go to the P.T.A. like everybody else's mommies, or they are up here at the theatre being exposed to people like you and me. Do they know you sleep with me?"

"I'm sure Kate has filled them in on that," he said sadly.

"Oh, Matt, why the hell don't you dump her? She's tearing us all to bits."

"I love her, Linda, that's why," he sighed.

HASTINGS, HEARTE & DANIELS

118 AVENUE OF THE AMERICAS
NEW YORK, NY 10013

Feb. 17, 1975

Dearest Annie,

Do you want me to send you money? Do you want me to come to San Francisco? Do you want me to say I love you?

I can't marry you right now, but I'll do anything else you think best. Only let me in on things. I <u>am</u> the father, and if a child of mine is to be alive, I want to know.

What <u>do</u> you want me to do or say?

Love,
Martin

---

430 Pacific Avenue
San Francisco, CA 94133

Feb. 20, 1975

Dear Martin,

Since you asked, there are a number of things you can say—about <u>Heritage</u>!

First, you could start with something like, "An unforgettable novel of our time! It is impossible to praise this book too highly! If you care at all about people who have blood in their veins"—I like that—"it is imperative that it be read by the world! If you are nostalgic for novels of plot and structure and commitment"—I like that too—"then you can't afford to do without it! It will break your heart, make you laugh, and make you weep! An extraordinary achievement!"

Or how about, "What from another author might have been banal is witty, perceptive, and"—get this—"deftly satirical!"

Please tell the editorial board you sat there "weeping, laughing, raging, feeling exalted and intensely emotional, and inspired!"

I could go on and on, but I think you get the idea. Too bad <u>I'm</u> not reviewing it.

Love,
Annie

The year before Mother insisted on moving to San Francisco and destroying herself, she took Holly and me on our first trip to New York. She announced to my father that she was going to visit Hollistor, and that would give him plenty of free time with Linda without having to worry about her "finding out."

"I haven't been worrying," he said.

"I could divorce you on grounds of adultery," she said.

"And do what?"

"Act."

"Would that really make you happy?"

"Shit," she said, "you got me there."

Because Linda had been pestering my father to take her away for a weekend, and he didn't exactly have the courage to tell his worldly wise wife that he was going to be away on "business" for a couple of days, he didn't object to the New York trip. He once said that the unfortunate thing about marrying one's mistress is that she knows all a man's tricks and they can't possibly be repeated. Mother said the trouble with marrying a man who leaves his wife for you is that he probably wouldn't be above doing the same to you. Holly once asked why the hell they got married in the first place, and Mother gave her some bit about the human being is a strange animal.

Old Linda was thrilled at the news that she was going to the Oregon coast with my father and that Katie would be three thousand miles away for an entire *week*. Because Hollistor had promised to take Holly and me to at least three tacky Broadway musicals, feed us at the Stage Deli, and take us to a store that sold real motorized swan boats, we were delighted too. Mother would be seeing people who "remembered what she was," so she was in a better mood than we had seen her in for a long time.

She selected a number of evening dresses with plunging necklines. "What the hell if I have no breasts," she said. "I have a perfectly gorgeous chest!"

"So do I," I said. "And you don't see *me* going around in a dress cut to my waist."

"You're *nine*," she said, "and I detest having people watch me while I pack." As I started to leave the room, she asked me to get a couple of plastic bags from the kitchen. As I walked by my father, he nodded at me. He was having a late-morning drink along with *U.S. News and World Report* (the magazine from which most of my elementary school themes were plagiarized). When I got back to the bedroom, my naked mother was checking stockings to see which ones were still perfect. She tossed her hair out of her eyes and smiled at me. "You excited, Annie?"

"Sure! Uncle Hollistor promised we'd go on a tour of Woolworth's."

She draped a scarf over one eye and said dramatically, "This trip will be a turning point in my life!"

"You aren't going to try to be a Broadway star again, are you?"

"No, no, no . . . that would be admitting I'm unhappy."

"But you're *always* unhappy!" I said.

"My marriage to your father has been the happiest time of my life!"

"God," I exclaimed, "I'd hate to think what the *rest* was like!"

She wrapped the scarf around her neck and said, "Annie, it's *all* behind me now. Perhaps I'll just fly away and vanish."

"We'd miss you," I said softly.

"Oh, Annie, I'd miss you *too*—all of you." She put her arms around me. "I'd miss your father . . . God, for everything in this world there is a fucking price."

"What price are you paying now?"

"Boredom," she said.

HASTINGS, HEARTE & DANIELS

118 AVENUE OF THE AMERICAS
NEW YORK, NY 10013

Feb. 24, 1975

Dear Annie,

Please don't be evasive. I asked you a direct question about your pregnancy, and you launched into a cliché-ridden series of puffs about your book. I want to know the facts about our child-to-be, and if there is in fact a child-to-be!

Please play it straight with me, Annie.

Love,
Martin

430 Pacific Avenue
San Francisco, CA 94133

Feb. 27, 1975

Dear Martin,
What do you _mean_, "cliché-ridden puffs"
about my writing? That is _credible_ criticism!
Most of it was copied off the back cover of
Exodus.
Also, you had better start making some
kind of talk show arrangements. Of course I am
very disappointed that Dick Cavett got shoved
off (next to Robert Redford, he is the love of
my life), but you've just _got_ to get me on
Johnny Carson. God, Johnny Carson!
I promise I will talk about my book as if
it were the greatest art in the world, make it
sound like I had outlined and researched it
ahead of time with profound "purpose," and most
important, make it sound as if I took the
entire thing seriously—you know, talk about
"women and creativity" or something. This will
give Carson something to bounce off of, so he
can make some good jokes, and I might get asked
back—might be a guest host—might get my own
talk show!! At any rate, it will definitely
help sales.
As an important publisher, you must make
sure that I don't get a guest host like Joey
Bishop or Joan Rivers. Do you realize that even
if Katharine Hepburn is the guest everyone
thinks twice about watching it if Joey Bishop
is the host? It's either Johnny or nothing!
Well, I would consent to be on Merv or Mike

Douglas, but as I'm sure you already know,
those fools who stay up until one in the morning watching Johnny Carson are probably the
same fools who will buy my book.

Love,
Annie

P.S. I'd rather be on Johnny Carson than go to
Heaven!

chapter **22**

On the morning we were supposed to leave for our 1965 New York trip, my father broke his wrist, which secretly pleased Mother, as she figured it would put a damper on the great weekend he had planned with Linda ("How many of those three hundred positions can you do with a broken wrist!" she had commented loudly.). Holly threw up in the car on the way to the Portland airport, and I almost left my plane ticket in the coffee shop. These were the only mishaps, for Mother was more organized than I'd ever seen her. She wore a black hat over one eye. "In mourning for my life," she had said.

"You're just quoting Chekhov again," I said.

"I'm not like you, Annie," she answered. "I can't write my own parts."

Since she was in such a good mood because she was going to "split this town," she bought us a variety of things to make plane travel more pleasant—Nestle's Crunch bars, *Modern Screen* and *True Story* magazines, a crossword puzzle book, etc.—and said she hoped this was enough crap to keep us busy because she intended to drink martinis all the way across the continent, drown her sorrow in alcohol, and contemplate her past.

"Are you sorrowful about your past?" Holly asked her.

"No, about my future," she snapped.

"He's not going to marry Linda," I said, hoping that would help.

"Christ!" she screamed. "Do you think I'm reduced to jealousy?"

"*Are* you jealous of her?" Holly asked.

"Hell, no," Mother said. "I just hate the idea of *anyone* thinking she is having one up on me."

"Why don't you have an affair?" I put in. "Then you'd be even."

"Annie," she said, "I'm not like your father . . . fucking and screwing. Jesus, he can do it with sheep for all I care. Sex is like going to the bathroom for him—he's just got to do it. He always paces around until he has had his one good dump of the day—with Linda . . . or whomever." She looked at her watch. "You know, Annie, I'm a romantic . . . I have to *love!* Shit, if I'd been like your father, I could have stayed in New York and fucked every director from here to East Jesus . . . there isn't room for us anymore . . . the romantics. People write us off as crazy."

"Romance messed up your life, Mother."

"Romance *made* my life," she said.

As soon as they called our flight, she gathered up our assorted junk, including the present for Uncle Hollistor: a woman's shoe sprayed gold, covered with shell macaroni and filled with plastic flowers—a find she had stolen from the mother of a fag actor she knew. We boarded the plane, Holly and I made it clear to the stewardess that we thought it was a bunch of horse shit to have junior stewardess wings, and Mother picked up Hermann Hesse, ordered a martini, and told us to amuse ourselves until Chicago, and then from Chicago to New York she would "have some conversation with us."

"Is that a threat or a promise?" Holly asked.

"It is a promise, my darling," Mother said.

Because Mother had wisely ordered a split of champagne for us, Holly and I both slept most of the way to Chicago. On the New York leg of the trip, Mother made good her promise and devoted her time to us. We worked on a present for Uncle Hollistor that Mother had started before we left. It was one of those blank books you can buy and write your own stuff in. Since Mother and Hollistor were addicted to Tastee Freeze hot fudge milkshakes (once it had got to the point that the greasy girl with acne, who worked there, would just start making them up when Mother and Hollistor arrived), she called the book *Disgustingness Is Being a Regular at Tastee Freeze*, and on every page, we thought of something else that was disgusting. She had "Disgustingness is when the guy you were feeling sorry for at auditions, because he was so bad, walks off with the lead." Holly suggested starting another section called "You know you're in trouble when. . . . " Mother said, "You know you're in trouble when everyone just laughs when they see Portland City University on your transcript." I thought up, "You know your in trouble when you say 'Oh, fuck it' at the dinner table and your grandmother's minister is there." Mother said, "You know you're in trouble when some jerk movie star says, 'It's nowhere at the top, the journey is what counts,' " and I said, "You know you're in trouble when someone is always using you as an excuse," Mother said (I think for Hollistor's benefit). "You know you're in trouble when Matthew Foster is the only person who can make you happy," and I added, "You know you're in trouble when you look at your ancestors on *both* sides."

"Yes," sighed Mother. "Disgustingness *is* being a regular at Tastee Freeze."

We went on with this for about a half hour, Mother wrote the best ones in the book, and Holly and I illustrated them.

Hollistor had taken a cab from the city out to La Guardia airport, and Mother, with scarf flying, trailed by two slightly tipsy little girls, lipstick smeared, hair in her eyes, and waving the gold shoe filled with plastic roses, rushed down the concourse to Uncle Hollistor, who was waiting with a gigantic metal ashtray shaped like the state of Maine.

"Hollistor!" she screamed.

"Katie, the model mother!" he yelled, hugging her. "I got Maine!"

They embraced and exchanged gifts with more pleasure than if he had bought out Tiffany's for her. She and Hollistor had collected those tacky tourist souvenir ashtrays in the shapes of states for years, and I think they were serious about someday getting the entire continent, putting all the states together, covering them with liquid plastic, and making a coffee table out of them. Holly and I never really could understand why they went into hysterics over such things, but then few people understood them.

Then Hollistor told us that "Gadge and the bunch" were throwing a little party for Mother, and he was *personally* going to escort Annie and Holly to Sardi's to wait for the reviews.

"What reviews are we waiting for?" I asked.

"I don't know," he said. "It doesn't matter . . . that's what one is *supposed* to do at Sardi's."

HASTINGS, HEARTE & DANIELS

118 AVENUE OF THE AMERICAS
NEW YORK, NY 10013

March 3, 1975

Dear Annie,
    Your letters, which at another time I might have found amusing, I now find painful. You go on and on in the nonsensical style that fills your writing and totally avoid my questions.
    It is unfair to me to ignore the fact that you are carrying my child, and then go on

about <u>Johnny Carson</u>! I don't think you're all
there, Annie.
Until you give me some straight answers,
I am not reading any more of <u>Heritage</u>.
Did you get either of the telegrams I sent
you?

Yours,
Martin

---

430 Pacific Avenue
San Francisco, CA 94133
March 5, 1975

Dear Martin,
You fucker! Not reading <u>Heritage</u> until I
tell you the graphic details about my uterus
being vacuumed out at the Berkeley Medical
School is blackmail. I'm aware of your tactics.
I just wanted to forget it, but the world never
lets you forget your mistakes, does it?
Our child is dead. I killed it. (I aborted
it? I got rid of it?) What else was there to
do? Don't bother with the money—the medical
school is cheap, and soon you'll be selling
the paperback rights for a million anyway.
Also, don't flatter yourself by thinking that
I was trying to "spare you." I was sparing
myself; and the kid. Look, I'm a writer. I'm
talented! <u>Anyone</u> can change diapers—let them!
Since you were the one who pointed out
that "bad characteristics tend to skip a generation," you must understand why I wanted to
save the kid from its inherited heritage which,
as you also pointed out too many times, cannot
be escaped.

Because I don't want to hurt children the way my mother hurt me, I did the best thing. And, as I said, what else was there to do? Just let me forget about it and get on Johnny Carson.

<u>Yours</u> (since we have apparently stopped saying "Love"), Annie

P.S. I hope your "separation" from your wife isn't too painful for you, you ass hole.

chapter 23

I really did fly off to New York—but by myself and not with Holly, who chickened out at the last minute. In order to avoid being sent to my Aunt Allison's, I went alone. Now, I had always counted on Holly because she kept me from following my mother's pattern of doing everything on the spur of the moment, but this time I decided "spur of the moment" was the only way we were going to get away with it.

At about eight o'clock on the night we were supposed to leave, Holly came into my room, where I was burying a bottle of J. W. Black in my suitcase for Uncle Hollistor.

"Uh. . . . " she said. "Uh . . . I. . . . "

"What, Holly, are you okay?"

"I'm not going, that's all."

"You know where they're going to send you," I said.

"If you were Uncle Hollistor," she said, "how do you suppose you'd feel if we suddenly just showed up?"

"I'd be thrilled."

"You're just saying that." She glanced at the J. W. Black and said, "Look, Mother was crazy, that goes without saying; Daddy is obviously nuts because no one mashes in someone's head for no reason at all; and *his* mother wasn't exactly normal; and Grandmother's in the State Hospital; and I don't want to end up there. Okay, so Allison is a bore—so fucking what? She's going to be my escape."

"Shit. You'll hate it."

"Maybe not. Anyway, I can always come to live with you as soon as I'm eighteen." She sighed. "Besides, I still somehow don't think this is legal."

"We're just simple innocent victims of our environment."

"How do you mean?" she asked.

"Don't you remember when we wished we had 'come from a broken home' because it would give us an excuse for doing poorly in school?"

"We were just joking," she said.

"Yeah, true, but all those kids with personal problems seemed to get away with a hell of a lot more than those from happy families."

"Did *ours* qualify as a 'happy family'?" she asked.

"On school records it did," I said. "I mean, our parents were *married*, we weren't poor, our father had a respectable job. . . . Hell, we didn't have any problems if you just read the basic statistics about us!"

"Yeah, so?"

"Well," I said, "now we can't possibly be blamed for our actions because we have 'been through so much,' don't you see?"

"Yes, I see, but I'm not going."

"Well, I *am!*"

"I'll ride out to the airport with you, and I won't tell anyone," she said as supportively as she could.

"You really won't go?"

"No . . . no," she whispered.

As soon as I got my baggage at Kennedy airport, I phoned Hollistor. He responded to my phone call with a rather sleepy, "What the fuck?"

"I'm here! I'm in New York! I thought I'd grab a cab and come over and give you a thrill!"

"What the fuck?"

"This is Anne Sarah Foster, the love of your life!"

"Jesus Christ! You sounded like Kate for a minute. . . . God, I was asleep, what time is it?"

"Ten-thirty A.M. Should I get a cab and come over?"

"Who's with you?"

"Uh . . . no one." I suddenly lost all my cool and started to cry. "Oh, God, Hollistor. . . . It's really so horrible . . . it's. . . . "

"Annie, what's the matter? What are you talking about?"

"Daddy killed Linda, and. . . . "

"He *what!!*"

"Killed Linda. . . . I don't know where they took him, and I just *can't* live with Allison . . . and Janet isn't a relative . . . and I knew if I didn't get the fuck out of S.F. . . . "

"Listen, Annie, take a taxi over here, and tell me then."

He heard a great gulping sound on the other end of the phone.

"Do you want me to come and get you?" he asked.

I got my cool back, and up to Kate's standard said, "No, and I won't let the damn driver take me three times the hell around Manhattan either. I'll get there okay."

"Okay."

"And, Uncle Hollistor?"

"What?"

"You won't send me back, will you?"

"We'll see, Annie. Now just get yourself the hell over here."

Hollistor lived in an apartment on Central Park West and wrote all his "great American plays" there. After he was "in the money" and moved to the apartment, it never occurred to him to buy new furniture, so it was tastefully furnished out of Woolworth's and the Union Gospel Mission. Uncle Hollistor had graying hair and dressed like a 1960 college boy—you know, the V-neck-sweater-cord-pants bit. He served food out of Cool Whip bowls, drank too much ("just like O'Neill," he said), ate most of his meals either out or on the coffee table with take-homes from Zabar's, and had all his books piled up, so his apartment gave the impression that someone had just moved in or was just moving out. Because he was a writer and all, his filing cabinets were very organized, and one entire room was devoted to them. He kept letters and clippings and things he might use in a play—including a valuable file of letters from my mother, which he never *did* let me see. He had an entire collection of original cast recordings from *every* musical that ever recorded an original cast album.

After telling the doorman Hollistor was my uncle, I went upstairs. Hollistor opened the door, hurried me in, and asked, "What the hell has that bastard done this time?"

"God, he really went bananas."

Hollistor laughed, saw my face, and suddenly sobered. I explained—and of course, true to the family tradition, making it sound just a little more dramatic than it actually was—what had happened yesterday.

"So you want to stay here?"

"Shit, Hollistor, you don't want to see a promising person, with a sense of humor in the advanced stage, get stifled by an aunt whose greatest achievement was a perfectly molded jello salad, do you?"

"It doesn't really matter what I want, Annie. I asked you a simple question. Do you want to stay with me?"

I started to cry. "I don't have anywhere else to go. . . . I want to . . . uh . . . I want to stay alive . . . and well . . . don't let anything happen to me . . . please? . . . "

He held me until I had stopped sobbing. "Christ," he said under his breath, "Katie . . . why?"

HASTINGS, HEARTE & DANIELS

118 AVENUE OF THE AMERICAS

NEW YORK, NY 10013

March 7, 1975

Dear Annie,

I wish I knew what to say. I'm so sorry
you had to go through it alone—you know I
would have come out, don't you? I can send you
money. Please don't be bitter, things like this
happen.

You would probably say if I felt any
remorse, it would be false. I would be lying if
I said I weren't sad at the loss of my only
child. Strange and sad—for you and the baby.

Write to me soon. Please send me another
chapter—write the way you would want me to
know you because it is through your writing
that I <u>do</u> know you.

All my love,
Martin

P.S. You did do the right thing, and I hope it
wasn't too hard on you.

430 Pacific Avenue
San Francisco, CA 94133

March 9, 1975

Dear Martin,

T. S. Eliot wrote a boring but very famous play about Thomas à Becket and martyrs for the Church. He talked about people doing "the right thing for the wrong reason." Is there anyone who does the right thing for the <u>right</u> reason? I did the wrong thing (morally?) because I killed the baby, but it was sure as hell for the right reason. I'm too young to waste nine months being pregnant and eighteen years raising a kid! (Is that the right reason?) Also, I was angry at myself for being so stupid. I'm not, you know.

Oh yes, T. S. Eliot reminds me of what a title can do for you. How many people do you suppose bought <u>Murder in the Cathedral</u> just because it had a great title? How many people bought <u>For Whom the Bell Tolls</u> because <u>it</u> had a good title? . . . Do you think <u>Heritage</u> is enough of a grabber?

You said some horse crap about "knowing me by what I write." Please don't "know me" by this commercially packaged art I'm planning to dump on the public—"know me" by my gorgeous legs because that's all you were interested in anyway.

Best,
Annie

P.S. Would it help if I dedicated this to my patient editor?

chapter **24**

Marlon Brando did not come to my mother's funeral. Of course, since my father was not in any state to carry out her "will" to the last letter, he didn't even try to contact Marlon's agent. The gathering at the service was made up of very ordinary people (if you can call our family ordinary). Uncle Hollistor arrived before the cremation, looking less grief-stricken than we had thought he would. With him he brought a huge, taste-less, horseshoe-shaped wreath covered with green plastic ivy that said on a wide orange ribbon across it, "Best of Luck in Your New Location!" He said he got it from a branch of Tie City that was moving down the block in New York because their building was being renovated. Naturally, my father was furious, until Holly touched his sleeve and said, "You know, Daddy, Mother would have *loved* that." Since he had always felt bad about the fact that Hollistor seemed to know Mother better than he ever did, he looked a little pissed off but shut up.

Because none of us could bear the thought of Mother rot-ting and molding in the ground and being eaten by maggots, my father had her cremated. We figured she'd much rather go up in flames and smoke than waste away in a coffin. My father said he would take care of the ashes. Uncle Hollistor told us privately that she had probably always had visions of Marlon Brando standing on the Golden Gate Bridge and letting her ashes blow in the wind across the bay, but most likely my father just dumped them somewhere in the backyard. We really couldn't picture him standing, as Marlon would have done, with the wind blowing his hair back and an affective tear running down his cheek like the Indian on the ecology commercials.

It's too bad Marlon Brando couldn't have been there, but Hollistor said that he really couldn't just phone him and ask him to come to some funeral for a has-been actress who wanted the "drama of her life" to extend past her death.

"Death's the end, Annie," he said. "Your mother believed it was the beginning." He put his arm around my black coat. "You've got to accomplish things in *life*, because after the ashes are scattered . . . well . . . people forget."

"They won't forget Mother," I said.

"People forget everyone who hasn't accomplished anything."

"I won't let them," I said.

At the funeral, my grandfather sobbed openly and said we all should have anticipated it. My grandmother was seventy-nine years old, and the doctors at the State Hospital said it was better she didn't attend. When my father informed her of her daughter's death, we were told she just smiled and nodded and said something about Kate's wanton life and that's what she got for taking someone's husband and ignoring the teachings of our Lord Jesus. Then Grandmother laughed hysterically and said, "May she rot in Hell!" As you can imagine, we were pretty glad she wasn't at the service.

My Aunt Mona ate the whole thing up. She was so sorrowful that we actually could see a little of Mother's sense of the drama in her. She was really playing "funeral." Aunt Allison flew all the way over from Hawaii with Uncle Insurance Man and used the occasion to buy a 750-dollar, black designer suit from I. Magnin. Aunt Caroline came on the ferry from Sausalito, very pregnant, and gave us all incense and gold signs of Allah to wear around our necks.

The only other people there were Janet, who kept patting our heads, and Mother's friend from high school who had married one of those Universal Life mail-order ministers. Since no one in our family had darkened a church in years, he gave a "simple nondenominational service." The ashes were put in a flour canister, we all went home and ate Janet's yeast cinnamon rolls, and Holly and I each got to drink coffee.

During the two days before the funeral, I had done all my "feeling sad," and my father had been very unfeeling and businesslike about the whole thing. I felt we ought to cry or something.

"What do we do now?" Holly asked.

"We go on," my father said, "a little more peacefully than the last few years."

"Do you believe in life after death?" I asked him.

"For your mother's sake, I hope not," he said.

"Huh?"

"Since your mother didn't love life at all for a short thirty-six years here on earth, you can imagine how horrible eternal life would be for her."

"That's probably what hell is," said Holly. "You know, making someone who hates life, live forever."

"She was very beautiful," was all that Janet could come up with.

My father sat stirring his coffee for a long time. Because I was only ten, I don't remember if he showed any emotion. I just wondered if it was somehow our fault.

"Let's make a reservation for dinner somewhere," he finally said.

Janet and Daddy took us out for pizza, and (although I didn't say it at the time) it was actually nice just to eat without hearing about the starvation in the world, how fattening it was, or having discussions about "life" with gigantic quotes around it.

HASTINGS, HEARTE & DANIELS

118 AVENUE OF THE AMERICAS

NEW YORK, NY 10013

March 12, 1975

Dear Annie,
    Christ, you're bitter. As your mother
would say, "Use it." That's the only thing I
can think of to tell you.
    I don't think you really know where this
book is going to go. Until you decide, I would
put in some more sex scenes.
    Also, if this gets published, I'd be
honored to be in the dedication.

Love,
Martin

430 Pacific Avenue
San Francisco, CA 94133

March 14, 1975

Dear Martin,
    Do you think Marlon Brando's agent will
make sure he gets a copy of this book? Do you
think Marlon Brando will even read it? Since
there doesn't seem to be too much else to do
in Tahiti except drink, eat, and fuck, he might
take a moment. Don't you think?

In this chapter, the fictional Anne Sarah Foster loses the old cherry. I think it is pretty good nowadays to get through three-fourths of a book and have your narrator still a virgin.

Best,
Annie

chapter 25

Before I explain how Uncle Hollistor and I became lovers, I feel it is very important to remind you again that he really wasn't my uncle. I mean, I'm not against being perverted, but incest isn't my bag. He was just my mother's best friend. That's all.

When I arrived in New York, I hadn't exactly planned on having an affair with him; he was simply my last hope for survival in this society of el-whak-o's. And I'm sure Uncle Hollistor didn't convince Janet to let me stay with him for a while so he could seduce and corrupt me and all—you know, turn me into a "shattered and neurotic person."

After Hollistor calmed me down, we discussed where I should sleep. Then he remembered that his Union Gospel Mission couch had a foldout bed. Although it was quite an operation, he finally got it unfolded. Even though there had been the folding bed bit in the first motel scene of *Lolita*, it didn't cross either of our minds as we struggled with the couch. "Will this do?" he asked.

"You ought to get some new furniture," I said.

"What would I do with new furniture?"

"Shit, Hollistor—sit on it, sleep on it."

"Okay," he said, "maybe I will someday. It used to be just me, and I could sit on this as well as something else, but if you care that much. . . . "

"I *do*," I said. "This is really pathetic."

He laughed, and then sat me down so I could explain exactly what had happened. After he poured me a shot of the J. W. Black, I told him the rest of the gory details about Linda, and then he sent me out for a walk while he called Janet to verify my story and let her know where I was.

I walked up Central Park West to the Natural History Museum and back again on the park side. Even though I was truly proud of myself for just packing up and leaving, I felt somewhat empty. Shit, I was practically an orphan; I had no high school diploma, no skills, and no real place to live.

After I got back to the apartment, Hollistor told me I could stay, he would find me a good private school in New York, and he would pay the tuition until everyone had figured out legally where the family money was at. I guess it was partly the jet lag, partly what they call "semi-shock recovery," and mostly my loneliness for past simple existence that made me cry. I felt much emptier at that moment than at any time since Mother kicked the bucket. Suicides are like that—they haunt the living. Maybe suicidals know that and somehow feel they can glorify themselves by dying. Shit.

"What do we do now?" I finally asked.

"You go on, Annie. You've got no other choice," he answered.

"Do you think I'll ever amount to anything, Hollistor?"

"Sure, you're Kate's daughter, aren't you?" He stretched out his legs on the opened Union Gospel Mission couch. "You look like her," he said. "Very much."

"Is that good?"

"Katie was beautiful."

"Shit, I'm not beautiful," I laughed. Because laughter and tears are so closely related, he thought I was crying again. He came over and put his arms around me . . . Well, what would any considerate man do with a sixteen-year-old girl who might be on the verge of a nervous breakdown?

"Hey, hey, Annie," he said.

I looked up at him and smiled, we both laughed, and then he gave me a real sure enough tongue-down-the-throat kiss on the mouth. Now, no one really believes the bit about "sweet sixteen and never been kissed," but I really hadn't been kissed before.

Hollistor stroked my hair and kissed my neck; that made me shiver. As he kissed me again, I slowly put my arms around his neck. "I love you. . . . I've always loved you," he breathed. He unbuttoned my blouse, kissed my shoulder, then my breast.

"Good God!" I cried.

He stroked my leg. "You've got her legs, Annie . . . long . . . I love long legs." As he removed my clothes, I started to breathe faster. My body felt so good—like warm red wine and Valium. I had read that it was supposed to really hurt, but as he entered me I felt only excitement and joy.

So I lost my virginity in probably the most poorly decorated, disorderly, ten-room apartment on the park. It wasn't the way I really would have wanted it. I had sort of visualized my fall from grace as taking place by some lake on a velvet green lawn in turn-of-the-century costumes—like *Smiles of a Summer Night*. We'd have champagne and liver paté, and as my breasts were suddenly released from my laced corset covered with ruffles, Mozart would swell up out of nowhere. Of course if not *that*, it should have been in a private dining room with red velvet and mirrors—like in *Dr. Zhivago*, with an element of mystery and danger in the air; or surrounded by gunfire in the middle of an unidentified revolution with a handsome Latin American dictator. But what the hell—it happened, didn't it? Even though imagination can conjure up great scenes of seduction, it can't really make your body feel the way mine did on the Union Gospel Mission couch. To put it bluntly, I discovered I loved to fuck! Maybe that was what Mother was talking about all the time under the name of "Love"!

HASTINGS, HEARTE & DANIELS

118 AVENUE OF THE AMERICAS

NEW YORK, NY 10013

March 17, 1975

Dear Annie,

Well, so that's how you (uh . . . I mean,
Anne Sarah) lost her virginity. Very interesting.

One of the things I have always liked
about your writing in the past is, despite the
bizarre nature of your family, it seems to be
written realistically. In Chapter 25, you're
not only unrealistic, but seem to be self-
consciously trying to be "different" (for my
sake?). I think it would be much more interesting if you told how it really happened. You
know I know.

Yours,
Martin

430 Pacific Avenue
San Francisco, CA 94133

March 19, 1975

Dear Martin,

I was being realistic! Shit, you really
do have your heart set on the fact that this
is one of those autobiographical novels, don't
you? Even if it was, do you think I'd write

that I'd lost my virginity to my _editor_? God, that would be just too fucking much. Besides, you were talking about sex scenes, and if my narrator goes through most of the book a virgin, what kind of hot sex are you going to get?

Real life, no matter how "meaningful," doesn't deserve to be spread around on a fictional page. Anyway, "real life" usually takes on the quality of "As the World Turns." Just think, I could have written:

The evening breezes blew softly through the balmy night, rustling the maple leaves near the fourteenth green of the Bayfield Country Club. The crickets chirped softly against the distant sounds of the dance orchestra drifting through the warm summer night.

The moonlight filtered through Darlene's gossamer-like, strapless evening dress, and the gentle breezes blew her soft hair around her angelic face. A whisper-like smile played in the corner of her mouth. "Chad?" she breathed.

"Yes, Darlene," he responded.

"I look over this moonlit golf course, and I feel sad."

"Why, Darlene?" asked Chad, moving closer to where she leaned against a tree trunk. His white, tuxedo-clad arm encircled her bare shoulders, and he inhaled the distinct yet subtle smell of her perfume, which mingled with the smell of the honeysuckle.

"Oh, Chad," breathed Darlene, "I feel there is something missing in my life. My feet are still rooted, so I can't die, but I lie helpless against the wind. Even though I am the most beautiful and popular girl in all Bayfield, I sometimes still see myself dead on the fourteenth green."

"But Darlene," said Chad. "There is so much to live for! Think of us. Think of my job with my father's gigantic multimillion-dollar oil corporation!"

"I feel so incomplete!" she answered.

"Darlene," Chad said, his lips pressing hotly against hers. "I love you so!"

Darlene was suddenly overcome with emotion. "Oh Chad," she breathed, "you and only you have made me realize the meaning of life!"

Chad pressed his lips against hers. "Oh, Darlene! Oh, Darlene!" he exclaimed, unable to control himself.

"Yes, Chad, yes, yes, yes!" she said, now in a state of wild abandon. She parted her lips to accept his kisses, and they collapsed into ecstasy.

Do you prefer that?

Love,
Annie

P.S. Hey, that was kind of fun, writing that. Do you think I should give up being a serious writer like J. D. Salinger, and write for Harlequin Romances? Do you have any contacts with Harlequin Romances? Don't feel bad about not being in my book. I'll never forget you—they say women never forget their first lover.

chapter 26

Hollistor looked through his piles of papers and newspaper clippings for a cigarette. "I don't suppose you smoke too, do you, Annie?"

"No."

"That was your first time, wasn't it?" he asked softly.

"Am I supposed to have lived as exotic a sex life as Mother did at my age?"

"I said *nothing* about your mother!" he said sharply.

"I'm sorry. . . ."

He said nothing and kept lifting things to look for his smokes.

"It doesn't really matter, does it?" I asked.

"Yes. I think I'm supposed to feel guilty . . . a guilty child corruptor or something."

"I'm not a child."

"Oh, Jesus," he said, then found his pack, lit a cigarette, and sat down.

"Well, just think of it this way: you've freed some man in my future from guilt."

"Are you planning to have many men?"

"Mother said I would."

"*I said leave your mother out of this!*" he shouted.

"I just said. . . ."

"It doesn't matter what you just said." He took a drag.

"God, Hollistor," I said, crying now. "Aren't you supposed to kiss me and say it was wonderful? Aren't you? . . . "

He stroked my hair. "It was, Annie. . . . I'm sorry." He kissed me, and I reached for a cigarette. "That will stunt your growth," he said, taking the pack away from me.

"You know I've always loved you, Uncle Hollistor," I said almost as well as Sue Lyon would have.

"Please, Annie, for the sake of my mental health, let's drop the 'Uncle' for the time being, okay?"

He put one arm around me, said nothing, and smoked his cigarette to the end. He stubbed it out and lit another.

"What are we going to do now?" I asked, remembering the scene in *Dr. Zhivago* where Lara and Dr. Zhivago have just screwed and she looks at him and asks very dramatically, "What are we going to do?" I don't think I did it as effectively as Julie Christie because instead of burying his head in my arms like Omar Sharif and saying, "I don't know, my darling, I don't know," Hollistor said nothing.

When I repeated the question, he still said nothing. Finally, I sat up and demanded, "Are you going to send me off to school as if nothing has happened, pick me up every day in my saddle shoes and cheerleader's sweater, and take me home and fuck the shit out of me? What are you going to do? Send me back to Allison?" I paused, and he kept on smoking. "I love you. It would break my heart if you didn't care at all. . . . It would."

"You're talking as if we had had a long and torrid affair."

"Look, Unc . . . ah . . . Hollistor, for a sixteen-year-old virgin, it was pretty torrid." He laughed, and I felt better. Because I had always known Hollistor laughing, I didn't feel so strange.

Hollistor walked over to the window, and I knew that if he hadn't known I had seen *Dr. Zhivago* six times, he would probably have said, "What are we going to do now?" ˙

Instead, he said, "You've *always* been my girl, Annie."

"Chip off the old block, huh?" I was suddenly pissed off. "Remind you of someone?" No answer. "A miniature version of Katie who just happens to *want* sex with you instead of thinking it would be hilarious?"

"Don't be so worldly wise," he said evenly.

"Look, you just screwed me. Big deal? *I* thought it was a big deal. I *love you*, Hollistor. . . . Mother believed in love. . . . I also really liked it . . . the sex, you know. You already said I could stay here, so sharing the same apartment with me obviously didn't upset you; I could think of ten thousand people who would be worse company for you; I'm much too young to think about getting my meat hooks into you, marrying you, and suing you for every flat dime you own when we split the sheets, and everything you own isn't much if you don't count the Union Gospel Mission couch. And as far as my being 'overly worldly wise,' that is the fucking fate of any sixteen year old: either everything you say isn't valid because you're so goddamned young, or if it is valid, then you're an overly worldly wise precocious child!"

"What's all this leading up to?"

"To what we're going to do."

He sat there and smoked two more cigarettes. Then he said, "Do you know how not to get pregnant?"

"Of course, you take birth control pills!"

He looked slightly bothered and relieved at the same time. "You're *taking* birth control pills?"

"I didn't say I was taking them. Why would some virgin be opening the door to cancer by taking pills when she didn't need them? I just said I knew that was one way how not to get pregnant."

He opened another pack of cigarettes, poured some J. W. Black into two Flintstone grape jelly glasses, and said, "I'll take you to a doctor. I know a doctor . . . and I'll teach you. I can't send you off to school—not now. My flat in London will be vacant soon, and we can live there for a while, I guess." He moved over to me and put his arms on my shoulders. "You must promise me something. I need five hours alone every day . . . to write."

"Sure . . . but do you love me?"

"I said you'd always been my girl."

"And I don't remind you of Mother?"

"Of course you do, but so what? She's long dead . . . and forgotten."

"I haven't forgotten her, and I don't think you have."

"We will . . . we'll help each other."

I sat there sort of smiling and not knowing what to do. "Isn't this a little perverted?" I finally said. "Do you think this will really screw me up?"

"Oh, Annie, if you aren't screwed up by now, nothing can hurt you." He ran his hand along my leg tenderly. "Besides, there is a chance . . . just a chance that I might be the best thing that has ever happened to you."

"You think I should? Mother did tell me never to trust a man . . . never to love one . . . shit. You know, she said just to *use* them."

"She said that?" he laughed.

"Yeah," I said, shrugging.

"Well, then use me!" he said cheerfully.

"I love you, Hollistor," I answered.

HASTINGS, HEARTE & DANIELS

118 AVENUE OF THE AMERICAS
NEW YORK, NY 10013

March 21, 1975

Dear Annie,

Although you have written a very quotable manuscript, I find the words—referring to men—"use them" the most memorable. Is that why your love, trust, and interest in me went down the tube as soon as you found out that I alone couldn't get your book published?

214

Even if I were able to publish it tomorrow, I don't want to believe you are the kind
of person who wants to have "made it on her
back."

I still would like to see you again. I am
very confused.

Also, I don't think the public will buy
the fictional Anne Sarah if she is simply a
user.

Love,
Martin

---

430 Pacific Avenue
San Francisco, CA 94133

March 23, 1975

Dear Martin,

If I had written Springtime Comes to
Darlene, and slept with you, and you published
it, yes, I definitely would have "made it on
my back," but no matter what F. Scott Fitzgerald, Henry James, Nabokov, or James Joyce
did with their editors, no one is ever going
to mention it. After reading Ulysses, no one is
going to toss it down and say, "Shit, he 'made
it on his back.'" Good writing speaks for
itself. Heritage is my gift to the world as
my virginity was my gift to you. I am not saying you sleep with someone to get something;
I am saying you don't sleep with someone who
will drag you backward.

Even if the fictional Anne Sarah were a
homosexual child molester, you can't say the
public won't buy it. America will buy, eat,
and digest anything that is sold to them in the

right way. McDonald's has sold over a billion shitburgers; the shops along Fisherman's Wharf have sold hundreds of thousands of foot-shaped ashtrays that say, "I got a kick out of San Francisco" on them; <u>The Valley of the Dolls</u> is the largest selling hardback book, followed closely by <u>Jonathan Livingston Seagull</u>, and <u>The Bible</u> heads the whole shebang; the movie <u>Airport</u> made box office history; Clint Eastwood is "the most popular American actor"; Charles Bronson gets a million dollars a film; Ali McGraw somehow wasn't thrown out after her first screen test; they keep on turning out commercials that have a ketchup bottle and a mustard jar doing a dance on a tablecloth; millions of people actually live in L.A. and have no intention of moving; Dean Martin is allowed to live; Nixon was <u>re</u>elected; universities have a "credit/no credit" system so students won't drop out because it is too hard; <u>Deep Throat</u>, <u>Wet Rainbow</u>, <u>The Climax of Blue Power</u>, and <u>The Blow Job Girls</u> play in neighborhood theatres; Helen Gurley Brown makes more money than the President of the United States; millions of people pay ten dollars for symphony tickets each week and fall asleep; and most newspapers give the Cub Scout Report before telling us we are at war with the Soviet Union.

Digest all that, Martin, and tell me if they won't eat up a significant novel like this, which is no less bizarre than any of these other things.

                                    To Success,
                                    Annie

Since Janet had a lot of polyester-doubleknit-Midwestern-conservative values, Hollistor and I decided not to tell her we were living in sin. She just thought Hollistor was really nice to "help out." Shit. After about two weeks, she wrote to tell us what was happening. I've really got to hand it to her for hanging in there. Because legally she could have just skipped out the second my dear father went bananas, I was grateful to her for dealing with the upheaval of an entire family that wasn't even hers.

When the mail arrived, I was still asleep. The night before, Hollistor had taken me to see *Ain't Supposed to Die a Natural Death*, which he thought was dog puke. I kind of liked this gigantic rat they had running around the stage, but Hollistor said he had once given Mother thirty cents at a carnival to see the "world's largest rat," and he had skipped the excitement *then*, so why would he like to see someone dressed up as a huge rat now? He turned to me, even before the break, and announced that he really couldn't stand any more of this, gave me five dollars, and at intermission told me to take a cab home.

Because I was slightly afraid of being murdered, I asked him why he couldn't stick this play out until the end.

"Because, Annie, I am a public figure, and it is noticed when I stay or do not stay, and my staying would be condoning shit."

"And buying *The Love Machine* even before it came out in *paperback* wasn't?" I teased him.

"Give me a break, Annie."

"God," I said, "you're really lucky you're not one of those Nielsen rating families. You'd have to watch all that 'good' stuff on PBS, so you wouldn't be condoning 'Bracken's World' and 'The Partridge Family' whenever you 'happen' to switch them on."

"I'm a writer," he said. "I have to keep my finger on the pulse of America."

"Tell me another one."

"Shit," he said. "Let's get out of here and get a beer. I know an 'actors' bar' nearby."

"Will I see stars?"

"Only out-of-work ones."

"Do you love me, Hollistor?"

"As much as you do me," he said.

We drank beer and sat until all hours of the morning in Charlie's bar waiting for the stars to arrive. We talked about my tender age. I was getting a little bored with hearing about my youth, but then when one is young, what else does one have to talk about except one's future, and that was treading on thin ice.

Because I slept late, Hollistor brought me some coffee in bed on a *tray* no less. I guess having a woman around brings out the elegance in a man. Even the Union Gospel Mission couch was gone, and we'd hit Bloomingdale's a number of times. Hollistor said the apartment was beginning to look like something out of the decorating section of *Cosmopolitan*, and I told him it was better than looking like those gleaming, waxed kitchens from *Family Circle*, and he laughed.

On the tray with my coffee was a letter from Janet. It said that my father had had a number of psychiatric examinations, and the results revealed he was absolutely unfit for any kind of a trial, so she put him back in the private hospital. She said our lawyer had a power of attorney to pay my father's medical expenses, and Allison and Mona would handle the family money until we were "of age." I asked Hollistor when "of age" was, and he said it probably meant when Allison and Mona thought we were mature enough to handle it.

"Shit," I said. "I'll be fifty before I see any of it."

"It doesn't matter," laughed Hollistor. "You told me you were going to make millions of dollars on your own."

"Yeah, sure," I said, sarcastically, and finished reading the letter. Janet said that Holly was in Hawaii with Allison (traitor!), enrolled in a private school, very tan, and hated it (no surprise to me), and that she hoped I was happy. Janet wanted to know if Hollistor had done something about my school, and said that the house was being taken care of by a rental agency, and as soon as they could get things packed away in storage, she and Ruth were going back to Chicago to live with her sister and her niece. She said if I ever needed a place to go, I was always welcome because after all I *was* Matthew Foster's daughter.

"Well," said Hollistor, "that's pretty nice of her."

"Yeah," I said, "she was okay. It wasn't her fault she loved my father."

"I still don't understand why Kate loved him," said Hollistor.

I decided to change the subject. "What am I going to do today while you have your 'five hours alone to write'?"

"Let's see," he said. "You can go to the Museum of Modern Art and pick out one thing you like best—and it can't be a movie because that's cheating. First you write why you liked it for me, and then go to the library on 42nd Street—probably you won't get to that part until tomorrow—and look up everything you can find about the artist, and write it all up. You can use the electric typewriter this time, it's your turn, and we'll read it together."

"Are we going to see a play tonight?"

"No, I thought we'd dine at Nathan's."

"Yeah, sure, really, what are we going to do?"
"Would you like to go dancing at the Plaza?"
"God," I said like Nina in *The Sea Gull*, "it's a dream!"

HASTINGS, HEARTE & DANIELS

118 AVENUE OF THE AMERICAS
NEW YORK, NY 10013

March 25, 1975

Dear Annie,
Regardless of your opinion of the American public, I think some careful reevaluation of your writing style is in order.
Your sentence structure leaves a lot to be desired. Parentheses should not be used as an easy device to insert afterthoughts. If you want to add something, material should be revised. In your correspondence, I find your thoughts most amusing, but I don't think this slapdash style will go over in book form.
Your subject matter is always interesting, but when the public reads a love story, they want, if they are not going to get graphic sexual details, a warm human relationship. Since you have presented a seemingly cold love affair, perhaps you could add love or passion.
Even though I'm getting the feeling your interest in me only goes as far as the publication of <u>Heritage</u>, I still think you are a warm person. Try to insert some of your per-

sonal warmth into your writing. If you are
convinced there is no real feeling in Annie's
affair with Hollistor, then it is absolutely
necessary to make it very sexual.

Yours,
Martin

---

430 Pacific Avenue
San Francisco, CA 94133

March 27, 1975

Dear Martin,
    You see no love in the affair because
obviously you don't understand the way I show
feeling. When we met I was a <u>fucking virgin</u>!
Don't talk to me about not feeling. If you
last it out as a virgin until you're eighteen
in 1975, you aren't going to be a cheap lay.
Does it ever occur to you that I may have just
lost interest in <u>you</u>—not in your lack of power
at Hastings, Hearte & Daniels?
    You are so full of shit! You come on with
this crap about "warm human relationships" in
novels which, in my opinion, are even more
boring to read about than hot sex. First of
all, <u>Heritage</u> is <u>not</u> about a love affair; it
is about the <u>effects</u> of heredity and environment on a person. Did it ever occur to you that
the narrator was so screwed up in her childhood
that she was <u>incapable</u> of a "warm human
relationship"?
    I have considered the possibility of put-
ting some porn into it, but decided against
it. Too much sex makes it unsuitable for those

huge college Freshman English classes. Ideally
(after we've cornered the Coffee Table and
Book Club markets), we can corner those Freshman English classes that have two hundred or
more people in them. If old J. D. can move in
there with <u>The Catcher in the Rye</u>, then certainly the "women's Salinger" can. Do you
<u>realize</u> how many copies of <u>The Scarlet Letter</u>
are sold to English classes alone? Nobody just
goes out and <u>buys</u> it anymore. Since English
classes ensure immortality for a book, too
many cocks and cunts are out. I hope this has
set you straight.

Sincerely yours,
Annie

chapter **28**

My mother and father were married in 1954 by the Justice of the Peace in Lincoln City, Oregon, on the weekend after the Tuesday my father received the papers that said he was officially no longer Janet's husband.

Janet had had six months to get used to the idea. When my mother told my father she wanted to have his child and all, my father finally decided to give Janet the axe. I bet it's really hard, after twenty years, just to go in and tell someone it's over. I always wondered how he had done it, and mentioned it to Hollistor. On one of his visits to the house in San Francisco, he squeezed the story out of Janet.

Even though grilling Janet for information was like squeezing blood out of turnips, he did get her to say that on that fated day, my father came home, fixed her a gin and tonic, and asked if she had ever thought of a separation—just like that!

"What?" she said.

"A separation . . . you know, what people have before they are divorced."

"Divorce?" she said, waited a moment, ripped up the lettuce, and then said, "You're joking."

"I was thinking," he said, "that it might be a good time for us . . . uh . . . to . . . well . . . maybe start on new lives . . . oh, shit."

Without thinking, she dried her hands on her beige knit suit (polyester doubleknit wasn't invented in 1954). "Are you unhappy or something?" she asked.

"Aren't you?"

"Why should I be unhappy? We've had a reasonably good life. . . . The Bureau of City Records isn't as great as . . . say, Katharine Hepburn's profession, but I can use my Library Science training. We've been together so long . . . you and I . . . I really can't imagine life without you . . . really."

"I was just thinking that maybe we should separate, that's all," he said casually.

"You're joking," she said again.

"You're putting me in a difficult situation," he said.

"*I'm* putting *you* in a difficult position!" she almost shouted. "You suggest, out of the blue, after twenty years, that we should separate, and then you say you're in a difficult position!"

He suddenly felt a wave of nausea. Because he had imagined himself saying these things so many times, it wasn't the words he was worried about. It was the sudden reality of the situation, and the lack of knowledge or even the slightest inclination as to what Janet's reaction would be.

"Well, you see . . . " he said, "I've . . . I mean, I believe . . . I mean . . . I have promised someone else I might marry her, and . . . Jesus Christ, Janet, I don't know how to say this!"

She didn't say a word. She just stood by the sink with a bottle of salad dressing in her hand.

"Well, I said it," he said, as if he were expecting congratulations. Janet carefully shook up the salad dressing, poured some of it over the lettuce in the bowl, and carefully replaced the cap. She put the bottle in the refrigerator, carried the salad bowl over to the table, and placed it by Matt's place.

"Do you want your drink?" he asked.

Janet put some butter in a saucepan and stirred it around with a fork until it was melted. After measuring out several spoonfuls of flour into the melted butter, she stirred it and poured in some hot milk from a small pan on the back of the stove.

"Can you leave that and come sit down with me?" he asked.

Janet just took a jar of chipped beef out of the cupboard and added it to the pan, stirred it, and opened the oven to check the baked potatoes by squeezing them with her oven-mitt pot holder with the checkered kittens on it. After replacing the pot holder on the hook over the sink, she stirred the beans in another pan.

"Janet?"

"Who?" she asked flatly as she drained the beans.

My father sipped his drink and folded up the evening paper and carefully slipped it under *Theatre Arts* magazine. As Janet took the two potatoes out of the oven, slit them open, and squeezed them apart, he filled his pipe. She spooned the chipped beef over them, dumped the beans on the plates, and set them down on the table with a bang. Nervously, my father brought the drinks over to the table and sat down at the same place where he had sat for twenty years.

"Who?" she asked again.

Stirring his potato and wishing he had never met Katie— something he was to wish many times in the future—he said, "It has been going on for a while . . . uh . . . I've known her for a long time."

"You sleep with her, I take it," said Janet bitterly, taking a sip of her drink. "For how long?"

"About six years . . . off and on." Silence. "Mostly off . . . I mean, she's been away. . . ."

"Who?" asked Janet evenly.

"Uh . . . one of my former students."

"My God."

"I knew her when she was a student."

"Who?" she asked again. My father didn't answer.

"You could have been a little more original," she finally said. "You could have gone somewhere else. . . . One of your students!! Good God! All professors have affairs with their students and secretaries! You could have found a whore, a waitress . . . someone not connected with school . . . someone who had no interest in marrying you. . . . You know, I really thought you would have been more original!"

"I didn't plan it."

"What a stupid thing to say. . . . " Janet was starting to cry. "You didn't *plan* it! You say you want to marry her, and then you say you 'didn't *plan* it'!"

"I didn't know I was going to love her . . . Janet? . . . I didn't know. . . . "

"People who have affairs with their students and secretaries don't *marry* them!"

"I never had an affair with my secretary," lied my father.

"Is this the first one?"

"Yes," he lied.

"And you want to *marry* her?"

"Yes."

"Jesus, how moral of you. You go to bed with someone and bingo, you want to make an honest woman of her—is that how you put it?—make an honest woman of her?"

"I think . . . I love her. . . . I really do think so. . . ."

"*Think?*" said Janet, and then flatly, "Oh, my God." She slowly ate her entire baked potato. "Who?" she asked.

"Her name is Mary Kate."

"Mary Kate? Mary Kate who?"

"McNeil. Katie McNeil."

"Katie McNeil!!"

"Yes." He was shaking.

Janet's tears were gone. "My God," she said softly. There was a deathly quiet. She got up, went over to the stove, and poured some more chipped beef over her beans. She came back to the table. "Good Christ, I liked her!" she shouted. "You *let* me *like* her! I *defended* her when you called her flighty and obnoxious! *You let me like her! You let me defend her!* Did you two laugh about it, huh? Oh, my God, I *liked* her!" She buried her head in her hands and sobbed for a moment, and then looked up and said quietly, "You are going to *marry* her?"

"I think so."

"Jesus." She picked up her plate, carried it over to the sink, and rinsed it off. "Get out of here," she said very softly.

"Janet?"

Picking up his full plate, she scraped it into the paper bag in the kitchen garbage can and rinsed it along with hers. "Get out of here," she whispered.

HASTINGS, HEARTE & DANIELS

118 AVENUE OF THE AMERICAS
NEW YORK, NY 10013

March 31, 1975

Dear Annie,

I'm sorry I doubted your feelings, but I just haven't met too many people who express love by saying, "You're full of shit."

I know I asked you to be realistic, but I'm sorry, Annie, who needs a recipe for creamed chipped beef?

Love,
Martin

P.S. Could you come to New York? I need to see you. I don't understand you.

430 Pacific Avenue
San Francisco, CA 94133

April 2, 1975

Dear Martin,

I resent the fact that one of my better
chapters is written off as "a recipe for
creamed chipped beef."

I have a number of reasons for having
Janet cook the chipped beef right there before
our eyes. First of all, I put in all the action
going on in the room, so the reader can
actually be aware of how much is going on during the time no one is speaking. The pauses
are important to show (a) the routine of twenty
years of marriage, and (b) the lack of real
communication between husband and wife. Harold
Pinter does this in all his plays by simply
writing, "Pause." In a novel, that would be
cheating because you're supposed to have all
this description and there are no actors to
interpret the length of time between the lines
for my readers.

If Heritage is turned into a screenplay,
it will give the actress playing Janet something to do instead of just standing there
looking shocked when her husband drops the
bombshell. If David Storey can have a whole
play take place while people are putting up a
tent, then I can have one chapter take place
while someone is cooking creamed chipped beef!

This chapter is an example of "Natural-
ism." When Strindberg had an entire fifteen
minutes of Miss Julie with a servant just
baking bread and puttering around the kitchen,

no one called it boring—they called it innovative. If Strindberg can get away with it in a <u>one act</u> play, I can certainly squeeze a bit of it into an epic novel.

Love,
Annie

P.S. I can come to New York only to receive the Critics' Circle Award.

chapter 29

Because Hollistor was so well known in New York, he felt more comfortable fucking me in London, so we spent most of 1973 getting cultured. Personally, I think London is sort of old, cold, gray, and settled in its ways. Hollistor, of course, loved London. He said he always felt he was walking around in a foreign film where everyone speaks English. Since the ambulances were always doing their European wailing in the background, I tended to agree with him, but who the hell wants to walk around in a foreign film? *Citizen Kane* would have done just fine for me.

We spent almost every night at the theatre. Now, I have nothing against theatre, and it is really exciting to see Laurence Olivier or Alan Bates in person, but to be frank, I would rather go to a movie.

When we first arrived, Hollistor's flat was not vacated, so we stayed in some hotel near Harrods (where Anne Bancroft fainted in *The Pumpkin Eater*), and then moved to his flat two stops up the Bakerloo line of the subway (*tube*, I was corrected).

During the first part of our stay, I kind of got a charge out of seeing the Tower of London, all the torture implements, and the "actual chopping block that Anne Boleyn was beheaded on." I also found out that there was no 221B Baker Street. Shit, the one thing I had wanted to see more than anything was Sherlock's actual house, and there was no fucking 221B Baker Street. Again disappointing was the discovery that

21 Oxford Street (which I knew as the famous whorehouse in *Threepenny Opera*) was just an English language school.

London was bloody cold, the theatres didn't have drinking fountains, and if you wanted to buy a jar of Skippy Peanut Butter, you had to go to the *gourmet* section of Fortnum and Mason!

Hollistor thought it would improve my mind to go to museums, so I saw the Victoria and Albert ("The old V and A"), learned all about period furniture and costumes, and spent one long boring afternoon sketching the history of wrought iron gates from 1636–1839 (I mean, *really!*).

Visiting the science museum provided a little more entertainment. I saw a Rolls Royce engine that had been running for twenty-five years, climbed around in a train, and watched the base two lights blink off and on on the computers. In the Natural History museum, I saw a model of a gigantic whale, studied charts (with photos beside them) on how humans get bubonic plague from rats, and sketched the different varieties of vultures and what bodily part each one attacks first in the event that someone is left dead in the desert.

And, God, the British Museum! I was just walking along and bumped right into the fucking Rosetta stone. And the mummies! God, I was mesmerized by those mummies. While I stared at an entire section of the Parthenon, I wondered why anyone even bothered to go to Greece. Hollistor took me to the manuscript room, and I saw the *original* manuscript of *Finnegans Wake*, where James Joyce had crossed out every other page.

After the British Museum, the rest of London was just a bunch of cold, old buildings. While Hollistor was writing—he found something very aesthetic about writing in England, maybe because Shakespeare wrote there—I visited the National Portrait Gallery and saw the gigantic picture of Queen Elizabeth II in her 1958 prom dress.

I'm telling you, after a month I wanted to see a McDonald's and a drive-in movie so badly, I was climbing the walls. I told Hollistor I wanted to go back to where the middle class lives like middle class instead of lower class, where they put butter on their sandwiches, and where you fear for your life in the subway and have a good excuse to take cabs. He told me I was crazy and showed me an article in *The Times* that told what was opening next week at the Aldwych Theatre, and I just sighed and said, "What's a play without a free program?"

"And what's life without 'Mary Tyler Moore'?" he teased.

"It's just a great place to visit, but I sure as hell wouldn't want to live here. Corrupted America at least gives you *ice* with your drinks."

"I came here for *you*," said Hollistor quietly.

"Don't put it on me," I snapped. "I just want to go, that's all."

"You want to leave me . . . or London?" he asked.

"Uh . . . London . . . I guess."

"Well, leave then!" he said sharply. "You can go to your Aunt Allison, sit in her hot tub, and get microwave poisoning from her oven!"

"Shit, Hollistor, I could get you fucking *arrested!*"

"For what?"

"Screwing a minor."

"The funny thing about the law, Annie, is that until you're eighteen you can't vote, drink, or fight for our country, but I'm sorry, as soon as you're sixteen you can fuck your brains out!"

"I'll see you later," I said. "I'm going to a movie."

My mother once said that all relationships go bad sometime, and maybe I was just blaming old London for what really was a combination of the flaws of love and the generation gap.

April 4, 1975

Anne Sarah Foster
430 Pacific Avenue
San Francisco, CA 94133

Dear Annie,
    The previous chapter about your London
visit was amusing, but I do remember you told
me London was your favorite city. I don't think
it adds anything to the story to spend an
entire chapter telling how bored you were with
everything you saw in London. Even though
Holden Caulfield was bored with the world, he
at least learned something from it.
    If you want your readers to have a sym-
pathetic attitude toward your narrator, then
you should have more respect for your readers.

Best,
Martin

430 Pacific Avenue
San Francisco, CA 94133

April 7, 1975

Dear Martin,
My narrator _did_ learn something: she
learned that maybe her relationship was on the
skids and that's why London looked so bleak
to her. Didn't you read the last paragraph? I
really wonder how you can keep your job as
an editor!
If you want the _real_ picture of the London
_I_ know and love, it would be a more colorful
book, but it would be even more unbelievable
than _Play Misty For Me_! For example, the best
evening of entertainment I had in London was
this film called _Frightmare_, which was about
a woman who goes after her children with an
electric drill, and the most astonishing thing
I saw was a film about a woman with a _seventy-
two_-inch bust (!) called _Chesty Nelson and her
Deadly Weapons_.
Now, I could go into all that stuff and
only reach a chosen morbid few, or I could go
into a bunch of plot summaries of dull West
End comedies like _No Sex Please, We're British_,
but you'd probably hate that and _never_ pass
this on to your editorial board.
You _couldn't_ want me to talk about how the
"red of the double-decker buses and the red of
the guards' uniforms added a splash of color
to the majestic gray stone facade of the Queen
Victoria statue," now _could_ you?

To success in your career
as well as mine,
Annie

My mother got pregnant six months after she married my father. Since the whole reason he had dumped Janet was because she "wanted to have his child," she couldn't very well back out.

As soon as they were married, Mother was dashed on the rocks of reality and realized that not only did they not lie around all afternoon drinking champagne, but she shopped for paper towels, washed sheets, and was supposed to be the cheerful light of his life when he came home from his hard day at school (and with a mistress).

Since this was bad enough, she could imagine cheerfully folding Matt's boxer shorts with a screaming baby in the next room. Good-bye, golden dream—she'd won, but she had to keep her prize.

After leaving her diaphragm on the bathroom shelf for a while and hoping she was sterile, and fearing that one of the little sperm had actually made it home, she decided to kill herself. Of course, it took her eleven years and two children to get around to it, but she succeeded at that too, and managed to screw up my father, Janet, and her children in the process. God, if only she'd swallowed some pills then. . . . I realize I wouldn't be here, but worse things have happened.

When she died, Mother was "in touch with reality" (meaning she knew day from night, which rouge didn't make her face break out, and which one of her kids was which). Both

Holly and I had to admit that it probably takes one hell of a nerve to shoot yourself, but was this a way to show bravery? For Mother, it would have taken more nerve to go on living.

Because Mother had once been sort of famous, my birth as well as her marriage were written up in "Milestones" in *Time* magazine. If she hadn't waited around eleven years to bump herself off, she might have got a death mention too. Poor Mother, even *Time* (which once said she showed "rare talent" in *Young Victoria*) had forgotten Mary Kate McNeil by 1966.

Katie was terrified of pregnancy, but during the six months it took her to *get* pregnant, she swore she didn't cheat and use her diaphragm. She read several books, hoping to discover that it really wasn't too bad, but the more she read, the more she discovered that "creating a miracle" was probably much, much worse than she had even imagined. She went to hospitals and looked at the new, red, shriveled babies and tried to imagine herself stretching open wide enough to expel something of that size. She went to football games down at Oregon State just so she could see eighty thousand people all crowded into one place. As she watched them, she tried to make herself believe that since all eighty thousand people had had mothers who had presumably lived through the experience, then she maybe could do it too.

After she had been married to my father for about two months, she interrupted him while he was correcting a group of papers on Restoration comedy and asked if he'd be really upset if she decided not to embark on motherhood just yet.

"Katie," he answered. "I love *you*, not just your potential for having my child, but we did agree. . . . I mean, we said the only reason to destroy Janet's life was to have a child."

"*You* don't have to give birth to it," she shouted. "*You* don't have to have your stomach stretched out of shape; *you* don't have to have the hemorrhoids; *you* will be able to shit easily all nine months; *you* won't have to have it kicking you in the ribs; and while *you* are out teaching your bloody Chekhov, *you* won't have to wipe up baby barf, roll the ball, and make peanut butter sandwiches; and *you* won't have to feel guilty if you neglect it; and *you*. . . . "

"Wait a minute, Kate," he said. "You should have thought of it before. . . . "

"*Women,*" hissed Kate, "are conned into believing that a baby is a cooing bundle of love in a basket with a swan quilt over it. *Women* are taught they aren't feminine if they don't spit out a couple of kids. *Women*. . . . "

"*Men,*" he said sadly, "are made to feel they aren't masculine if they don't father a child . . . and earn the money to support it."

"The system is fucked! Christ, I'm frightened . . . and I always sleep on my stomach," she said.

"What does that have to do with anything?"

"You can't sleep on your stomach when you're pregnant, your hair falls out, you, you. . . . "

"I loved you so much," he whispered, "I wanted *you* and only you to be my child's mother." He paused and then said, "And I thought that's what you wanted."

"Okay!" she snapped. "We'll have a child together, and then, whether you like it or not—no matter what happens— you will *always* be connected to me in some way until the day I die. . . . It's your grave!"

She went into the bathroom, squatted, wrenched her diaphragm out, and put it on the bathroom shelf. "You gave me six extra months," she said sharply to it. During the next four months she tried to learn to cook things that kids like: you know, crap like macaroni and cheese, meat loaf, hot dogs, etc., not knowing she'd have two children who preferred liver paté. After trying to write poetry, she gave up when Hollistor told her it sounded like early greeting card rather than early Auden. Then, until she actually got pregnant, she ran an acting workshop at Portland Civic Theatre for all those jerks who thought that studying with a "former Broadway actress" was a big fucking deal.

Hoping she was sterile, she fucked my father with all the sighs and screams of her student days and wondered why knowing his brand of toothpaste, seeing his hair on the bathroom sink, and buying his laxatives made the moans of ecstasy only an acting exercise rather than the joy of her life.

Well, Katie wasn't sterile. She knew she was pregnant even before she missed her period. Because she had been flat chested in the breast-worshipping forties and fifties, and an actress that costume designers were always putting high necks on, stuffing Kleenex down, and putting uplifts under, she was very breast-conscious. I swear, if a tit expanded *one tenth* of an inch, Mother noticed it. "Is nine months having tits worth it?" she wondered. Then she fainted—really fainted. She thought this was very dramatic, as she had never fainted before, and when all the concerned shoppers gathered around her on the floor of Meier and Frank, she just said, "It's nothing. I'm just going to have a goddamned baby!"

"Please tell me," she said to my father, "not to move anything very heavy and to stay off my feet."

"Okay, Kate, go easy on the house, and above all don't move anything heavy."

"Oh, God, I wanted someone to say that to me. Oh, God, I love you . . . and I'll love the baby, won't I?"

"More than you love me," he said sadly.

And thus I was born: part of everyone who went before me— destined to carry on the family tradition and fill the earth with children having the superior (inferior?) genes my father the loser and my mother the madwoman passed on to me. Shit.

Hollistor and I sat in a London theatre watching the R.S.C., and Hollistor turned to me and nudged me awake. "Annie," he said at intermission, "don't you like this? It's terrific!"

"Mother would have loved it, huh?"

"You might say she would rather see *Richard III* played this well than go to Heaven."

"You said the wrong thing, Hollistor," I said quietly. "I'll see you at home." I walked out of the theatre—not hating Hollistor for making me see it, but hating him for loving Mother and not me . . . for being disappointed in me when I wasn't a carbon of her. And hating myself for thinking that going against one tiny piece of my heritage was going to save me.

I laughed to myself. "I'll have to 'use it,' not rebel against it," I thought. As I walked to the tube, I laughed and kicked the puddles. "How," I thought, "I don't know, but I *will*."

HASTINGS, HEARTE & DANIELS

118 AVENUE OF THE AMERICAS

NEW YORK, NY 10013

April 9, 1975

Dear Annie,

    Because I was under the delusion that Heritage was a true story, I was fascinated. Now, since I do know one important fact is fiction, I am beginning to wonder if the rest of it is. Let's just cut the rest of the flashbacks and find a conclusion.

Yours,
Martin

P.S. I must admit I was hoping I'd be a character in it. . . .

430 Pacific Avenue
San Francisco, CA 94133

April 11, 1975

Dear Martin,

Why does _everyone_ want first-person novels to be about the author? Erica Jong said that after she wrote _Fear of Flying_ all these people she knew came up to her and were pissed they weren't in it, and just the other day, I ran into an old friend, told him I was writing a novel, and _without even knowing what the fucking thing was about_, he said, "I can't wait to read the chapter about me." Shit. If people want to be immortalized, they should write their own books! I bet you were the main character in your crappy novels about navy life, weren't you?

About the flashbacks: we _want_ those English class sales, and they always like it when the narrator reflects on things. I just _know_ the part about how I was a part of everyone who came before me will, in the future, be underlined with that transparent yellow marker in thousands of student copies across the country!

Best,
Annie

P.S. Do you think _Time_ magazine would put _my_ death in "Milestones"?

chapter 31

Because I did a really idiotic thing, Hollistor and I left London on the day after Christmas, 1973. Hollistor wanted to stay into April because *Life Class* was opening at the Royal Court, and he had already read it along with a privileged few and thought it was "important." Of course, even though Alan Bates was going to be in it, I could see no reason on earth to stay another *four months* just to see a bunch of actors standing around on stage in an art class. Being a real bastard, Hollistor said that if there was any trouble between us before I was eighteen, I would go straight to Pasadena, Mona, "Air Force One," and their *Time* magazine "Man of the Year" mirror in the bathroom. The only threat I had over Hollistor's neck was to "expose" his lust for minor girls, but he said all that could happen was that my aunts would be upset with him, and he just didn't give a shit whether Allison and Mona were upset or not. I saw his point.

So, every day I left Hollistor alone for his five hours, and I wandered around the streets and haunted the tubes of that great and historical city, London. I kept writing papers for Hollistor, so he could be assured I was being educated and he couldn't later be blamed for my maladjustment to life (does one automatically adjust to life because one is educated?).

Because London bathrooms are all so goddamned freezing, I was constipated the whole time I was there. I mean, if you can't comfortably read the cartoons in *The New Yorker*, you lose all desire to even *try* to shit. The toilet paper is so non-absorbent that one night, just to prove my point, I left a piece with some water in it on the bathroom counter, and in the morning the water was still there. Now, I've never been hung up on shit before, or never really thought about it except for a few times that Holly and I went into hysterics when in a TV commercial this middle-aged, eye-glassed lady stares out at you and says, "Do you mind if I say a few words about laxatives?" Did we *mind*? I mean, *really!* However, all the time we were in London, I was obsessed with shit. I memorized the hotels that had warm bathrooms in the lobbies, so after a play, I could sit comfortably, read *The New Yorker*, and hope.

Because of this, I had abdominal aches and probably wasn't too pleasant to live with. Hollistor rented a car, so we could drive up to Stratford, Nottingham, etc. to see more fucking theatre. When in London, even though I had a goddamned international driver's license, I *refused* to take the car anywhere—partly because I could never get used to that idiotic custom of driving on the left side of the street and also because normally civilized and polite British citizens suddenly become homicidal when turned loose behind the wheel of a car.

If you decided to save your life and not drive, it was just as dangerous to *walk!* Drivers in London don't accidentally run over people, they aim for them. Because people are smaller than cars and will ultimately come out second place in any collision, they really are at a disadvantage . . . and the drivers *know it.* Of course, once, as my life was passing before my eyes in the middle of a Zebra crossing, I decided that if you have to be killed, it is better to be run over by a bus in London than just knocked off by some Chevy on the L.A. freeway. "How did it happen?" people would ask, and Hollistor could say, "Oh, Annie was just run over by a double-decker bus in London," and that would have made a *much better* story.

Because I spent a good deal of my time figuring out stage settings for my death, I must have been sick or, because of what my father had done, still in shock. Some of my favorites were, of course, falling in front of a subway train and being mashed on the tracks; freezing to death in an underground tunnel—found the next day frozen, huddled over, with my blue, stiff finger tracing down the "Lonely Hearts" section of *Time Out;* drowning and having my sad body, including stringy wet hair, pulled out of the water at the Camden Lock; or simply freezing to death in my own bathroom while trying to take a shit—dying of the cold and exhaustion.

Christmas Day was the real kick in the tit. Now, for all my mother's faults, she really did try, even her last year, to pull herself together enough to do *something* special for us on Christmas. After she died, my father didn't look forward to Christmas with the same relish she did, but he usually managed to make it over to Baskin-Robbins or Joseph Magnin for us.

In London, Christmas Day is the worst goddamned day of the year unless you have a big fireplace, a Christmas goose, champagne, and Robert Redford. I had Hollistor, who just thought Christmas was a commercial and religious venture, and since he hated business and was an atheist, what was the point?

"It was the only day we knew Mother would be happy," I said.

"She was a child," he said, "and liked the presents."

On Christmas morning Hollistor *did* come through with a present: copies of most of the plays we had seen (real page turners . . . I mean, I already knew the endings), and I gave him several books on the history of circus freaks that I had picked up at Foyle's. One of them actually had a *foldout* of the genuine three-legged Scotch man in the nude! Because he was so thrilled with that, I was surprised when he expected his usual "five hours alone" to write.

"On *Christmas!*" I yelled, pulling on a sock and hoping he was kidding.

"Art and artists don't conduct themselves in the normal commercial tradition."

"What about all those religious painters?"

"I'm not a painter, and I'm not religious."

"I thought we might go out to eat or *something.*"

"Restaurants aren't open on Christmas—except for those bread pudding, tough turkey, and chips places at hotels."

"Shit, well, let's go to Brighton then."

"Trains don't run on Christmas. The best day to write . . . quiet everywhere."

"Who runs this city, the Pope?"

"Most English people aren't Catholic."

I was just about to tell him to take his play and ram it up his ass, when I thought of my Aunt Mona in Pasadena with her white, fake, grotesque-looking Christmas tree and the California sun streaming in through the smog and shining over the sickening Christmas paper with Rudolf the Red-Nosed Reindeer on it. I thought about "Air Force One" slapping me on the back and giving me a "special Christmas Drink" (Rum and Fruit punch . . . vomit) from his portable, black, fake leather bar, and Mona giving me Christmas bell earrings. That would really be puke city.

"Sure," I said as cheerfully as I could. "I'll go for a walk and come back in time to throw something together for dinner."

Hollistor had already hauled out the fucking portable type-writer, was busy at work, and didn't hear me. Well, no matter how desolate I felt, it was sheer elation compared with how I would feel in Pasadena hearing "The Little Drummer Boy," with stereophonic sound coming from the ten speakers of "Air Force One's" wonderful P.X. stereo system.

In London, our flat was a fourth floor walk-up—not because we were poor, but because all those British jerks walk up (I bet the elevators in the *Savoy* are only there for the Americans). The first two floors of our house were a bed-and-breakfast place, and the top three were flats owned by Americans who made a fucking fortune renting them to other Americans. It was just this side of being a dump, but by English standards, it was pretty swell. The lady who ran the bed-and-breakfast place and did once-a-week cleaning of the flats thought I was Hollistor's daughter (or wanted to think that); was from New Zealand; was very anti-American, anti-English, and anti-Irish; and apparently didn't believe in working on Christmas day, as all the people renting rooms in the bed-and-breakfast were standing around looking hungry and complaining in several languages.

Since it was raining a very chilling rain, I decided to take the tube down to Piccadilly Circus or Leicester Square and see some movie (maybe even a double feature to make Hollistor wonder if I had been murdered while he wrote his latest morbid comedy hit).

After sitting in the St. John's Wood tube station for several eternities, feeling as if I were in the advanced stage of being preserved in ice forever, a southbound train finally came along and slowed down, as if it were doing me a big favor, since I was the only one at the stop. I guess people in St. John's Wood all have fireplaces and Christmas geese and don't need to sit and look at Kentucky Fried Chicken ads in a London subway.

I got off at Piccadilly Circus and came up from the Underground into what looked like London during an air raid alert. I swear, there was nobody there. Except for a few fat Americans standing outside the front door of the Piccadilly Hotel staring out at the rain, and a few skid row types hanging around a soup kitchen, the goddamned place was totally deserted. The only other thing that looked open was a hopeful souvenir shop selling plastic policemen's hats, scarves with Buckingham Palace on them, and the postcard of the Queen in her 1958 prom dress.

I was amazed. I walked down the middle of the Haymarket just to see what it felt like, and suddenly I knew how the Israelites felt walking along the floor of the Red Sea—weird!

I took a walk down to Leicester Square, appreciating the fact that no one was trying to run me over and hoping Alan Bates would pop out and whisk me off to a meal of roast goose and sweet almonds. I'm telling you, the *only* goddamned fucking movie open in the entire city of London was a soft-core porn flick called *Murder in Her Thighs*. Because soft-core is so boring and it was Christmas and all, I decided to skip *Murder in Her Thighs*. I walked up Tottenham Court Road, feeling utterly depressed because I was completely dependent on commercial enterprises like movies, restaurants, and man-made happiness. I was so American it made me puke. Shit, even in *Pekin, Illinois*, they print a newspaper and show a movie on Christmas Day. I finally understood what the nonseparation of Church and State meant.

Life gives you one hell of a choice. If you live in America, you hate yourself because you are one of the plastic-mass-middle class, and if you live in London, you either are rich and everyone hates you, or you are a goddamned little match girl trying to scrape together 50p to go see *Murder in Her Thighs* because it is better than freezing. I had always wanted to be in London and in love, and I was in London all right, but the whole world looks fucked when you realize you've done the wrong thing for the wrong reason: Hollistor didn't love me—he loved my mother, and I—shit—just wanted to be wanted.

Since I didn't really know where I was going, I decided to take the tube home, warm up, and improve my mind in some way while Hollistor finished writing. Well, another bitter blow was about to come: the tubes stop running at 3:00 P.M. on Christmas Day, and *all* the taxis are off duty.

I decided to wander along a bit and see whether or not I froze first or came to someplace that was open so I could give Hollistor a call. The first place available was about three blocks down the road. Even though the Bedford Corner Hotel didn't have what I'd exactly call "charm," it advertised a bar, so I figured I could wait for Hollistor with a glass of whisky and feel sorry for myself this Merry Christmas.

Of course, the bar was closed, so while I waited for some American to finish using the one pay phone, I wandered over to the other side of the lobby, checked out the menu of "The Happy Casserole Restaurant," and wondered why Britishers were such terrible cooks and who in their right mind would ever name a restaurant "The Happy Casserole."

"You're an American," said the American using the phone who had come up behind me.

"So," I said, wondering why all Americans in Europe act like soul brothers when they wouldn't give each other the time of day back home.

"Just noticing," he said.

"I see you speak French," I said. "I overheard you on the phone." God, what a boring thing to say, but what else could I say unless I resorted to "Pretty cold out there, isn't it?"

"I teach French," he said. "At the University of Wisconsin."

"Really? My father got his Ph.D. there."

"Oh," said the man who looked sort of like Art Carney. "Is he here in London?"

I loved to drop the bombshell. "Oh," I said as cheerfully and as casually as I could, "he is in a mental hospital in California because he murdered his mistress in a fit of insanity."

"What!" said the poor innocent man who was just trying to strike up a conversation with some fellow American.

Feeling bad, I just said, "Don't worry about it. . . . I don't." He frowned, so I said, "I'm traveling abroad to 'forget my past.' "

"How old are you?"

"Twenty," I lied.

He laughed. "You staying here?" he asked. "At this hotel?"

I was too polite to say that I wouldn't stay at this dump on a bet, so I just said, "Oh, no—at the Savoy. I was just in here to phone for my car."

Since he didn't say anything, I figured I'd better resume the conversation, because if anyone were going to do the snubbing, I wanted it to be me.

"Who were you talking to in French?" I asked.

He shrugged.

I decided to try again. "You know, I didn't get your name," I said.

He smiled. "You're not going to believe this, but it's Redford. Robert Redford. Professor Redford."

"You're kidding!"

"Everyone says that when I tell them."

"Shit, I just finished wishing I was with Robert Redford. He's my favorite actor, you know—*Butch Cassidy* and all."

He didn't answer. I started again. "Were you talking to Paul Newman on the phone?"

"I . . . uh . . . was breaking it off with my French mistress. . . . She wanted me to leave my wife."

"Oh, I'm sorry."

"Well, I'm not. She was a bitch."

"That's really exotic, you know," I said. "I knew someone once who had a real Chinese mistress, but never a French mistress. You must love your wife."

"She's in Wisconsin," he said meaningfully as he put his hand on my waist.

I decided that now was the time to end the conversation, so I didn't say something ass hole like, "You must be lonely so far away without your family on Christmas." That would only lead to trouble. I'm not a common pickup—Robert Redford or no Robert Redford.

He cleared his throat. "Care for a drink?"

"The bar's closed."

"For hotel guests there is a booze machine—like a Coke machine, only it sells whisky for 50p."

"No kidding?" I said. "And I suppose we drink it in your room, huh?"

"Would you rather 'The Happy Casserole'?" he asked.

Now, if I hadn't been pissed at Hollistor, I never would have gone up to his room. I must also say something about my philosophy about being "picked up." I've never believed in the "strangers on a train" bit, or *even* Erica Jong's famous zipless fuck. Passion never entered into it; just revenge. That's how I rationalized my wanton behavior while Robert Redford (really his *real* name—he showed me his passport) kept inserting 50p coins into the booze machine and collected a number of miniature whisky bottles for us to take up to his room.

One healthy pickup is good for anyone if you get a good lay and a good meal. The one problem with my first wanton pickup was that this middle-aged French professor turned out to have a stocking fetish. Now, being still relatively inexperienced with sex except for Hollistor's variety, I really didn't know too much about weird sex. During early high school I had read *Wet, Wild, and Wonderful, Body and Fender,* and *Airline Cockpit,* and I had found them boring but sort of informative. I was told by Janet, who was horrified after discovering my under-the-mattress reading collection, that things like that "didn't ever go on in real life." Well, shit, on Christmas Day, 1973, I found out differently.

Now, Robert Redford was a pleasant enough conversationalist, if you call a conversation about the Wisconsin winter landscape and how New York City was really going down the tube pleasant. We downed two of the whiskies, and then talked about "education," and how *it* was really going down the tube. Then the pervert showed me his stocking collection. At first I thought he might be a salesman or something—he showed me all different colors of women's stockings, ballet tights, opera hose, but when he got out the black ones with the seams and the garter belt, I knew he was a fucking pervert.

As he explained to me all about how he liked to see women wear different varieties of stockings and walk around on the bed while he sat on the floor and beat his meat, he got very excited. Now, I figure that I have more natural curiosity about the bizarre than your normal person, but I'm sorry, I just wasn't curious enough to see some sickie jack off while I cavorted around in a pair of opera hose.

When he started to remove his clothes, I decided to run for it. He chased me out the door, waving the ballet tights, and yelling that I owed him two pounds for the whisky.

Since the porter sensed my urgency, he let me use the house phone. The operator gave me an outside line, and I dialed

Hollistor. He answered with a you-interrupted-me-sounding "Hello."

"This is Annie," I said, breathing hard. "I . . . just . . . met this guy named Robert Redford . . . who had black stockings . . . with seams . . . and. . . . "

"Wait a minute, Annie."

I explained a little more slowly. I don't know if he was more pissed off at Robert Redford with the stocking fetish or at me for going to someone's room, but he was real ticked off. He came right away in the car.

At first he didn't say anything, but when we got back to the flat he said, "We'll leave London tomorrow."

"I'm sorry, Hollistor."

"I'm sorry this had to happen to you," he said bitterly. "You were very lucky."

"I'm sorry. I'm so very sorry," I said, realizing I was getting a tad bit redundant.

"Look," he said angrily, "if you don't want to be with me, okay, but whether or not you're involved or mad at *anyone, don't ever* go up to a strange man's room—ever again!"

"I'm sorry. I'm young."

"You use your youth as an excuse for a lot of things, yet you want to enjoy all the privileges of an adult."

"Okay, then, I was stupid. . . . Is that okay . . . to be stupid?"

"As long as you learned something," he said curtly.

By his attitude, I couldn't tell whether he thought he was punishing me by taking me away from fun city, London, or whether he thought he was doing me a big favor because I had had such a bad experience, but I decided it was better not to ask.

I knew I could have said to him that he was getting the privilege of screwing a seventeen-year-old girl and shouldn't be pissed because she didn't act as if she were thirty, but I thought that was pointless too. Poor Hollistor: all he really did was love Kate.

We left London the next afternoon. God save the Queen!

HASTINGS, HEARTE & DANIELS

118 AVENUE OF THE AMERICAS

NEW YORK, NY 10013

April 14, 1975

Dear Annie,

I am very curious as to the origin of the expression, "A kick in the tit." Wouldn't "a kick in the ass" do?

Also, I feel the entire episode with a man named Robert Redford, who happens to have a stocking fetish, should be cut. You could simply use dissatisfaction with London as your reason for leaving the city. I don't find a pervert named Robert Redford either amusing or informative. I think it is just a little far-fetched.

You must not hate me, Annie. Everyone has to lose her virginity to <u>someone</u>, and at least it was in a suite at the Mark and not on a Union Gospel Mission couch. Maybe we should just forget everything and have a professional relationship.

Sincerely,
Martin

430 Pacific Avenue
San Francisco, CA 94133

April 16, 1975

Dear Martin,
    I've been _trying_ to have a professional
relationship with you! _You're_ the one who's
been saying, "I don't understand you," and
"I'm confused." I'm not confused—we were both
in it for what we could get out of it: you
used your power, and I used my legs and youth.
I don't hate you; you're no worse than I am,
and we may _both_ get something out of this—
providing you play your cards right.
    If I'd said "kick in the ass," it would
be less original than "kick in the tit," and
neither is as offensive as three-fourths of the
language in _Manchild in the Promised Land_,
which has made it to all the Sociology classes
and uses expressions like "motherfucker" all
the time. I could have used one of my _awful_
expressions like "three-day-old period blood
clot," but I respect my readers as you told
me I should.
    And who the hell cares if the story of
Robert Redford with a stocking fetish is far-
fetched! The idea of _Ada_ taking place on
another planet that is very much like Earth
but measures time differently seems farfetched,
and no one gave Nabokov a hard time! Shit,
when Jules Verne wrote _20,000 Leagues Under the
Sea_, everyone thought _he_ was farfetched. Are
you looking for excuses not to publish this?
People don't want to read about things they see
in their own backyards! Don't you remember
that perversion is a recurring theme?

Would it help things if I were in love with you? If I gave my narrator a "warm human relationship" with the man with the stocking fetish, would it move this along? You'd <u>better</u> publish this, or you may regret it.

<u>Sincerely</u> yours,
Annie

Sometime during the early winter of 1974, Hollistor and I terminated our relationship. There wasn't just one day when he sat down and told me to get the fuck out of his life, but I think London and my not living up to his memories of Katie sort of made it wither up and die.

When we came back to New York from London, my hair was so greasy it looked like someone had soaked it in Wesson Oil—really Crisco city! English bathtubs just weren't designed for washing long, greasy, American hair, and I was too young to think of going to a beauty parlor. During the plane ride, Hollistor had been unusually silent. I guess he was still pissed off at me for almost getting raped by a fucking guy with a stocking fetish. Shit. In all our love making and confidence sharing, we had never promised to be faithful to each other. I mean, that's just too corny. We were both awfully careful about being corny. All I wanted was respect, and maybe a little passion, but when you're trying so hard not to be corny, it is hard to get passionate—especially when your knowledge of passion is from movies like *A Summer Place* and *Ryan's Daughter*. When you are only seventeen, it is hard to get respect from *anyone*.

On the flight back, Hollistor gave me the headphones so I could watch *The Way We Were*. He told me that I'd live to regret it, but it was just the kind of shit I liked. Robert Redford was a writer instead of someone with a stocking fetish, and Barbra Streisand looked into his eyes and said, "I love the way you write." It was one of those "artistic" movies that had the credits in the middle. It was so terrible, I loved it. Naturally I cried in the end when Barbra Streisand is passing out her "Ban the Bomb" leaflets in the middle of the street in New York, and just happens to meet Robert Redford after all those years. Just as she was gently brushing his blond toupee away from his eyes, Hollistor turned to me, lifted my earphone off my ear, and said very calmly, "You make me awfully sick, Annie."

I pointed out to him that I was only seventeen, and I hadn't developed sophisticated tastes yet, and he just mumbled something about wishing we had remembered that fact when we first became lovers.

"I wish you had loved *me!*" I said.

"I thought you were amusing."

"Look," I said, now thoroughly pissed off, "did you expect this fucking affair with a goddamned minor to be *simple*? Take her to London, and when you're tired of her, just go on with your life?"

"I don't know what I expected," he said. "It just seemed like a good idea at the time."

"Just like Mother thought it might be a good idea to knock herself off—you know, for all the glory and grieving—and didn't realize that she'd be dead for good?"

He got really angry then. "Annie, your mother has nothing to do with any of this!"

"Good Christ, Hollistor, she has *everything* to do with it. . . . You wanted me to be more like her. She never loved you, Hollistor, and you were really stupid and insensitive to think that hitting the rack with me was going to make up for it!"

"Your mother *loved* me," he said quietly.

"*Not* the way you wanted her to," I snapped.

"I don't believe that's so, Annie."

"Believe what you want," I said sharply. "I know the truth!"

"Your mother rarely told the truth," he said evenly.

"I didn't say Mother told it to me," I said. "I just know it, that's all."

"Oh, God," he said sadly, "God. . . . "

"You never loved me, then?"

"Let's say I was attracted to your caustic wit. You had the humor of your mother without her self-worship."

"You're fucked," I said.

He didn't answer.

"Why don't you write another play about her?" I asked softly. "You could keep her alive that way. Don't use me; I'm not her."

"I tried to," he said, "but—now that she's dead—it takes a better writer than I am to capture her—-how do I put it—her joy and pain, genuine love of that pain, and well . . . I could never capture her love for your father. I'm not the right one to understand it."

"It was the sex, that's all," I said and returned to watching *The Way We Were.*

April 18, 1975

Anne Sarah Foster
430 Pacific Avenue
San Francisco, CA 94133

Dear Annie,
    No publisher, as you say, "looks for
excuses not to publish something." If we don't
intend to go on with a piece, we simply say,
as you know, that "it doesn't fill our publishing needs at this time." When I make sug-
gestions to you, it is simply because I am in
the business and have a better idea than you do
as to what sells.
    I'll not ask you to come to New York any-
more; any contractual arrangements can be made
by mail if necessary.
    I think the book has reached a good stop-
ping point. Why don't you wind it up, and I
will submit it to our editorial board.

                It has been nice working with you,
                Martin Goldsmith
                Senior Editor

MG/ht

April 23, 1975

Dear Martin,
    "It's been nice working with you." (!!)
Do you always have such a pleasant working
situation with your writers? Since you are much
too professional to lose interest in my book
the minute the possibility of bouncing the
springs with me is out of the question, I'm
sure you mean Heritage should be short to keep
publication costs down. I understand economics
. . . I hope.
    I have some ideas for an ending. Since we
are "no longer involved," I'm sure you can be
objective and help me select the best one—
knowing the market as well as you do.
    My first idea was for the narrator to go
into some piano bar in New York and take up
with the fag piano player. She would get into
the "gay scene" and finally commit suicide in
some grotesque way because she is "following
the family tradition." Because the fag won't
screw her, she thinks the "fault lies within
herself." With homosexuality really big now—
you know, Staircase, Boys in the Band, The Lion
in Winter, etc.—it will sell, add some dirt,
and prove how liberal I am as a writer. (She
could get raped in a gang bang. . . .)
    The next idea I had was to have her go
"on the road," like Art Carney in Harry and
Tonto. Even though that movie sucked raw eggs,
the American public eats up stories about
wandering souls who meet all kinds of odd characters along the way and groove on them. Also,

when someone is homeless, he becomes vulnerable. A lot of Tennessee Williams' "sensitive"
characters are wanderers. Having the narrator
roam around the country would give me a good
excuse to add a bunch of characters I've been
meaning to write about. If you insist, I could
even give her a darling little animal. The
narrator can commit suicide because she is
"unable to find roots."

I could have her be a "lovable kook" like
Goldie Hawn in _Cactus Flower_, or Sally Bowles,
and she could commit suicide because people
don't see the deep sensitive person underneath
it all.

Then, I was thinking about having her go
back to San Francisco and write the "Great
American Novel" about her life, but then it
really would be a bit too artsy-fartsy autobiographical to pass as good commercial
fiction.

I guess it _is_ possible to have a narrator
who _doesn't_ commit suicide. . . .

Sincerely,
Annie

Our first night back in New York was really the beginning of the end. When Hollistor and I arrived at the apartment, there were several messages with the service from a woman who called herself "Alexia." Now, I have nothing against the name, but you can understand that if your lover or husband receives messages from someone named "Gladys" or "Edna," you don't worry too much, but you *always* distrust messages from people named things like "Alexia," "Angela," or "Gloria." Of course I inquired as to who this "Alexia" was, and Hollistor said she was "the finest actress in New York City." Shit. "Superlatives are always a matter of opinion anyway," I said.

"What about your mother?"

"That was different . . . I was just a kid, and kids believe their mothers about things like that."

"Alexia is almost as good as your mother was."

"Christ," I said, "you just like actresses."

Hollistor didn't answer. He just hoisted his suitcase up on the bed and unlocked it. "What does she want?" I asked.

"Oh . . . uh . . . she just wants us to come see this experimental production of *Macbeth* in some church. She directed it."

"How did she know you were coming back today?"

"I sent her a card."

"Then you were planning to leave London *before* Robert Redford. Shit, I was reeking with guilt all the way home, and you were *planning* to come back! You made plans without telling me. . . . Just like I was a doll . . . a toy. Jesus!"

"Cool it, Annie," he said. "She's just a friend. She invited *both* of us."

"Well, I wanted to take a shower and watch Johnny Carson —you know, if you've been away from Johnny, Ed, and Doc for eight months, you really feel like you *have* to tune in and see how they all are."

"Okay," said Hollistor. "Don't go. I'll go myself."

"Not on your fucking life!" I yelled. "I'm coming!" I softened. "Maybe it will provide a few laughs . . . we could use some laughs."

Hollistor looked through the dirty clothes in his suitcase. Coming home from a trip always reminds me of laundry, and his suitcase was living proof. I remembered once Mother had complained about dirty laundry at the end of a trip. "Why don't you just burn it?" my father said, and she *did!*

"Do you think this *Macbeth* is going to be any good?" I asked. I really couldn't imagine an "experimental production" of *Macbeth* in a church being any better than Johnny Carson knocking down dominos.

"It takes place in South America," said Hollistor.

"Shit," I said. "I'm fed up with those productions of Shakespeare that take place in South America, in the South during the time of the goddamned Civil War, in Chicago in the thirties, in a mining town, in Nazi Germany, in. . . . "

"Come on, Annie!"

"You used to be the last person in the *world* who'd go see that crap!"

"You watched *The Way We Were*," he said, "so don't talk to me about taste."

"But I *laughed* at it," I shouted.

"And cried in the end," he sighed. "I'll go alone. Alexia wanted us to stop by for drinks before. . . . "

"I *said* I'd go," I snapped. "Shit," I thought, "Alexia. . . . "

HASTINGS, HEARTE & DANIELS

118 AVENUE OF THE AMERICAS

NEW YORK, NY 10013

May 5, 1975

Anne Sarah Foster
430 Pacific Avenue
San Francisco, CA 94133

Dear Annie,
Autobiographical novels are in now. Why
don't you stop worrying about it, have the
narrator go back to San Francisco, write a
novel about her strange family,and commit
suicide because her editor throws her book into
the wastebasket instead of sending it to the
editorial board?
Does that sound like a good idea to you?

Sincerely,
Martin Goldsmith
Senior Editor

MG/ht

430 Pacific Avenue
San Francisco, CA 94133

May 9, 1975

Dear Martin,

I think that idea is a real snoozer. Since there naturally would be at least ten publishing houses who would kill to publish my narrator's manuscript, I don't think any reader would believe she'd have to kill herself to become famous. Sorry, Martin, Annie can make it! If her editor scrapped her book, she'd just send it off to all those other publishers who are beating down her door with sticks.

Oh, yes! I can just see <u>Heritage</u> in Safeway stores across the country with "Soon to be a Major Motion Picture" written in bold letters across the back! I can just see Darlene, now married to Chad, with a greasy baby who pulls things off the shelves in the supermarket, pausing before the paperback stand and seeing <u>Heritage</u> right there between <u>Jaws</u> and <u>Working</u>!

I already know what I'm going to wear to the Academy Awards!

<u>Sincerely</u> yours,
Annie

P.S. Do you have to have written more than one great work to qualify for the Nobel Prize for Literature?

chapter 34

We took a cab and picked up Alexia, who lived in the west seventies, had "tasteful" furniture, hanging plants, classical music playing on the stereo, and black walls in the bathroom. Because she was British, she served us whisky out of stemmed glasses with no ice in them, and worst of all, she looked quite a bit like the impression Mother wanted to give: dramatic and exotic. She had Katharine Hepburn-like cheekbones, frizzy hair, and long fingers that gestured beautifully, and she kept making comments in my direction about how she would give anything to be young again. She also referred to Hollistor as "a great artist." Although I'd have rather been home watching "stump the band," I refrained from saying so. Alexia looked about thirty-two, but I suspected she was at least forty. Of course she was *very* pleased to meet me, and was too charming to even give my jeans a side glance.

"So you're Hollistor's . . . uh . . . friend," she said.

"My *mother* was his friend," I stated.

"Oh," she said, rolling her whisky around in her glass, "I see." She gave a little chuckle under her breath.

While she was out taking a leak, I asked Hollistor right out if he had the hots for her, and when he said, "Oh, I think she's just enormously talented," I knew he did.

During the first act of *Macbeth*, I was convinced that at intermission Hollistor and I would be back on our old ground. Since it was really el-puke-o, I figured we'd laugh about it and leave. Then I looked over at Hollistor, and he was actually watching that piece of dog shit and not even trying not to laugh. One minor point against this attitude was that there wasn't a single good actor in it. Particularly bad were Banquo (who looked like the guy who does the Doritos commercials) and the black man who played all three watches. Lady Macbeth looked like this girl who lived upstairs from us in London named Jill who threw up in a cake pan the only time Hollistor and I had met her, and she must have been a four point student at the Sandra Dee School of Dramatic Arts. Because it took place in South America, they had all this Latin Moo Cha Cha music playing in the background all through the production. And the costumes! Jesus! In her first scene, Lady Macbeth came out in a red and orange bikini and sat around her pool waiting for news of how Macbeth was doing helping Duncan put down this unidentified revolution. Now, I'm all for inventiveness in the theatre, but Lady Macbeth in a bikini just isn't my idea of a good costuming job—particularly when your Lady Macbeth looks like Jill who threw up in the cake pan.

Another hit were these giant Inca statues that were supposed to be Macbeth's apparitions. About twenty of them (about eight feet tall) walked around saying, "Macbeth, beware Macduff." The real scream came when the Inca statues played trees—well, they were okay as trees (they just stood there), but when it came time for Macduff to kill Macbeth (which he did with an enormous machete—also cause for a big laugh on my part and a jab in the ribs from Hollistor), the trees started moving in to mask the killing. I screamed with laughter at this, which was okay since most of the audience had already left. I wondered why Hollistor failed to see the humor in it. Since he was usually the first one to laugh at horseshit in life, I thought I could count on him.

After the show, Alexia was throwing a party, and since I was jet lagging, I threw Hollistor a "let's not go" look, which he ignored. I will hand it to him for not going the whole hog and saying he *liked* that piece of dog puke, but Alexia directed it, so he decided to be polite. I looked at Hollistor so we could secretly smirk, but he was intently listening to Alexia talk about how she was "process-oriented" rather than "product-oriented" when she directed. When Hollistor said that he "knew exactly what she meant" without one *bit* of sarcasm, I decided to give up. He didn't even laugh when she said she had liked *A Little Night Music* so much that she went out the next day and bought two boas.

Hollistor was a traitor. He was like everyone else. He had sold out to the other side: to the people who endorse *Macbeth* set in South America; to the people who buy Sugar Frosted Flakes for their kids; to the people who use Frost-and-Tips on their hair; to the people who buy matching living room suites; to the people who say, "Put that in your pipe and smoke it"; to the people who won't say "fuck" yet swap wives; to the people who say *Ulysses* is their favorite book and never finished it; to the people who say nothing at all; to the people who always talk about changing the world and then flip on Dean Martin's "Celebrity Roast"; to the President; to the culture vultures; to the people who think everything is "far out"; to ladies with poodles; to the people who do "last-minute Christmas shopping"; to the women who wear false eyelashes; to the people who actually like being dentists; to the people who refuse to watch television because it is the "downfall of America"; to the people who say, "It must be good because it's on PBS"; to the contestants on "The Price is Right"; to all the people in the retailing and banking business; to all the people who overuse the word "creative"; to the people who believe everything they read; to the people who don't read at all; to the people who refuse to believe that all the media are paid to be pro-Arab; and to all the people who sit back and let life squish them to death. I couldn't believe it. Hollistor had sold out to all the people at Alexia's party—to all the people he couldn't tolerate. I had loved that bastard because he was the one person who wouldn't put up with horseshit, but at Alexia's party, he swallowed her drinks and spouted out as much dog crap as anyone else.

Alexia, too, reminded Hollistor of Mother. To get my love, he had pretended to laugh at the world; to get hers, he pretended to get sucked in by it.

I walked out to the street and went up to Central Park West. Since I'd be eighteen in a few weeks, there was nothing forcing me to stay. As I walked up the street to our building, my tears mixed with the rain. "Fucking bastard," I thought. "Fucking *man!*" Because I was too young to be so bitter, I cried harder.

HASTINGS, HEARTE & DANIELS

118 AVENUE OF THE AMERICAS

NEW YORK, NY 10013

May 13, 1975

Anne Sarah Foster
430 Pacific Avenue
San Francisco, CA 94133

Dear Annie,
    I have submitted your manuscript to several members of our editorial board. So far, they are not sure as to the salability of your book. You must send the last chapter right now, because they are almost ready for it.

                    Yours,
                    Martin

MG/ht

                              430 Pacific Avenue
                              San Francisco, CA 94133

                              May 21, 1975

Dear Martin,
    Here is your last fucking chapter!
    You spoke of your editorial board. Are
you sure it really exists, you lying ass hole?

                              Piss on you,
                              Annie

Because Hollistor and Alexia became "an item," he didn't make a fuss when I told him I was going back to San Francisco. He even took an almost "fatherly" interest in my welfare. I think because he felt pretty guilty about the whole thing, he went to California with me to help me get settled.

There was only one little thing I couldn't solve: what I was going to do with my goddamned *life!*

Hollistor arranged for me to take the California State High School qualifying exam (which was ridiculously easy), and stuck around in San Francisco until I decided what I wanted to do. He made some vague noises about college, but being a daughter of a college professor, and knowing you have a pretty good chance of paying thousands of dollars a year and then getting some jerk to teach you, I thought I'd do something productive until my "right direction" hit me.

I became a "temporary" personal shopper for Joseph Magnin, and Hollistor said that I could have got a Ph.D. from Harvard, but with the way the job market was going, I would probably end up a personal shopper at Joseph Magnin anyway. He said, "Disgustingness is doing the crappy job after you have your Ph.D. that you could have done when you were in the sixth grade."

The job consisted of walking around the store with a folder. Once in a while, you got a call or letter from someone and had to actually go out and shop for something for them; but most of the time you spent eight hours a day trying to *look* busy, which actually takes more energy than *being* busy. No one in the store knew exactly what I did there. Since I had a folder, they assumed I must be important. Hollistor called it my good sense of props.

I had this boss who used to sit right at the next desk, but instead of telling me anything, she would send me an inter-office memo. After reading it, I had to sign it in the correct place and put it back on her desk so she could file it in her gigantic inter-office memo file. One day she sent me this god-damned memo, everyone in the office signed it, and about two minutes later we heard fucking Mrs. Abernathy let out this primal scream. Naturally, I thought something really drastic had happened, such as her daughter had died or that her files for 1970 were missing. We rushed to her side, only to find out that the cause of her pain was that we hadn't signed in the right order on the lines she had provided for us. Well, I had the bright idea of covering the portion we had signed with white paper, taking it to the Xerox machine, getting it copied, and resigning it in the correct order. When she got it back, she placed it in her drawer with the same kind of sigh of relief that I might utter if I suddenly found myself in a nice, safe, Midwestern college, greeting my nice Mom and Dad from Ohio on Homecoming Weekend. I actually sort of envied Mrs. Abernathy because she could get that same sense of peace from a simple inter-office memo.

About five minutes later, I did the Doris Day routine, threw my papers up in the air, and said, "I quit!" I slammed down my folder and walked out. No one even seemed disturbed.

As I walked home, I realized I needed a reason to be alive, and Joseph Magnin sure as hell wasn't going to give me one.

I walked into the house and yelled at Holly, who was visiting me.

"What are you doing home?" she asked. "Are you sick?"

"I quit," I said simply.

"Why?"

"Because I want to be remembered when I die."

"Like Mother?" she asked sarcastically. "The way she just got up and quit?"

"No, like Shakespeare—for what I *did*, not what I didn't do."

"So you quit your job," she said. "That's just something else you didn't do . . . didn't go back to school, didn't do the dishes this morning, didn't make it work with Hollistor, didn't ever finish your paint-by-numbers when we were kids. . . . Shit, Annie."

"I am like Mother. . . . Frightening as it is, Holly, I'm like her."

"Nobody says you have to be."

"Huh?"

"Use it, Annie," she laughed. "Write a novel."

"No," I said, thinking that novels involved an awful lot of work. "I haven't lived long enough to write a novel. . . . I'll write a short story."

HASTINGS, HEARTE & DANIELS

118 AVENUE OF THE AMERICAS

NEW YORK, NY 10013

July 20, 1975

Anne Sarah Foster
430 Pacific Avenue
San Francisco, CA 94133

Dear Ms. Foster,
    We regret to inform you that your novel does not meet our publishing needs at this time. We wish you success in placing it with another publisher.
    Thank you for letting us read your manuscript.

Sincerely yours,
THE EDITORS

```
                              430 Pacific Avenue
                              San Francisco, CA 94133

                              July 25, 1975

Martin Goldsmith
Senior Editor
HASTINGS, HEARTE & DANIELS
118 Avenue of the Americas
NYC, N.Y. 10013
```

Dearest Darling Martin (Senior Editor),

By the time you read this (don't you love that beginning?), I will be dead, zapped, kaput, "pushing up daisies," and most of all, "just a beautiful memory to those who knew me."

I have just downed thirty "reds" (with a double shot of J. W. Black for courage), and am about to walk up to the attic, slit my wrists, place a rope around my neck, tie it to the beam, put "<u>The</u> Gun" to my head, and pull the trigger just as I kick the stool out from under me. That should do it.

Now, you bastard, you must realize what the market for this goddamned novel is <u>now</u>!

To love, death, and whatever you make off this!

                                        Annie

P.S.   A suicide you think is queer
        At this high point in my career;
        But just a word in my behalf:
        Look what it did for Sylvia Plath!

HASTINGS, HEARTE & DANIELS

118 AVENUE OF THE AMERICAS

NEW YORK, NY 10013

July 29, 1975

Dearest Annie,

Although I found no obituary in the San
Francisco newspapers, I was genuinely frightened by your note. Please, Annie, write and
assure me you are still alive. I phoned you a
number of times and received no answer. I
called the San Francisco Police, who said
they'd check on things and get back to me, but
I haven't heard from them. Please just let me
know. I'm almost positive you are not dead. You
wouldn't die this easily.

If you are angry about the form letter,
it wasn't my doing. When a novel is rejected
by the board, the manuscript is supposed to go
back to the editor, but yours got into the
form-letter-reject pile instead.

I did want to publish Heritage—I just
have no control over the board's decisions.

Please write to me.

Love,
Martin

430 Pacific Avenue
San Francisco, CA 94133

August 4, 1975

Dear Martin,

    So all it takes is a little suicide note,
and you start using the word "love" again.
Well, well, well.

    Do you really think I would bother to
write a whole fucking novel and then blow the
whole thing because of one stupid rejection
notice? There are other fish in the sea, baby.

    As you should know by now, unlike old
Kate, I am a survivor. From reading my novel,
you should <u>know</u> I'd never stoop as low as
suicide. Unlike my mother who wanted to die,
I want to live. Although Mother gave up her
work as an actress, I want to make millions of
bucks off my work as a writer!

    Katie managed to turn victory into defeat,
but I will take not defeat but only a small
disappointment, and turn it into victory. You
see, Martin dearest, as your form letter
advised, I have submitted <u>Heritage</u> to another
publisher. <u>However</u>, I figured it would be much,
much better if I submitted our scintillating
correspondence along with it. Because I knew
my letters were too good to waste, I made sure
to keep carbons.

    Of course I'll change the names, but if
you even <u>try</u> to sue me, you will only be admitting guilt. Since you are "in the process of
getting divorced," I'm sure your wife's lawyer
would be very interested in your admission of
adultery—especially with a girl under twenty-
one.

274

So you see, my dearest, <u>Heritage</u> will now do for the novel what Pirandello did for the drama. Thank you so much for your help.

I wish you best of luck in meeting your alimony payments,

> Love,
> X X X X X X X X X X X X X X X X
> Annie

SWENSON-ROLANDS PUBLISHERS

220 PARK AVENUE

NEW YORK, N.Y. 10017

October 17, 1975

Anne Sarah Foster
430 Pacific Avenue
San Francisco, CA 94133

Dear Ms. Foster,

I have just heard from our editorial board that they were impressed and entertained by <u>Heritage</u> and are recommending it for publication, along with your interwoven correspondence with Martin Goldsmith.

Before sending you the contract, I would just like confirmation that everything in <u>Heritage</u> is completely fictitious. Or did another editor really write you all the letters?

> Warmest regards,
> Amanda Stewart
> Senior Editor

AS/ge

430 Pacific Avenue
San Francisco, CA 94133

Oct. 21, 1975

Ms. Amanda Stewart
Senior Editor
SWENSON-ROLANDS PUBLISHERS
220 Park Avenue
NYC, N.Y. 10017

Dear Ms. Stewart,
    As I wrote to "Martin" once, "Fiction is
much more interesting than real life."

                  Warmest regards to you,
                  Anne Sarah Foster